9/25

SMOKE JIMI

A NOVEL
BY CHAD PEERY

Angie — Thanks for being a Racking Reader!

Chad Peery

This is a work of fiction. The events and characters portrayed are imaginary. Their resemblance, if any, to real-life persons, places, or counterparts is entirely coincidental.

Copyright © 2009 by Chad Peery. All rights reserved under International and Pan American copyright conventions. Printed in the United States of America by Create Space. Cover work: Chad Peery

ISBN-13: 978-1442112896
ISBN-10: 1442112891
First Edition
www.chadwrite.com

~Dedication~

I wish to express my gratitude to all, present and departed, whose patience and support helped me keep faith in myself, and to tell the story held within these pages. This is for Janet, Jan, Susan, Lynda, Jace, and especially for you, Bonnie.

~Acknowledgements~

Special thanks to John Dufresne and his writers' group for conveying the craft of writing in a kind and thoughtful way. If I were better at names, I would have a long list of fellow writers and mentors who have come and gone through the years, all leaving the mark of their wisdom.

I do wish to thank John Kay, Bob Welch and Mick Fleetwood, all of whom gave a young Chad Peery the opportunity to experience worlds only imagined by most of us. Oh yes, and Christine McVie, for choosing my audition tape on that night so long ago. I also wish to honor the work and the lives of the many incredible musicians and support people who shared the path of my life.

Gassho.

~ *SMOKING JIMI* ~

by

Chad Peery

1

It was 1999, the year we were supposed to party, the year I almost lost my life. It started with a 6 a.m. phone call from Mitch Damian, our old band's ex-manager, who hadn't been heard from since he ripped us off back in the '70's. He told me he was dying, and begged me to meet him, to "break bread one last time."

So, there I sat in a Wendy's restaurant across the table from Mitch, whom I could only describe as a bundle of human embarrassment with his fake mustache, blond wig, and gold chains. I prayed no one would recognize me.

"Are you hearing me, man? One million cash! C'mon, Brad, you're killing me here." Mitch's cynical leer and off-center jaw gave him the gravitas of a weasel. As if to drive his point home, Mitch bit into his cheeseburger and chewed furiously, glaring at me with the expression of a cannibal.

"Look, Mitch, tell you what, it's been great seeing you but I've got a photo shoot to get to and I'm a little short on time today."

Before I could get up, Mitch launched into a weepy rant about how we'd been through so much together and how I should consider all the things a million dollars would buy.

While Mitch rambled on, my stomach soured. If it weren't for him, two people I loved would be alive, and my old band would still be together. I took a drink of Diet Pepsi to quench the angry coals, while Mitch, with a gluttonous thrust, packed his cheeks with a fist-full of fries.

"Mitch, c'mon man. What comes next? You gonna ask me for my credit card number? Isn't that how these scams work? Tell you what, it's been real— see you around."

Mitch gulped his wad of fries and dabbed his fake mustache. "Brad, man, sit down. I don't want *your* money. I'm here to bring *you* money, my friend. Enough bigtime, big-cash money to gag a calculator!"

"Mitch, just stop. There are no million-dollar gigs for washed-up, one-hit wonders. Besides, Frank died a long time ago.

Stick this in your calculator— no keyboard player, plus no band, equals no scam."

Mitch held up his palms as if he were directing traffic. "Brad, C'mon now, I just learned about Frank. Why didn't somebody— you know?"

"Why didn't somebody tell you?" My stomach coiled as I leaned into his face. "Last time anybody saw you was nineteen-goddam-seventy two. Frank died right after you ran off with our money. Should've been *you* in my Porsche that night instead of him."

"Hey, c'mon, Brad, gimme a break here. Like, what was Frank's problem, you know, why'd he do himself? Brokenhearted over a guy? What?"

"I'm looking at the reason why."

Mitch recoiled. "Who? Me? C'mon, everybody knows Frank was a fag, but he was OK. I never did nothin' to the guy, honest."

"Like hell!"

Scornful faces turned my direction and I lowered my voice.

"Frank's whole life was the band. After you ripped us off things turned ugly, fast, especially for Frank. He got real quiet, withdrawn, I should've known. Borrowed my Porsche one night— said he had to get out into the desert, do some thinking. The Highway Patrol said he was doing over a hundred and forty when he hit that wall. Wasn't enough left of him to have a funeral with. All because of you."

Mitch shifted his eyes. "Look, Brad, like I just didn't know. I mean, I'm sorry. That whole thing was just— a business deal that went wrong."

"Stealing our money— that's your idea of a business deal? You gonna sit there and tell me the cops aren't looking for your sorry ass?"

Subdued perversions flickered at the curves of his mouth, just like back in '70 when he conned us into signing that one-sided management contract.

"C'mon, that's old news. I'm living the clean life now."

"You? Clean? Give me a break."

Mitch craned towards me, his breath heavy on the onions. "Brad, listen, don't shut the door on this one, you don't get a lot of chances in life. None of us are as young as we used to be."

My fists slammed the table. "Young? You ripped us off! You turned our best years into living hell."

Heads turned. My words seemed to flitter around in the silence, like bats trapped in a chamber. The murmur of conversations slowly recovered.

"Let's just take a breath, here," Mitch said, and took a delicate nibble from his cheeseburger. Children at a nearby table snickered as they flicked french fries at each other, and Mitch gave them a disapproving glance.

"Brad, let me give it to you straight. You guys were just like those dumb-assed kids over there. If you'd have gotten your hands on all that money, you would've screwed yourselves up. I've seen it before— drugs, cars, women— wow, you know, come to think of it, I actually did you all a big favor."

Blood roared in my ears. "Favor! *Favor?*"

"Well, yeah, sure, I— I mean, I guess you could say I did you guys a favor. Sort of, anyway."

"I'll show you a goddam favor!"

Cat-quick, I grabbed Mitch's hamburger and shoved it into his face with such force that his chair toppled over. Arms flailing, Mitch crashed onto his back and laid still, his eyes blinking, his hairpiece dangling. The ice in the soft-drink dispenser made a ghostly click. Shocked diners stared.

"Sorry everybody, I guess— I don't know, I'm sorry."

Heart pounding, I made for the door. South Florida's heavy breath steamed my face, while the sky had darkened and soured beneath an approaching thunderstorm. As I made for my car it occurred to me that I'd never done anything as crazy as decking Mitch in a public place. If only the guys could have seen this! Too bad I didn't have one of my cameras ready. Too bad none of us kept in touch anymore.

"Wait," Mitch called from the doorway. With the gait of a penguin he shuffled along, trying to catch up to me. "Brad, man, I'm sorry, I was wrong. I screwed up, OK? You guys all think I flipped out and stole the band's money, but I didn't. I just made a bad investment, that's all. Hey, don't give me that look, I did it for the band, man, I did it for you and the band and everything. Brad, think about it. If things would've worked out, I'd have been everybody's hero. All my life I wanted to make it up to you guys. Is that so much to ask?"

Mitch's head gleamed beneath wisps of blond hair— the remnants of his once-thick mane. His liberated toupee resembled a soggy rodent, and he jammed the thing into the pocket of his sports jacket.

"Some people from up north might be looking for me, gotta be careful till things cool down," Mitch said, fingering his phony mustache.

"Who'd your rip off this time?"

"Look, man, I gotta eat too. And I'm telling ya, this deal's gonna set us up for life."

"Mitch, there's no goddam band. Find another meal ticket."

"This your Honda?"

"Screw you."

"Aw, geez," Mitch said, scowling up at the boiling storm clouds. "That looks bad. Let's book."

Like the turbulent sky, my mind must have clouded over, and for some reason I unlocked the door for him. As we drove out of the parking lot, I formulated at simple plan— dump Mitch off a few blocks away, make him walk back to his car, and by then I would be long gone. At that moment, a great bolt of lightning froze before us, suspended between earth and sky, and then released with cracking roar.

Hoping to avoid the deluge I headed south onto Federal Highway, a wide boulevard that cut through Fort Lauderdale's car lots and tourist traps. Like probing artillery, dollar-sized raindrops smacked the windshield, and then the fusillade cut loose for real. The staccato drumming on the Honda's roof became a hammering roar, while all around us wind-whipped palm trees vanished behind curtains of rain. The downpour became ridiculous even for South Florida— it was like driving through a carwash gone berserk.

"Brad, pull over, just pull over, will ya? Man, I can't take this, you gotta stop."

"What's your problem?"

Mitch crossed his arms over his chest like a corpse in a coffin. "Please, man, just please!"

I pulled over to the curb. "You losing it or what?"

He gestured at the storm. "Brad, look, we gotta talk. How can you think straight if you're driving around in all this crazy stuff? Christ, you can't even see where you're goin'!"

Disgusted with myself, I killed the ignition. "It doesn't rain in Buffalo or wherever you're hiding out these days?"

Lightning flashes drew skeletal shadows along Mitch's face— a roadmap of his crooked perversions. Footfalls of thunder rumbled as he turned his mug towards me.

"So, looking good there, Brad. You dark-haired types age better than us blond guys— I'll bet you dye your hair, right? Ha, just kidding, but least you still got hair. Know what? When I saw you walking into Wendy's, I said to myself, 'Wow, there's Brad, man, he's the dude, he's still happening, he's still rock 'n roll!' You work out? How's your health?"

While he prattled on about how my hairstyle made me look like a studly version of Jim Morrison, I had this lovely vision of shoving Mitch into the rain-swollen gutter. Then, I remembered his condition.

"When you called, you said you had cancer. I'm sorry. Really. And I apologize for getting violent in Wendy's. That isn't like me."

"Cancer? Well, actually, I don't have the big C, but I am startin' to put on a gut. Does that count?" Mitch chuckled and rubbed his belly. Thunder mimicked the grumble of indigestion.

"I can't believe this! I should've known that cancer thing was a pants load. Lies are like farts, there's never just one. Especially with you."

"Hey, I had to come up with something, you weren't even going to meet me, remember? Besides, what I'm tellin' you ain't no lie. Last week, I got a call from an attorney with this wealthy client who's a huge fan of the Jammies. This dude got totally freaked when he saw that where-are-they-now Jammies' special on MV-1. Called his lawyer, who called the producers, who called me, and bingo, hello bigtime!"

Mitch paused to nod in agreement with himself.

"So, like I was sayin', this, uh— client, he wants to book a personal appearance by the band, paying one million bucks apiece. You guys'll hang out at his ranch, get treated like kings, play a few of the old songs, maybe get laid, ya know, party down a little, and everybody goes home rich and happy. This dude's a real fan. He knows how that record company screwed you guys over, and he wants to take care of things. Think about it my friend: one million bucks, tax-free. Besides, it's my chance to make things right, know what I mean?"

I shook my head at the rain-blurred windshield. "And I'm supposed to fall for this? What's your angle?"

"Me? Angle? Look, I bumped the price up for you guys. Know what the original offer was? One mil for the band, period. I told 'em we're talkin' about a bigtime band here, it's one mil apiece, or no deal. I got 'em to pay me a million bucks too, so you guys don't have to take my commission outa your share. See how I went to bat for you guys?"

Mitch coughed up a laugh. "Besides, I'm the one who got it all started: I talked MV-1 into doing that piece on you guys. Those punks didn't even know who the Jammies were before I pitched 'em. Now I got you guys a million bucks apiece. Me."

A truck swooshed past, blanketing my Honda in a wall of water which made the car shake like a wet dog. Mitch cursed all rain and all trucks. Muttering, he pulled a cigarette pack from his plaid jacket, tucked a cigarette behind his ear, and tapped the pack again. A paper worm tumbled into his palm.

"Is that a joint?"

Mitch scowled as if I'd asked a really dumb question. "What, this? Just a pinstripe, you know, a little something to take the edge off. Hey, you and I used to get high together, remember?"

"Nobody, especially you, smokes anything in my car, understand?"

Something inside felt good as I watched Mitch put away his joint. It's not that I cared one way or the other about pot. I smoked it in the old days, who didn't? But I quit that sort of thing a long time ago when a soul-shuddering tragedy destroyed my heart, and drowned my joy down to the last ember. Pot can be an amplifier, and I never wanted to turn its funhouse lens upon the grief that smothered my life.

The wind had let up some, but in its place the rain came roaring down, pummeling the car with newfound vigor. Denied his smokes, Mitch pouted like a child, which made me despise him even more.

"Why don't you just go? Haven't you screwed my life up enough?"

Mitch's eyes narrowed. "Brad, you ever seen a million bucks, cash, ever? That's gotta be one, sweet sight."

"Why should I believe that some rich— moron wants to pay us that kind of money?"

"That's true, he's very rich," Mitch said, nodding.

"Who's the guy, Mitch?"

"Him? Oh, he's harmless. He just likes to party and spend money, you know, like one of those connoisseur guys."

"The name, right now, or you're walking back to Wendy's."

Mitch swallowed. "Pablo Lupa," he said softly.

"Lupa? Where have I heard that name? This guy isn't some sort of drug dealer, is he?"

Mitch cocked his head like a curious dog. "Excuse me? Mr. Lupa is *not* a drug dealer. He just happens to be one of the wealthiest men in South America. Hangs with a lot of big-name European bands. Everybody who's anybody knows him."

"Where'd he get his money?"

"Like, I'm supposed to know? His cash is green, ain't it?"

"And you expect us to stay at this guy's ranch? In South freakin' America? Do you know how weird that sounds?"

"Brad, all that matters is that this cat's rich and he's paying cash money. Lots of people have flown down there and partied with the dude. Iggy Krotch and his band just made the trip. I'm tellin' ya man, it's cool. It's gonna be one righteous week full of gettin' high, gettin' laid, and gettin' rich. And that, my friend, is called livin' the good life."

"I can understand why this Pablo Lupa would want to fly Iggy Krotch's band down there, but why us? The Jammies had one hit that barely cracked the Top-10, and our second album tanked. Nobody plays our music or even remembers us, thanks to you."

Mitch scowled at the windshield, as if the driving rain had scribbled curses upon the glass. "Well, maybe I forgot to mention it, but you guys had bigtime record sales in South America. Especially that second album, where you played all that heavy rock and jazz stuff— what was the name of that record?"

My stomach tightened, and it wasn't due to fast food. "*Jamrods.* In case you forgot, that was also our band's original name. Know what burns me? The Jamrods could have amounted to something if we would have stayed true to our music, we were damned good. Should have told you and that record company to take a flying leap. But no, we listened to you, we got greedy. And the kicker? We changed our name to the Jammies, sold out, got a hit record— and ended up broke."

Mitch heaved a sigh. "Look, OK, I screwed up, but I saw an opportunity to invest the studio advance money, so I went for it. I did it for the band." Mitch shook his head. "Besides, those record company assholes had it in for you guys. Tried to kill your second album, but they forgot to get the word down to their South American distributors. Your LP sold like crazy down there. Pablo Lupa was a huge fan— yours were the first two records he ever bought. Played 'em till they wore out. Knows every song by heart. To him, you guys were as big as the Stones."

"The Stones' manager never ripped them off. What ever happened to the royalties from all those records we supposedly sold down there?"

Mitch flinched as thunder cracked.

"Well, you know how those record companies are— you got yer expenses, yer advances, yer this and yer that, but hey, we're talkin' peanuts compared to what we're gonna make off this one gig. Think of it, man— fly to South America, jam for this cat, and bingo, it's the 70's again. Only this time, we're instant millionaires. All of us."

"We're short one keyboard player."

"So? You still play guitar, don't you?"

I hesitated.

"You were the best. Jimi Hendrix asked about you once. Said you were hot."

"C'mon, Mitch, Hendrix was dead way before we got to Hollywood."

"Well, must have been Clapton or one of those cats. You know how I am with names, right?"

Although I knew Mitch was lying, how I wished Jimi Hendrix would have noticed me. When I was still a teenaged, three-chord-playing, growing-his-hair-long, punk-assed wannabe, I saw Hendrix perform in San Francisco. I couldn't believe anyone could do that with a guitar! It was as if a musical god had descended to earth to show us mortals what could be— if only . . . .

"Still got your old axe?" Mitch asked.

"Maybe." My Fender Stratocaster was tucked away in my closet. I couldn't recall the last time I'd touched my old friend.

"Talk to Jon or Danny lately?"

"No, I haven't. On that MV-1 show they said Jon was living in a Colorado monastery and Danny was holed up in the Rocky Mountains in some militia camp. Sounds like they're both wigged out, and I doubt if either one plays anymore. That's what you did to us. We ended up hating everything— the music, those record company jerk-offs, and especially you. At Frank's memorial, Danny swore that the next time he saw you he'd kill you with his bare hands. Still want to get the band back together?"

A brilliant flash cut the gloom and a snapping roar rattled the car. Mitch grimaced as the boom faded into the wail of wind and rain.

"Danny— said that?"

"Yeah, said he'd squeeze the life out of you nice and slow. And he meant it, too."

Color drained from Mitch's face.

"Brad, c'mon, that's ancient history, right?"

"Seems like yesterday to me."

"I'll bet Danny won't even remember. Besides, he was always sayin' weird stuff. But he was a damn good drummer. And you know what? I'll bet Jon can still sing and handle a bass guitar. Gotta be like riding a bicycle, right?"

"Frank fell off his bike a long time ago."

Mitch took a deep breath. "Here's the deal— Pablo Lupa plays keyboards and he wants to jam with you guys, so he must already know the songs, right?. Tell you what, I'll make a call and arrange your cash advance tonight. Five figures. Is there a problem with me bringing you that much cash money?" He waited with smug, spidery patience.

I exhaled through clenched teeth.

"Brad, what do you have to lose? You got something going on in this town worth a million bucks? Look at you, you take pictures for a living, you're driving around in a beater. Where's your threads? C'mon, man!"

I stared at the churning windshield. No, I didn't have a thing to lose, especially compared to the promise of that kind of money. Actually, the photography business hadn't been too good lately. I glanced out the window at the ghostly image of a lone car, slogging past my Honda, struggling through the deluge. Thunder banged overhead.

"Brad, let's make this real simple. Yes or no, may I bring you a large amount of cash tonight?"

"Knock yourself out."

Chad Peery

2

I unlocked the door to Carol's house, a ranch-style cocoon. Carol sat on pillows near the muted TV, hunched over a book. She was an agoraphobic, and concealed the windows behind heavy drapes, as if she feared being sucked through the panes into the vast horror of the outdoors. Perhaps her edgy vulnerability was what attracted me to her— I suppose every man needs to be someone's hero.

Home. And the children. Three-foot-tall dolls, dressed in colonial-era children's garb sat in miniature chairs, while others gazed stoically from display cases. Carol's favorite doll, dressed in royal blue and leaning on a cane, stood on a pedestal next to a rubber plant. The dolls' faces carried the inane imprint of bliss, which lately, had begun to creep me out.

A wrought-iron banister flowed into the sunken living room with its brass-and-glass fireplace, which had never held a fire. From the walls, photographs of Carol gazed down with an expression of attractive pain and mock concern.

"Finished up early," I said, as I set down my camera bag.

Carol glanced up from her novel, all blonde hair, glasses, and sweet curves. She wore her favorite silk robe, and flashed a reflexive smile.

I sank into the black-leather sofa and rested my eyes on the television. Wide-eyed reporters, using their best game-show expressions, were aghast at the latest scandal. I clicked off the remote.

That afternoon, I had taken some shots of a decaying, art-deco dump in South Beach. A Hollywood film company was considering it for a movie location, and this was the first decent-paying job I'd had in a while. All I could think of at the photo lab was Mitch's offer. It now occurred to me that greed and the prospect of easy money wasn't really what had me fascinated to the point of distraction— it was the idea of playing music again, of getting it right this time. And being free— really free.

"You had some disturbing calls today," Carol said, while pretending to read her book. "A man with an odd accent asked a lot of annoying questions about that old band of yours. Right after that, a dirty-sounding man phoned. He told me that you took pornographic pictures and wanted to hire you. He was so rude I had to hang up on him. Brad, is there something you're not telling me?"

"Hire me to do *what?*"

Carol slammed the book shut. "Brad, are you taking porn pictures? Are you that desperate?"

"Dammit, you know better than that. Who was this guy? Did you get his number?"

"Caller ID said the number was blocked. Pornographic photos, Brad?"

"Gotta be somebody connected with Mitch."

"Mitch?"

"My old manager. Saw him today. Offered me a million dollars."

Carol dropped her book. "For what? To take dirty pictures?"

"No! He wants us to put the band back together. Some rich guy in South America supposedly wants the band to play for him."

"And you said yes?"

"Not exactly."

Carol threw down her reading glasses. "Brad! Are you insane? You said no to a million dollars?"

"I'm thinking it over. It's for some guy I've never heard of, and it seems like there's always some sort of trouble going on down there. Besides, this deal may not be on the level. Mitch is a lying thief— I can't believe a thing he says. He might be trying to pull some kind of scam to save himself from loan sharks."

"See? That's your problem. You always go negative."

"Negative? You don't really know me every well, do you?"

"All I need to know is that you're stuck taking pictures for a living, if that's what you call it." She gestured at the dark television screen. "Haven't you've seen what's going on out there? Do you know what Y2K is going to do to our economy, the banks, everything? On what you earn, it's a good thing you don't have a family to support."

"Not much chance of that around here, is there?"

She gave me a spiteful stare. A familiar, dark feeling juiced up inside me, seeping from the wound where I used to love her.

"Brad, quit playing these games. I was up front with you, wasn't I? When we first met, I told you I never wanted children. Sometimes you have such a loser's attitude."

"Attitude? At least I don't pretend that a bunch of stupid dolls are the real thing."

A timid rapping at the front door interrupted our argument.

Carol grimaced. "If it's kids peddling something, get rid of them, I'm getting a headache. And don't give them any money—they'll just keep coming around."

I opened the door. A neatly dressed boy and girl shifted on their feet, their eyes cast downward. I figured they must have overbearing parents, just like I once had. If these were my kids, they wouldn't behave like beaten-down dogs. The little girl mumbled something about raising money for band uniforms. I traded a twenty-dollar bill for a candy bar.

As the kids walked down the driveway, I noticed a blue Ford Taurus parked across the street. Shadows obscured the driver's face, but I could tell he was watching us, and not in a very friendly way. I figured it was probably the kids' father, one of those overbearing types, and I felt his glare of disdain as I shut the door.

Before Carol and I could return to our argument, the doorbell chimed again.

I expected more kids.

Mitch!

"Man, it's happening, I'm carrying." He glanced over his shoulder at the blue Taurus, and then pushed past me into the foyer, cradling his wadded-up coat it as if it held a newborn.

"Excuse me?" Carol said, getting to her feet.

"Carol, this is Mitch, our old band's manager."

"Oh, yes, Brad has told me so many wonderful things about you, I've been dying to meet you, welcome to our home."

I led Mitch into the living room where he flopped on the black-leather sofa and patted the cushions, inviting us to sit, as if we were his guests.

"Just met with Pablo's attorneys and they were absolutely amazing. Told them to give us a few days, and we'll be ready to rock." Mitch unfolded his coat and fat packets of hundred-dollar bills tumbled across the tabletop. Carol gasped.

Mitch smacked his lips at the packets of cash, as if they were Danish pastries. "Check this out, Brad! Should've seen these guys, dishing out a hundred and fifty thousand bucks in cash. Unreal! This is your advance of fifty K, and there's going to be nine hundred and fifty thousand dollars more for each of us."

Carol released an orgasmic squeal.

"Did you sign an agreement?" I asked.

Mitch chuckled. "Man, that's not how these people do business. Not at all."

"Where's Jon and Danny's share? And what happens if we can't find them? Are these characters expecting their money back?"

"Don't sweat it, we'll find 'em. I put Jon and Danny's share in a safe place, and I had Pablo's attorneys wire my cut to Bernie up in the city. That should keep the ginkster off my back for a few days, if you know what I mean."

"So, if this thing falls apart, you're going to split for Buffalo, and these so-called attorneys are going to come looking for me. Same old Mitch."

Carol put her hand on Mitch's knee. "He didn't really mean that, you know."

"Brad, check out the goods. Nothing says it better than fifty thousand dollars in good-old, American greenbacks."

I picked up a packet. The hundred-dollar bills came fifty to a stack— crisp and new, smelling strongly of money. Were they real? What should I check? Serial numbers? A haunting feeling crept from the currency, up my arms and into my heart— that this would turn out like every other event in my life— badly. Still, a part of me wanted to believe, to play music again, to pull my old Stratocaster out of the closet, make those strings come alive, and then walk away with all that cash.

"Ain't it great, man?" Mitch put a five-thousand-dollar packet to his nose. "Smell that ink, right from the vaults. This is righteous beyond belief. Look," he said, getting up, "I'll meet you first thing tomorrow at the studio. Why don't you see if you can find Jon and Danny?"

"Hold on. Exactly how are we supposed to get down there and back?"

"Pablo Lupa's private jet. The lawyers said we shouldn't sweat a thing, it's all arranged. Brad, I'm telling you, these guys are hooked up with the right people. The fix is in. These days, you gotta be connected."

Smoking Jimi

"Mitch, listen to me, and listen good. We get paid in full before we step on any damned airplane, right?" The moment I heard myself say the words, I knew it was over— we were going.

"Absolutely. You'll get confirmation of the transfer, the whole nine yards. If it doesn't happen like they say, you guys walk, and the deal's off. And don't worry about your passport— they said you won't need that kind of stuff, everything's taken care of. Pablo Lupa's really excited that we're coming down. He's already practicing your songs. Ain't that something?"

"That's wonderful news," Carol said.

"We're on, buddy," Mitch said, as he headed for the door.

"Hold on," I said. "Did you give my phone number out to anyone? We've had some weird calls."

"Not me." Mitch picked up the candy bar from the hall table. "Hey, check this out, my favorite."

"Please, help yourself," Carol said.

Mitch pocketed the candy bar. "Cool. Tomorrow then?"

As I let Mitch out the front door, I noticed that the blue Taurus was no longer parked across the street. In its place, a shadowy, malignant vibe remained.

Chad Peery

3

I blinked awake to Carol's collection of miniature carousels, frozen mid-twirl beneath the poster of a couple close dancing, printed from a series I'd sold to a national magazine. Last night Carol had argued and she locked herself in the office— which kept me off the computer, so that I wouldn't check out Pablo Lupa or find anything to dissuade me from going to South America. Even though a large insurance settlement had padded her way through life, she had always said, "You can never have too much money."

Last night, after arguing with Carol, I had dug out my old address book and called Jon's mother, who lived in my hometown of San Jose, California. After giving me Jon's Colorado address and phone number, she explained that that my old bass player lived in the monastery of some secretive religious order. "He run off with them damned Vituscans, whoever the hell they are. My son, my own flesh and blood, he never writes, you know it's been years."

I couldn't bring myself to call Jon's number. If he refused to go, it would all be over— no South America, no million dollars, and part of me wanted to keep the dream alive. I couldn't get a lead on our drummer, Danny Dugan. I finally found one Dugan in the San Jose phone book who recalled Danny: "I knew that punk," the elderly man had said, "always in trouble, gettin' in fights. He was one of them rock musicians, always high on something, you know how those people are."

The MV-1 Jammies special had described Danny as a mountain-bound hermit. I formed a mental picture his cabin— a paranoiac's lair, bristling with guns and strung with booby traps. I figured that Jon would be able to find him, since they had always been close, at least back in the band days.

Carol drifted into the bedroom and sat next to me on the bed. Mornings used to be our favorite time for lovemaking. When we first met three years ago, she made me feel like the hero I'd always wanted to be. I immediately fell into the deep end of the love pool, sold my condo, and moved in with her. But now, I was just another of her oversized dolls, a part of her insipid collection, and this doll was ready to walk. Restless thoughts tugged like little fiends. What if we couldn't find Danny? Could any of us still play? What about the dangers?

"Any requests for breakfast?" Carol asked in her cutest voice.

"Pancakes sound good." She hadn't made breakfast in months. It's amazing how the prospect of money changes things.

Carol put on a satisfied air and walked out the door with extra movement in her curves. Her shape still reminded me of Gjerna, the only woman that I had ever loved with both body and soul.

As I showered, I reviewed a mental checklist. Which cameras and lenses to take? I had a few nickel-and-dime portrait sessions on the calendar. Reschedule? I laughed, thinking how I could be returning from South America a millionaire. Millionaire! Then, I'd show the world what a real photographer could do.

As I shaved, I felt a familiar disappointment. Sure, I could pass for a worn-out thirty-something, but I still thought of myself as twenty-five, and it wasn't fair that the mirror didn't reflect that. I threw on a black polo shirt with khaki trousers, smiling as I recalled Mitch telling me I resembled Jim Morrison.

In the living room, my guitar case sat upon the tiled floor, its velvety interior yawning open. Reclining in its velvet bed, my sky-blue Fender Stratocaster still bore the scars where I used to strum, and the fingerboard's finish was worn through where I learned my first chords. I picked up my old guitar, hefting the familiar weight. Corroded strings dug into my fingertips, and when I plucked the E-string, it snapped like a rotten rubber band. A great sadness came over me.

"Brad, honey, I thought you might like to practice, so I brought out your guitar."

I promised my Stratocaster a new set of strings, and gently laid my old friend to rest.

As I ate pancakes, I counted out forty thousand dollars. With the calmness of a bank teller, Carol watched me spread crisp, hundred-dollar bills next to the empty fruit bowl and my cluster of vitamin bottles.

"I'm taking ten thousand with me, and I'll leave forty thousand with you for safekeeping, just in case something happens. OK?"

"You mean—" She blinked, as if pushing back unpleasant thoughts. "Don't worry, honey, you'll be fine. Last night I couldn't sleep, so I went on the Internet."

I ignored her obvious lie. "Find anything on Pablo Lupa?"

She gave the money a devious glance. "Not much, really."

"What's that mean?"

She shrugged. "Well, I did learn that Pablo Lupa inherited a lot of money. He's a free spender, likes the company of musicians, and lives in a big South American estate. That's all there was."

I took another sip of coffee. It had turned cold.

"Why do I get the feeling that's not all there was?"

"Brad honey, don't be negative, you'll be amazed how different things will be if you just believe. You know I'm behind you one hundred percent." She sat back, all smiles and sweet curves.

* * *

Fort Lauderdale traffic was crowded with the usual mix of beaters and luxury cars. I sang to a Sam Cooke tune on the Oldies station, and then laughed out loud, thinking of all the money I was going to earn playing a few lame songs for some rich eccentric. It seemed as if an ancient, stone wheel had begun turning, and this newfound momentum made my heart shine like the sun after a storm. No more portrait work! I had always dreamed of being free to do creative photography. Money meant freedom— real freedom, like I had known only once in my life, so long ago. I had earned that million dollars, every cent of it, by swallowing the slow poison of the empty years of my life.

As the sun dimmed the Stones' *Paint it Black* came on the radio, and the creepy feeling of being stalked cast a shadow. I checked the rearview mirror. Who could tell in all this traffic?

I parked at the rear of my photography studio behind Las Olas Boulevard, and checked things out. Nothing unusual— just the butt-ugly backsides of trendy storefronts. When I reached my studio's backdoor, my stomach fell. The alarm was off! Had I forgotten to set it? Were those fresh scratches? I unlocked the deadbolt. Insurance covered my equipment— lighting, flash pods, a computer, a medium-format Mamiya, plus a few older Nikons and lenses. Luckily, my top-line Nikon and best lenses were safe in my bag. As I entered the studio, I sensed that my sanctuary had been violated, but also that the intruder had vanished, leaving only his breath's exhaust— a vapor trail to nowhere.

Enough foolishness. It looked like everything was where it should be. As I set my camera bag on the desk, languid models gazed from the walls along with creative baby shots and a few artistic black-and-whites. At one time, I reasoned that if I'd come close to making it big in music, then why couldn't I find success as a photographer? As always, I had an artistic vision, but that creativity was under appreciated. I often took a unique, imaginative approach to wedding or portrait photography, but lately, my referrals were falling off.

I turned on the computer. In a few minutes, I'd hop onto a search engine and see what I could discover about Pablo Lupa. A check of the answering machine revealed three hang-ups, and then came an irritating voice with a Miami accent, claiming to be a photographer who had met me at a party. He bragged about how much money he'd just made doing porn, offered to get me in, and gave his cell number. My heart raced as I scribbled down the information. Now I would find out who the hell had been calling my home with porn offers. I felt as if I were scrubbing graffiti when I hit the delete button.

Someone pounded the glass of my front door.

Mitch!

The comedic wig and phony moustache provided a clownish frame for his panic-stricken scowl. I unlocked the door. Clutching a briefcase, Mitch pushed past me into the studio.

"Where the hell you been, man? I was parked out there damned near an hour. We're not alone, either. Check out that blue Taurus down the street. These guys just showed up, and they're checking us out."

I peered out the window. "Looks like the car parked across from my house last night. Thought it belonged to those kids' father." I snapped a 400-mm telephoto lens into my Nikon, and used the viewfinder as a telescope.

"Two guys," I said. "Maybe fifty yards out. Looking this way. That's odd. The passenger appears young, but he has white hair."

Other than those two strangers, the street seemed normal for that time of morning— the occasional Lexus, an in-line skater, and old man Pierce washing his antique store's windows. The sensation of being watched was intense.

"Dammit," Mitch said. "Gotta be Bernie's boys from the city. But why? I called him last night, told him Lupa's lawyers

Smoking Jimi

were sending him fifty grand, and now he does this. Can't trust nobody."

"How much do you owe this guy?"

"A few bucks. No big deal."

"How much?" I asked, as I led Mitch away from the door.

"Oh, what, two hundred fifty thousand, plus interest. Probably up to three by now. Hey, I hit a bad patch, got on the wrong side of things, then my partner backed out of a deal, ripped me off."

"Imagine that. Great feeling, isn't it?"

"Hey, look! The white-haired guy's gettin' outta the car!"

I framed him in my lens. The man was my height and build, trim, perhaps six feet tall, and in his late twenties. Strands of snow-white, shoulder-length hair lifted in the breeze as he walked toward us. Watching him, I felt an air of familiarity, and then the sickening jolt of a prey's premonition.

Mitch punched his palm. "Let's ditch these guys. Got your car?"

"Out back."

Mitch grabbed his briefcase. "We're outa here. Go."

I locked the front door, threw some film into my camera bag, grabbed my cell phone, and hustled Mitch out the back door. I was so nervous that when I started the car, I twisted the ignition so hard the key almost snapped off. As the engine roared to life, I checked the alley. A scruffy dog barked at a Dumpster near the street. What could be in that container? Someone hiding? Watching? One way to find out. I put the Honda in gear, punched the gas, and when we reached the Dumpster I hit the brakes hard and sounded the horn. The lid of the trash container rose. A face like a crumpled beer can peeked out. Dead eyes cringed. The dog chuffed, greeting the bum with a wag of his tail.

"What's with you?" Mitch shouted at me. "Move this goddam car, for Christ's sake!"

I tore onto Southeast 10th and floored it. Mitch scrunched around in the seat, watching for the blue Taurus, his eyes gone wild. We sped past crowded rows of homes, and then I cut a quick left, squealing onto Southeast Second Street. I saw an opportunity, and so I braked hard, skidding into the driveway of a private residence, nearly throwing Mitch into the windshield.

"What the hell?"

"Shut up and stay down," I said.

We had pulled onto a driveway that separated two houses. I drew the Honda up to a garage at the rear of the property and yanked the emergency brake. From the street came a flash of blue as the Taurus sped by. I cursed as I let out a long breath, aware that my heartbeat was racing faster than that Taurus.

"Jesus, man, those guys must really want my ass," Mitch said.

"Probably have to wait in line." I made sure the Taurus was out of sight before I pulled onto the street, and then doubled back toward Las Olas. "They'll get dumped onto an eastbound, one-way street. We'll be long gone by the time they figure it out."

Mitch snapped open his briefcase. "Bastards would like to get hold of this, wouldn't they?" Rows of hundred-dollar bills stared at me, crisp and green.

"Who's in the Taurus, Mitch? That car was parked on my street last night when you came over."

He cleared his throat. "Don't know. Guy with the white hair kinda looks like Edgar Winter, you know, that cat who plays the—"

"I know who Edgar Winter is. You rip him off too?"

Mitch gave me a look.

"How do we know these guys aren't Pablo Lupa's pals, keeping an eye on his little investment? And some creep's been calling my house and my studio. You were in such a rush that I left his number behind. What the hell you got me mixed up in?"

Mitch snapped his briefcase shut. "Maybe those guys are after you instead of me. Ever think of that?"

"After me? For what, decking you in Wendy's?"

Mitch took out a cigarette, and then grimaced as he cradled it in his palm, unlit.

"I'm callin' this whole thing off," I said. "It's getting too damned weird."

Mitch gestured at the dash. "Man, think! What do you have to lose? You got something cooking in this stinking town that I don't know about? You gonna walk away from a million bucks just 'cause of two guys in a Taurus? Tell you what we're gonna do. We're gonna make tracks and leave these pecker heads in the dust. Screw 'em."

I crowded my Honda onto Sunrise Boulevard, and headed west toward I-95. Mitch was right. What did I have to lose?

Portrait photography? Carol? Wasn't life supposed to be more than just a lame excuse for not being dead?

"So, you ever get a chance to find Jon?" Mitch asked.

I took a deep breath. "He lives in Wort Rock, Colorado, in some monastery. Couldn't find Danny."

"Jon'll know where he is. Let's get our butts down to the airport."

"I have Jon's phone number."

"You didn't call him, did you?"

"No."

"Good." Mitch heaved a sigh. "We gotta handle things the right way— in person. No telling where Jon's head's at. We might need the old persuader," he said, patting his briefcase. "Gimme your cell phone, I'll get us a flight outta there."

"Right now? Today?"

Mitch rolled his eyes.

"What about your car?" I asked.

"You mean that delivery van? Borrowed it from a guy up in the city."

"You can't leave it in front of my studio. It'll get towed."

"You gotta think large, man, we're millionaires now. I'll take care of him later."

"Remind me to never lend you anything."

Mitch cocked his head. "Hey, I gotta do what I gotta do. Let's just get our butts out to Colorado before something goes bad. I got a feeling, and my feelings are never wrong."

"Yeah, Mitch, you're a regular psychic hotline." I turned northbound onto I-95, keeping watch in the rearview mirror. My cell phone rang.

Mitch turned white. "Don't answer!"

"It's just Carol."

She sounded as if she were lonely, making up a reason to call. "Brad, honey, I wanted to let you know I put the money away safely."

"Carol, something's happened, and I have to leave town right away. If strangers come to the door, don't answer. Watch the caller ID. If you don't know who it is, let the answering machine get it. Tell anyone who asks that I'm out on a shoot somewhere. There were some guys waiting for us at the studio. I think they know where I live."

"Brad, honey, your guitar?"

I pressed the mute button. "Mitch, what about my guitar and passport? I could zip back home—"

"No! Why take a chance? Christ, we'll buy you a new guitar, we're millionaires, man! And forget your passport, I told you that you don't need it, didn't I?"

"C'mon, you gotta have a passport."

Mitch fingered his fake moustache. "These people are connected. They'll get us down there and back, no problem."

"Getting back's the part that worries me."

"I'm tellin' ya, it's no big deal. Sometimes, you gotta take a chance. That's life, ain't it?"

I returned the phone to my ear. "Carol, I'll call you tonight."

I handed the cell phone to Mitch. "Get us a flight out of West Palm Beach, I doubt if anybody will be watching for us all the way up there. I can't believe those two bastards were hanging around my studio, and my house too! Who are these people?"

"I honest-to-god couldn't care less. Let's just blow town, get the band back together, and get this show on the road."

4

As the Boeing leveled off, I reclined my leather seat. I should have known better than to let Mitch call in our reservations. With wrinkles of concern pasted over his lying face, he had told me that only first-class seats were available for the flight to Atlanta, and the same for the connecting flight to Denver, so we'd need to reserve them right away before they were gone. The connecting flight to Denver was the same as the one out of West Palm— two of us sat alone in the first-class cabin, while the coach section behind us was half-empty. On the good side, we had left South Florida and White Hair behind hours ago, and even though I had paid for the first-class tickets with cash, my wallet still bulged.

Mitch pressed the call button. Our flight attendant, a redhead around my age, greeted us with a professional smile.

"I'll have a Bloody Mary, and my friend will have one too," Mitch said.

"Make mine Diet Pepsi, please."

Mitch grabbed my arm and whispered, "Order a real drink for me and we'll get you a damned Pepsi later."

"Sir, I'll bring you two drinks if you like, it's not a problem," she said, with an attractive kind of amusement. "Anything else I can get for you," she asked, as our eyes met.

I lingered in the dreamy folds of her gaze for a moment, before I managed to tell her no thanks.

As she walked away, Mitch tugged my sleeve. "She's a hot one, I think she wants me."

"Mitch, you could count the women who want you on a hand with no fingers."

I had to admit, she was easy on the eyes, and come to think of it, I had never been with a redhead, which made her all the more intriguing. But this wasn't the time or place.

Mitch tilted his head towards me. "Gimme some money."

"Money? What do you call that stuff in your briefcase?"

"That's Jon and Danny's cash. Gotta keep that hundred K for them. Can't be short, they gotta think this is on the level. Lemme borrow, say, you know, twenty of them benjies for some walking-around money. Hey, don't give me that look— you're a millionaire, man! Gotta start thinking large, living large, you know?"

"What do you need that kind of money for?"

"Hey, it's just a loan. No problem, I'll pay you back before we get on Pablo's jet."

"Oh yeah? And who's going to pay me back after Danny kills you with his bare hands?" I stifled a grin as Mitch blinked back unpleasant thoughts. Counting twenty of my hundreds into his palm, I tried to think of it as play money.

After the drinks arrived, Mitch poured both mini-bottles of vodka into a glass and topped it off with tomato juice. After several swallows, he let his head fall back against the headrest.

"Hey Brad, got any kids?"

"No."

"How come?"

"Don't know. Suppose I put it off for later, or the women I was with never wanted any, or, well, it was always something. I thought one day there would be a time for that, but it just never happened." The rest was none of Mitch's business, how each passing year hung heavy with a longing for the son or daughter I never had, and probably never would. Why did I always end up with the same sort of women? Why didn't I learn?

Mitch drained his glass. "Family's the most important thing. I got two kids, both with my ex-wife. I don't see 'em much, but they know who I am. At least I got that."

While Mitch ambled about the aisle, stretching his legs, I gazed out the window, contemplating the women of my past. Thinking back, it was hard to tell one from the other— three years and out was the pattern. At one time, I believed Carol would be different. Now, just as I knew Mitch was a lying thief, I understood that Carol and I had reached our time. She had turned out like the others— it was as if I had been a beat-up doll handed down from one uncaring sister, to the next, to the next.

The plane bucked through an air pocket, reminding me of that bumpy ride in 1971 when the Jammies went on a European tour. We were the opening act for the Electric Butterfly, and our three-week tour went by in a wild flash of sold-out concerts across Europe, finishing up in Denmark.

I smiled in a sad way, recalling those two weeks in Copenhagen with a beautiful blonde named Gjerna. I keep her letters and one precious picture stored in a safe-deposit box. That faded photo is all that's left of her now— and it represents the one time in my life that really meant anything.

I thought back to that Copenhagen concert, and how we had just begun playing when I noticed her sitting in the front row. While other fans did their ridiculous carrying on, she looked straight into me, as if we were the only two people in the room. Time after time, I was drawn to her soft, blue eyes, so entrancing that once I even slipped up and forgot the chord changes. When I motioned her to meet me at the side of the stage, she nodded with a sly smile. Yes! I was going home with this one! Grinning to myself, I fantasized about the night I was about to have. When the encore finally ended, I giddily rushed to the side of the stage to claim my prize.

There she stood.

She was somewhere in her late teens, but so what? Scandinavian countries view things differently, I told myself. I led her backstage to the dressing room where we talked for a while. She was so attractive that even Frank, our gay keyboard player, seemed to be admiring her. Soon, Gjerna and I shared the backseat of a taxicab, on our way to the hotel, and I congratulated myself. What an incredible night this was going to be! Sure, pulling chicks was easy back then, I did it now and again. But this one, I thought as I stifled a chuckle, just wait till I get her back to the hotel, I'm going to slowly unwrap her like a Christmas present, take my time and really enjoy her.

When we got to my room and Gjerna removed her jacket, I almost bit my tongue. This had better not be a dream, I chortled to myself. We sat on the bed and talked, getting to know each other in simple English phrases— hers colored with a charming Scandinavian accent. I offered her a drink, and in her sweet way, she said no. As we talked, it dawned on me that I was in the presence of an intelligent young lady, which left me feeling awkward and ill at ease. Here I sat, next to a stunning woman who could easily have defined female perfection for the next hundred years, and I was tongue-tied! Hadn't I brought her to my room as a prize for my youthful hormones, her body mine to ravish and brag about the next morning? Then, why had I become a kid on his first date, frozen by her light, intoxicated by her closeness?

That night was a gift for which I was totally unworthy. Through the fog of memory, I can still see the mist of our souls making love, swirling, intertwining, leaving the empty shells of our physical forms behind.

The first glow of dawn opened the most beautiful day I've ever known. Even though I'd only been with Gjerna a few hours, I marveled at how we bonded so completely, as if we'd drawn upon a familiarity brought forward from a past life. When we held each other and watched the sunrise, it was the most powerful moment of my life.

Now, she's just a precious memory, and God, how many times have I wished that I hadn't left her there? Every cell in my body still longs for that woman, my sweet Gjerna, Now, she's gone forever, at least until the next life finds us again. Perhaps then we won't be cheated the way we were this time.

I gazed out the jetliner's window at puffy clouds, as soft and unique as her, floating beneath a deep-blue sky. I smiled, recalling our first few days together, and how the two of us floated like clouds through that timeless city, adventure and romance at every turn.

When I told Mitch I was staying a few more days in Copenhagen and wouldn't be flying back with the band, he went ballistic:

"So, she's a babe, the world's full of babes, and I got this deal cooking that'll take us right to the top. Brad, don't be a jerk, you're gonna have babes like that one lined up outside your door every night. I can just see it now: ya got yer blonde, yer brunette, yer redhead, and ol' Brad's got 'em all mixed up together in bed to where ya can't tell who's doin' what to who, and man, he just gets this big ol' grin and jumps right in the middle a' that ol' pussy casserole! It don't get no better, am I right? Huh? Ya ever done that? No? Then why would you want to get yourself hung up on just one babe? We got that big California gig coming up, and we gotta go back in the studio. This ain't the time, man. Tomorrow, your ass is on that plane, or else!"

On the return flight to America, Mitch's rump sat next to my empty seat, while Gjerna and I spent another perfect day in Copenhagen. We strolled past blooming gardens in tranquil parks, and explored quiet streets along peaceful canals. We watched the world go by from a sidewalk cafe, where passers-by smiled at this young couple so in love. I'd never been so high. For those few, precious days, I had something beyond love with Gjerna, and it will stay with me until my last breath.

Smoking Jimi

On the phone earlier that day, Gjerna had a tense conversation with her parents. She told them everything was OK and she was fine, but they were furious: "Seventeen is too young," they told her. "Come home now."

We just didn't care. We were the whole world, and nothing else mattered— the band, parents, Mitch, nothing. Some might say I was a young fool, after all, I was only twenty. But I know better. Those incredible days flowed from eternity, and she will always be my forever.

The clock, in its cruelty, pared away the hours, and soon, it was time to leave. We agreed that we would get married, live in California, and have three, maybe four children. I promised I would come back for her as soon as I finished recording our third album. She explained that calling her from America would be impossible because of her parents, and that once she returned home, they wouldn't let her out of their sight. We promised to write to each other every day, and vowed to never forget a single moment we had shared.

Upon my return to Hollywood, all hell broke loose. The big California gig fell through, and Mitch disappeared along with most of our money, including a big recording advance from the record company. The band had bitter arguments— the guys saying that it was my fault, that I should have been there, and it was my idea to sign Mitch as our manager. Despite that, Gjerna and I wrote every day. At least I had her.

The record company filed charges and started a lawsuit over the missing advance money. I became depressed, proceeded to get exceptionally drunk, and then did an ugly, stupid thing. I wrote Gjerna a letter. Through a haze of alcohol, I told her that I'd made some bad choices, I was broke, and I didn't know when I would be able to get back to Copenhagen. I'm not sure if I even remembered to tell her I loved her. God knows what else was in that letter, if only I could remember.

After that, her letters stopped. I wrote her daily, apologizing again and again. I even tried calling, but her parents refused my calls, pretending they couldn't understand English and hanging up.

Some days later, I received a terse letter from her parents: Gjerna is dead. Suicide. Damn you Brad Wilson. Burn in hell.

I frantically tried calling— disconnected, no forwarding number. I sent a telegram— no response. I wrote letter after letter. All were returned, marked "deceased." I even called the hotel I had stayed at in Copenhagen. They checked the newspaper for me, and found her name in the obituaries.

Jon, Danny, and Frank helped me survive those hellish weeks. I don't know what would have happened if I had been alone— I desperately wanted to join Gjerna, for without her I had no reason to live. Jon jumped ship and signed with an independent label that promised him a solo deal. The lawsuits raged on and our lawyers burned up what little money we had. Jon's record deal fell through. Our band was finished. I didn't care. My Gjerna was dead, and all because of me.

When Frank, our keyboard player, died in my Porsche that night in the desert, I had already been spending long days in my apartment, alone, drunk, and depressed. That night, before I knew of the wreck, I woke in a cold sweat. Frank's voice came to me through the darkness, clear and cold, whispering in my ear: "Death is music, and music is death."

That was the end. I quit drinking. I quit music. I quit life. I despised myself so much, that for many years I wouldn't allow myself a drink or anything else that would get me high, since that would only dull the pain. Honoring that emotional anguish was a sacred debt I owed to both Frank and Gjerna.

The shriek of an alarm startled me.

Above the first-class restroom a red light flashed. Cursing to herself, our flight attendant fumbled with a key at the restroom door. Amidst a cloud of smoke, Mitch opened the bi-folded door, his face crimson.

"What the hell's goin' on?" Mitch shouted over the alarm. "I was in there, and like, wow, everything went crazy!"

"Sir, that's the smoke detector. You were smoking in there."

Mitch cupped his ears against the screeching alarm. "Smoking? No way. I wasn't smoking!"

She leaned into the lavatory and silenced the alarm.

"Sir, I smell smoke. Where's the cigarette?"

"What do you mean? Look, I'm a smoker, my jacket smells like smoke. What?"

While she inspected the lavatory, Mitch smirked and showed me a crumpled cigarette butt. With the expression of a high-school truant, he sneaked the evidence into his jacket pocket.

Smoking Jimi

She rummaged through a disposal bin, gingerly feeling the refuse with the back of her hand. "Sir, that cigarette is a fire hazard. Where is it? The cigarette. Now!"

"This is crazy. That alarm thing's busted, that's all."

"Sir, what you did was a federal offense. I'm going to have to report this."

"Come on, honey, it's all just a misunderstanding, a malfunction, you know? Look, I got one of these old things if that's what you want." Mitch handed over the cigarette butt. "And I got these puppies, too." He unfolded several hundred-dollar bills. Her expression hardened.

"It's a tip. OK? You've given us great service today. How about another round of drinks and we'll call it even?" Mitch slipped the hundreds into her skirt pocket, and then slunk back to his seat, doing a decent imitation of an underaged kid sneaking into a pool hall. The flight attendant stood her ground, her eyes conflicted as she smoothed her uniform. Another attendant joined her, and they walked into the coach cabin, talking quietly.

"Idiot!" I whispered. "Don't you know the planes have smoke detectors?"

"C'mon, you wouldn't let me smoke in your car, I couldn't have a smoke in that damned Atlanta terminal, what am I supposed to do? I had a paper towel over that stupid smoke detector. It worked before. It's no big deal. Besides, money talks. She'd rather pocket them Ben Franklins than have to fill out a complaint form. Wouldn't you?"

"You're insane. They're going to report your ass, and when we land, the police will be all over us. How are you going to explain that money? Dammit! I flew with you before, you never did anything this stupid."

Mitch scoffed. "They used to let you smoke on these damned planes. It's the world that's gone crazy, not me, pal."

Chad Peery

Smoking Jimi

5

I drove our rented Lincoln sedan west on I-70, picking up speed as the four-lane clog of traffic thinned out— mostly supersized SUV's— grownup, toy-box dreams carrying their owners home for dinner and TV. Each exit scooped more of the lunch-box shaped vehicles into Denver's suburbs, while the Interstate took our Lincoln sedan higher into the mountains west of the mile-high city. The thin, dry air parched my Florida throat and my ears popped from the altitude. I checked my watch. Seven fifty-five local time.

"I still say you're an idiot."

Mitch laughed and shrugged. "Hey, didn't I tell ya? You got money, you got a free ride. And you and me my friend, we are on our way!"

Back at the airport terminal, no one at the security checkpoint had even given us a second look. I just wanted to get out of there, but Mitch insisted we stop at a clothing boutique to buy jackets. "Ya gotta live large man, if you don't look like you're somebody, then you're nobody. Besides, you freeze your ass off at night in these mountains." Mitch had bought himself a natural-hued leather sports jacket, while I selected a black bomber jacket, heavy on the hardware.

"This one's on me," Mitch had said, pulling out a wad of my hundred-dollar bills. "Keep the change, sweetheart, I'll be back for you later," he had told the butch-haired, tattooed saleswoman. Now, our new jackets lay in the back seat, reeking of fresh cowhide.

Denver's brown air reminded me of LA, back when the Jammies were a happening band. After the release of our hit single in 1970, our tour bus had taken this same route, rolling through Denver to get to the nation's breadbasket. The terrain still looked the way I remembered it, except much of it was now cluttered with tract homes, strip malls, and motels.

Mitch leaned forward, squinting at stubborn patches of snow that clung to imposing mountaintops, a snuggling white foam along the craggy skyline.

"How the hell can they have snow here in the summer? What a dumb-assed place."

I turned down the Lincoln's air conditioner. Mitch had insisted we rent the best car available. I didn't argue, I didn't need another living-large lecture.

"Places like this— we're talking a penal colony for the brain-dead. There's nothing out here but rocks and trees, and the people are so damned stupid you gotta wonder if the aliens haven't taken over and fried everybody's brains."

"How far before we hit Highway 72?" I asked.

"Get off here."

"This exit?"

"Yeah. Ya got yer Wendy's, ya got yer Holiday Inn, I say we get some dinner and drive up to Wort Rock in the morning. You won't find me on some hee-haw highway after dark. Jon can wait till tomorrow. Know what I mean?"

"What happened to living large? A burger and Holiday Inn?"

"Hey, that's as large as it gets," Mitch said, rubbing his belly.

The village of Dew Knot Pass, population 26, consisted of a cluster of motels, grease joints, and gas stations— a neon leech affixed to an asphalt artery.

Minutes later, we sat in green vinyl chairs in room 211 of Mountain's Best Motel, munching from bags of Wendy's fare. Freeway traffic droned past our gritty windows, while in the distance, the sun ate into a rugged mountain, chewing a glowing edge along the fading skyline. Mitch closed the drapes, releasing a pall of dust into the air conditioner's updraft. He fiddled with his moustache, which had come loose again.

"Why are you wearing that lip crawler?"

Mitch tossed the hairy thing into the wastebasket.

"What about that wig, I mean, who's going to see you?"

Mitch patted his toupee. "I'm kinda liking it, you know? I'm hanging on to this."

With that cheap hairpiece he did resemble his old self of thirty years ago— sort of. I took another bite of hamburger and sat back, savoring the salty tang of forbidden grease.

"So, what do you think old Jon's up to in that monastery?" Mitch asked between bites. "Think he's a rump ranger?"

"I think you are."

Smoking Jimi

Mitch threw a french fry.

"I owe you one," he said, pointing at me.

"You owe me a lot more than that," I said, and took a long drink of Diet Pepsi. "Last I heard anything about Jon was back in the early eighties when he was in law school. Guess he gave that up to become a monk."

"I don't care if he's a goddam monkey, he's back in the band. Afterwards, who cares how he wastes his life?" Mitch threw his crumpled sack at the trash basket, missing badly.

"We're just assuming he can still play bass and sing. And me, I don't even have a guitar."

"Y2K Disaster Looms!" was the headline on our complimentary Denver Times. Mitch tossed the front section aside and went for the classifieds. He dialed the phone.

"How much for that Stratocaster guitar and practice amp, and also the Fender Precision bass . . . that much, huh?" Mitch winked at me. "We're outside of town . . . ."

* * *

After the tattooed teen had dropped off the gear and pocketed a wad of my cash, Mitch hunkered down in the bathroom while I examined my new axe. The burgundy guitar wasn't my old Stratocaster, but it wasn't bad, either. I grabbed a pick. The fingers of my left hand formed chord patterns, and I strummed a bit, making tinny, thin sounds. Although today's stings are lighter and easier on the fingers, my non-callused fingertips were already getting sore. I pressed the whammy bar to dip the pitch of the strings, and it snapped back into perfect tune, unlike my old Stratocaster. I plugged my guitar into the Taxi amp, an amazing little practice amplifier the size of a small wastebasket. It had a rechargeable battery or could be wall powered, and was bright yellow with a black grill. I buried the wedge-shaped amp beneath the pillows so I could crank the volume, yet hold down the sound. These pickups made it easy to control the sustain and attack of the speaker, smothered as it was beneath pillows.

What a thrill to play again, and to have a reason for playing again. Melodies, riffs, and lines I hadn't thought of in years came with increasing ease, and while the dingy film of my wasted life peeled away, my heart sang out with a joy I hadn't felt in years. After a few more minutes, I stopped to shake cramps from my fingers.

Carol! I almost forgot I'd promised to call her. I grabbed my cell phone from the camera bag, and a moment later, Carol's tense voice came through the earpiece.

"Brad, honey, just after you called to say you were leaving, the phone rang again, and caller ID said it was your studio. But when I answered, it was the same disgusting man who called about porn yesterday. Wanted to know where you had gone, so I told him you were out of town, I didn't know where. Did I do OK?"

"You did fine, but what did the caller ID say?"

"It said, 'Brad's Photo Studio.' How could that be?"

My stomach pulled tight. Someone was either using some very sophisticated gear, or someone was calling from my studio and wanted me to know it.

"Did he have an accent, maybe from the Northeast?" I pictured her scowling in thought.

"No, he sounded like he was from somewhere ugly, like overseas. Brad, after he asked where you were, he asked if I knew that you were out chasing around with other women. I hung up on him."

"Other women?" I stifled the urge to curse. "I've been with Mitch all day. Carol, from now on, let the answering machine screen all the calls, and don't open the door for strangers. I'll call tomorrow."

I shut off my cell phone. Did White Hair and his friend break into my studio? Who the hell were these two? I had no enemies, and I didn't believe in coincidences. Mitch appears, and trouble follows. What could he be mixed up in— feds, cons, a drug deal gone wrong? Now, I had become one of the actors on Mitch's warped little stage. A part of me wanted my old life back, to just go home and be with Carol, although I couldn't think of a decent reason why.

I laughed. What a load. My life would never be the same. I stretched out on the bed, releasing a satisfied moan. Someone had punched a fist-sized dent in the ceiling, and I wondered why anyone would vent their anger up there. I took out my Nikon and framed hole with my lens, steadying it as the shutter went click-clack. My first shot of the tour. There would be more. Lots more.

Something, possibly someone's head, thumped the adjoining wall hard enough to rattle my bedpost. Perhaps the party-hardies next door could use a good photographer. Whatever they

Smoking Jimi

were up to, it called for the occasional war whoop, punctuated by a woman's belly laugh.

I examined the fingers of my left hand, their tips red from pressing the strings. If only my parents were still alive, or if I had a brother or sister, it would be nice to have someone to call, someone to share the news with. But outside of a few elderly aunts, there was no one. My ex-girl friends, like snakes, had been cast from the house of my life. My golf buddies were just that, buddies for golf, and I'd never told them about my years with the band, it was not something I was comfortable sharing.

On second thought, it probably wouldn't be good to tell anyone what was happening, not with these two goons snooping around.

Mitch emerged from the bathroom, an invisible cloud of malodor tagging along like an eager puppy.

"Geez, you eat too many of those damned hamburgers."

"Hey, Brad, some of that stuff you were playing sounded great. I'm going out to pick up cigarettes and toothbrushes and razors— ya know, stuff like that, maybe grab a beer on the way back. Want anything? Keep an eye on my briefcase while I'm gone, will ya?"

I tucked the briefcase between my bed and nightstand, while I told Mitch of the phone call to Carol and the stranger's foreign accent.

Mitch shrugged. "Tell you what. We're here, and those two idiots are playin' grab ass down in Florida. Color 'em gone."

* * *

Several hours later, Mitch was still gone. I considered how all hotel rooms are the same— the muffled laughter and slurred voices next door, the whir of the air conditioner, the distant rumble of the freeway. I had taken a hot shower, and now, with eyes closed, I floated upon the murmur of traffic. In the twilight of dreams, I sensed a malicious shadow darkening the stars, hunting me. I retreated into my secret refuge— beautiful visions of Gjerna. She came clear and real tonight— her perfectly formed lips, her eyes bright blue within blue, her sweetness beyond perfection. Still conscious, I reached into the dream, stroking her soft hair, reassuring her that this time I would not fail her, I would stay with her and love her forever. If you could cry in dreams, mine would have been tears of joy.

Chad Peery

6

Two a.m. came early. The door burst open and the lights flashed on, blinding me. Had the noisy party from next door invaded our room? I focused. Two loudly dressed women. Mitch, swaying and grinning, swigging from a whiskey bottle. I cursed. Hookers. Mitch had gotten drunk and brought back hookers.

"Hey, Brad," Mitch slurred, "this is Cindy— and this is Laura— and we're here to *party!*"

Everyone but me laughed and snickered.

"Mitch, you stupid shit. Oh hell. Just hell."

The three of them giggled. The door slammed. I gathered the blanket around my waist and sat up. The moron! Hookers. Why did this surprise me? They were hookers all right, probably making a good living servicing truckers and salesmen marooned on this sorry island of motels and gas stations. Most likely thieves, too. My pants with my wallet were draped over a chair, and the briefcase was tucked between my bed and the nightstand, with my camera bag next to it. I wanted to use the bathroom, but no way was I going to leave that stuff unguarded. It could wait.

The younger of the two sat at the foot of my bed, smiling. How old was she? Nineteen? It was hard to tell behind all that makeup, with her jet-black hair and bedroom eyes. Mitch and the older hooker whooped it up on the other bed, their backs to us, making yummy sounds as they took turns drinking from a bottle.

I squeezed my eyes shut, wishing that this were some bizarre dream. My hooker rustled on the bed. She had opened the front of her top, exposing her bare chest. My eyes locked upon the peaks of her breasts, and something inside me awoke, wanting to ravish those pert mounds. There's something about that uniquely female shade of pink that is designed to genetically evoke a mindless, reflexive craving in men, and my mind followed that well-worn path, loading up on the lust. I smiled and motioned for her to cover up. Why did I do that? Because I was angry with Mitch? Nobody would know, would they? Maybe I just didn't care for the idea of buying and selling human beings.

Hooker or not, she did look good. I mentally sighed as she buttoned up and gave me a smile that almost made me change my mind. Now, she seemed uncomfortable and not sure what to do next.

"You know, like your friend paid for me, you can have me if you want. Whatever you like, you know?" She batted mascara eyes with an impish flair.

"I'm fine. Don't really want anything."

She shrugged, using body language that said I was missing something really good. The smell of burning alfalfa came from the next bed. Pot. Great. I could imagine sheriff's deputies kicking down the door because some concerned citizen smelled suspicious odors wafting from our room. Busted with a prostitutes, drugs, and armloads of cash.

Calling Carol for bail money.

Mitch for a cellmate.

I buried my face in my hands.

My hooker nudged me, raising her eyebrows, her chest puffed out from holding in her smoke-laden breath. She offered me the joint.

I waved her off. I wasn't in a mood to party.

"Don't wanna get high?" she asked, blowing out two lungs' full of cannabis smoke. She took another hit and passed the joint to the other hooker.

"Haven't done that for a while," I said.

"Who's 'a while?' Is she cute?" The hooker sniggered smoke through her nose. "Sorry. Just sounded funny."

I almost smiled. "Now what?" I asked.

She told me her name was Cindy. While she listed her favorite bands, Mitch and Laura tossed their clothes on the floor, giggling, smoking, and swigging.

"You don't drink?" I asked.

"My father drank a lot, mama too," she said darkly.

I told her I was a rock musician. No, she hadn't heard of the Jammies, or the Jamrods either. Yes, I'd been with a lot of girls back in the day. No, I never counted how many. I didn't ask how many men she'd been with, and she didn't say.

The covers from Mitch's bed flew onto the floor. His hooker was a lustily built woman with pasty skin, and Mitch buried his face in her chest like a desert-parched man with two water balloons. "Yeah, baby, yeah," he cried out, his words muffled between great white bosoms.

"What brought you to this— line of work?" I asked Cindy.

"Don't know," she said with a shrug. "What made you become a musician?"

"Don't know," I said. "Guess we're all looking for something."

She sat up, her eyes brightening. "Everybody's looking for something. Problem is, most of us never find it, because we don't really know what that something is."

Her sophomoric notion struck close to the place where I hid uncomfortable thoughts.

"You must love someone very much. What's her name?"

I told her the story of Gjerna. For some odd reason, I had no problem spilling my guts to a hooker while her partner serviced Mitch in the next bed. It seemed the natural thing to do. It had been a long time since I'd told anyone the whole story of Gjerna, and it felt strange to say it out loud. And now, being forced to connect the dots of my life, the patterns made sense, in a sad way.

As I finished my story by saying I wished I'd had children with Gjerna, Cindy dabbed a tear with the sheet. "Why didn't you just take her back to America with you?"

I blinked back tears of my own. "That's a question I'll live with for the rest of my life."

"Fear is the greatest enemy of love, you know that don't you?" She leaned forward and caressed my face with the back of her hand.

"I'm not afraid," I said, uncomfortable at her touch.

"Don't you see? Ever since then, you've been afraid to be with anyone you could love enough to have children with." She gazed at me through misty eyes. "You're afraid you'd lose them, just like you lost Gjerna. But it's OK. We're all afraid. And we all deceive ourselves a little." She glanced at the other bed. "Some of us deceive ourselves a lot."

I took a long breath. "I guess, I suppose I could fall into that second group." Tears formed in our eyes as she leaned over and we hugged and rocked gently, this sweet young woman and me. She wasn't the first to accuse me of obsessive guilt over Gjerna. But those who haven't lost a loved one the way I had lost Gjerna could never understand. That heartache, that precious pain was the only thing of value in my life. It was my connection to her— it kept me alive, and in a way, it kept Gjerna alive too.

Mitch and his partner had finished their rutting frenzy. While she dressed, Mitch slumped on the edge of the bed, swigging more liquor. The whole episode reminded me of the old days on the road, with Jon and a groupie doing their business in the bed next to mine. Sometimes Jon and I would both be getting laid at the same time, and that was cool, but other times, either Jon or I would be the only one doing the deed, and that could get old, especially if the other was trying to watch a good movie on TV. Things were casual back then. Who could say if the groupies were our prizes, or we were theirs, and really, who cared? We were just kids, it was a good time, and that was the way things were.

Laura was dressed now, if you could call being clad in hooker chic being dressed, and she motioned to Cindy it was time to go.

"I hope you find what you're looking for," Cindy said, as she gently touched my cheek. "Or, you never know, sometimes it has a way of finding you."

* * *

While Mitch snored, I stared at the shadowy ceiling, unable to get Cindy out of my mind. The sexuality of my manhood lusted after her body, but my intellectual self found her thoughts intriguing. Cindy reasoned that since I had never stopped loving Gjerna and blamed myself for her death, I wouldn't allow myself to truly love anyone else. What she could never understand was that my painful devotion, my overpowering grief, was something I couldn't live without. To do so, would have meant letting go of Gjerna, and I could no more do that than walk on the moon.

The seeds of her childish honesty sprouted a sudden, disturbing thought. Not allowing myself the one thing I wanted the most, to have children and to be a father, was the ultimate self-punishment for leaving Gjerna behind. Did some vengeful part of me feel that I owed endless debt, the kind that could never be repaid? The more I lingered on such thoughts, the darker the night became.

I pulled the covers close and listened to the murmur of traffic. Who could be out on the highway at this hour? People with hearts as heavy as mine? Perhaps lonely souls who never had a chance, like Cindy. As I drifted off to sleep, I sent fatherly thoughts to her. She was too sweet to be in the bitter business of selling flesh.

7

Somewhere after dawn the snoring drunk on the other bed woke up and banged into the bathroom door.

"Do you have to be so damn noisy?"

Mitch threw open the toilet seat, called out to some deity, retched, and then kicked the bathroom door shut. The shower came on, and he moaned in agony. I smiled. The near-empty whiskey bottle lay on the floor, so I rolled it out of sight before Mitch found it and did a hair-of-the-dog act. He deserved every sweet sliver of pain a hangover could bring.

Perhaps it was Mitch's misery that put a smile on my face as I strolled to the motel office to check out. My breath steamed in crisp, cool air, while the sun, little more than a red disk in the sky, struggled with the clouds. The motel office reeked of cheap bacon, and cartoon racket blasted from a TV. The same goofy desk clerk who had checked us in last night emerged from the back room, pulling a T-shirt over his greasy self. Upon seeing me, he dropped his smile. While he clumsily shuffled paperwork, his eyes went all sneaky, glancing about like a druggie watching for cops. As I walked back to our room I checked things out, and noticed a gray Chevy Blazer parked across the street beyond a hedge. The Blazer's two occupants were looking my direction— White Hair! How the hell? Damn that Mitch! Wherever he goes, trouble follows.

Back in the room, Mitch, now fully dressed, had passed out on the bed and was snoring with his mouth gaping. I kicked his heel. He woke with a start.

"God dammit! Look outside! Your loan-shark buddies."

"What?" Mitch wobbled to the window and peeked through the curtain. "Crap." He scratched his ass thoughtfully.

"That's it," I said. "I'm going down there and tell them to piss the hell off."

"Wait," Mitch said. "I've got a better idea. You go first and take our stuff down to the car. Wait for me there." He ducked into the bathroom and returned with a dripping-wet hand towel. "Be ready to haul ass. Go."

Minutes later, I sat in the Lincoln, wondering where Mitch had gone. After he and his wet towel had disappeared behind the motel, White Hair and his partner had remained in their Blazer, unobtrusively watching me. Then, I spotted Mitch in the bushes, sneaking up behind their vehicle. My hands gripped the wheel, and I checked the ignition, ready to fire up our Lincoln the second Mitch made it back. If he made it back.

* * *

We sped north on State Highway 72, leaving the freeway behind. Our two-lane road swooped and climbed, then temporarily widened into a gracious avenue as we passed the yuppie enclave of Clairvue, with its affluent homes crowded upon the hillside. A glance in the rearview mirror revealed only clean road following our ascent. I laughed out loud, as Mitch adjusted his sunglasses.

"What?"

"Your palm."

Mitch's right palm bore the mark of a black oval the size of an exhaust pipe. He laughed.

"Wonder if those two guys ever got that Blazer started, I really rammed that rock and towel up their tailpipe. I'd like to stuff it up their butts. Bastards."

I had to admit that Mitch was good, the way he'd snuck up behind the gray Chevy Blazer and done his deed, playing the role of a delinquent teen out for mischief on a Saturday night. I wish I'd taken some shots of his escapade.

Mitch puffed his cheeks. "Brad, how'd this happen? Didn't you pay cash for the hotel room?"

"I paid cash, I swear. I used my Visa card, but only to guarantee the room. I also had to show my credit card before they'd let me have a rental car, remember? But I made sure nobody charged anything on the card. I told them I was paying cash, and they said OK."

Mitch backhanded the air. "Dammit. That's how those two goons found us— even if you don't charge anything, they still run your card through to make sure it's good, and they reserve part of your limit. That activity gets reported and the rest is easy. And God, this bloody headache."

"Think those guys are cops of some kind?" I asked.

"Who cares? They're back there scratching their butts, probably thinking we're still on the freeway. Couldn't know we turned off or where we're headed, and we're not going to make any more mistakes with those damned credit cards, are we?"

I gave the steering wheel an angry squeeze. "I should have walked up to that Blazer and told those two sons-of-bitches to stay the hell away from me. I'm sick of this crap, I haven't done anything. Now you, you're a different matter."

Mitch sniffed his armpit. "We need clothes, these threads are gettin' kind of ripe. And I'm starving, must be a Wendy's somewhere. What's that up ahead?" Mitch gestured at an approaching road sign. "Great. Now entering Pulsifer County. Home of your inbred, knuckle-dragging, born-again shit-for-brains and their doublewides with big-haired women and skinny drunks. Saturday-night wrestling. Six packs. Bug zappers. Outhouses. And check out that green, piece-of-shit pickup, they got a gun hanging in their rear window. God, I hate this place."

"What's with you? Didn't you grow up in Oklahoma?"

"Yeah, and I beat feet out of there when I was twelve. I mean, check out those losers in that pickup! Why do you think I live in the city?"

We sped past an elderly Indian couple in their battered green pickup truck, and then slowed for hairpin turns that cut deep into the mountain, our Lincoln's tires squealing in protests. Ranks of evergreens crowded the roadside, their trunks standing guard against civilization.

"What if Jon can't find Danny? What if they're both crazy? What then?" I asked.

"Jon'll find him," Mitch said, craning his neck to peek over the guardrail. "God, that's a long way to the bottom. Danny and Jon always hung together. So first, we get Jon into the program."

I pulled the Lincoln onto a turnout that overlooked the valley we had just passed through. Mitch strolled about, swinging his arms across his chest in little exercising motions, a cigarette dangling from his mouth. I grabbed my Nikon and joined him at the edge of a stone wall, where we pissed over the edge, darkening the sharp-edged rocks below. How different from Florida. The air here tasted virgin and clean, carried upon a sweet breeze that whispered through the boughs of trees.

My photographer's eye framed a series of shots— looking down upon a mosaic of restless treetops immediately below, then on to a steely-blue stream that tumbled down a canyon and rushed over rocks where it smoothed into a mirrored path along a lush meadow. Filling out the distance, like watchful parents, stood a pair of craggy mountains with great hunks of rock flecked in white, the likes of which had given the Rockies their name.

I looked into the Nikon's viewfinder. The 400-mm lens had the magnification of strong binoculars, and I played it along the rocky creek that wandered the valley floor. I let out a happy chuckle as I spotted a buck, a doe, and two fawns drinking from the water's edge. Suddenly, their heads turned in unison. I swung the camera toward the object of their attention. On the highway, a gray Chevy Blazer veered into view.

"Dammit!" I focused again and glimpsed the image of White Hair before the vehicle disappeared around a curve. That horrible feeling clenched in my gut.

"What?" Mitch asked, as the old green pickup truck chugged past us.

"Let's go. They've found us. Coming this way, maybe five miles back."

"Oh, man, how the hell? They had no way of knowing where we were headed." Mitch hopped in and slammed his door.

"What, you think I left a crumb trail?" I punched the accelerator. The Lincoln kicked gravel and tattooed the pavement as we roared onto the highway.

"Maybe they found out we were heading to that stupid town, Wort Rock. Maybe they got a homing beacon on our car. They got something." Mitch sat up straight. "Hey, see that old green pickup? Pull 'em over. And gimme all your cash."

8

I shifted the ailing Ford pickup into third gear, fighting its sloppy steering and limp shocks, working hard to keep the damned thing on the road. A mile or so behind us, the truck's previous owners, an elderly Indian couple, drove our Lincoln rental car, while White Hair's Chevy Blazer was still some distance behind them.

"Mitch, what the hell did you do back there? I can't believe how those two hopped out of their pickup so fast, like you pulled a gun or something."

"I pulled money. You should'a seen! No sooner did I give that geezer the cash, than his wife snatched it, jammed it into her purse, and gave him a look that would kill. Ha! Now they'll drive that Lincoln all the way to the reservation and those bastards in that Chevy Blazer won't have a clue. Sons of bitches. Gotta be Bernie's people."

A pothole jarred my teeth as the pickup bucked and rattled. I struggled with the steering wheel.

"Mitch, you're paying the charges when that car rental company doesn't get their Lincoln back."

"Brad, Jesus man, you're thinking small again. Tell 'em to shove it. I'll buy 'em ten of them cheap-assed cars when we get back."

Mitch jammed his briefcase under the seat, and struggled to roll down his window. "Wish this pile of junk had air conditioning. Where's that damned monastery? I'm starving."

The highway led us into a narrow valley populated by a small cluster of weathered wooden buildings, some of which appeared never to have been painted.

"They call this piece of crap Wort Rock? Maybe they should call it Fart Rock. Ha! You got your regulation trailer court, some falling-down shacks up the hill, and I suppose that dump over there is a gas station. This the whole town?"

"Looks that way. We need to stop for gas. Besides, I want to get a good shot of those two in the Chevy Blazer. I'll focus a telephoto lens on their windshield when they go past, get a shoulder shot of those bastards."

I drove into the gas station and pulled up to an aging gas pump. When I turned off the ignition the engine chugged, and then, with a final knock, collapsed.

"Ain't that Indian Charlie's truck?" an old man called out, sitting near the gas station's door. His grubby clothes defied description. With great effort, he rose from his oil-stained chair. I stared in disbelief. A face like a crumpled beer can. From the Dumpster? No. This man's eyes were sharp and alive.

"Charlie sold us his truck," I said. "Fill it please, hi-test, we're in a hurry."

The old man shuffled off to fill the tank, and I checked my Nikon with its telephoto lens, and made sure it was loaded with high ISO film.

Mitch leaned out of the way. "I know what kind of shot I'd like to take." He rapped his knuckle on the battered shotgun stock in the window rack. The attendant gave Mitch a strange look as he rubbed our bug-crusted window with a rag.

"Here comes the Lincoln," I said, and focused in on the Indians' faces. The driver sounded one long blast after another on the Lincoln's horn, leaning out the car window, smiling and waving toward his old truck. The gas attendant let out a hoot.

"Oh shit," I said, "it's them. Get down."

The Chevy Blazer cruised along behind the Lincoln, the two men peering in our direction. I crouched low, fear squeezing my stomach. Using my leather jacket as a blind, I aimed my camera, and rapid-fired frame after frame. White Hair passed by the cross hairs in my viewfinder, and I almost wished I had my finger on a gun trigger instead of a camera button.

I lowered the camera and released my breath. "You can get up now."

"Did they see us?" Mitch asked, panic in his eyes.

"I'm sure they didn't see you, hiding on the floorboards."

"Cop troubles?" The attendant stood alongside my door, wiping perspiration from his sunken face with the bug rag.

"No, no troubles, we just need to get to Denver to catch a plane to— Salt Lake."

"Yup, that's what I'd do, get myself off to the big city, if I didn't have all these here assets and responsibilities. You got guitars back there. You boys musicians?"

"Well, yes." I handed him a fifty-dollar bill. "Keep the change."

Smoking Jimi

"Ain't full yet."

"Doesn't matter. Where's the Vituscan Mission?"

He pointed down the road. "First left. Hardly nobody goes up there that I know of."

The road to the monastery snaked along a dry creek bed littered with boulders and bleached snags. As the monastery came into view, I was struck by how it seemed so out of place— it resembled a modern office building with turreted windows and lime-green walls. Several windowless outbuildings hid behind it like blind offspring. A tower bearing an antenna array sat atop one of the outbuildings next to a satellite dish. VITUSCAN CENTER was hand painted below a cross positioned over the main building's entrance. I parked next to a late-model SUV.

"This is a monastery? I was kinda thinkin' of an old castle, or a big-assed church," Mitch said.

"I'm surprised you weren't thinking of a whorehouse."

I tried the windowless, metal door. Locked. I pushed an intercom button just below the security camera.

"May I help you?" the intercom's speaker said.

"We're here to see Jon Nealy," I replied to the video camera.

Silence.

"He's supposed to be a missionary, a Vituscan."

Pause. "Yes. Jon. And you are?"

"An old friend, Brad Wilson. I've come a long way."

Silence.

"So, is he here?"

"He has a place in town. In the trailer park. Lot number six. I'll call ahead so he will expect you. God bless."

* * *

We found Jon Nealy's doublewide at the rear of the Happy Trails Trailer Park, at the end of a gravel driveway bordering a field of brush and scrub trees. Rusting and mildew stained, the trailer sat upon concrete blocks partly obscured by an overgrown flowerbed. The place had a rustic, comfortable air.

"Must be his car," I said, parking next to an old yellow Mustang with racing stripes and a ragged convertible top.

"Missionaries have cars? I always thought of a guy with a brown robe riding a donkey. And sandals. You gotta have sandals. And those beads around your neck. Should we call him Brother Jon?" Mitch let out a scoffing laugh.

I switched off the ignition and the engine stopped cold. Some of the keys on the ring obviously didn't fit the truck, and it seemed strange to put someone else's house keys in my pocket. I slammed the pickup's door to let Jon know he had visitors.

Dogs barked from several trailers away. An angry stream of music poured from an open window of Jon's trailer. I reached through a rip in the screen and pressed a mechanical doorbell. I rang it a second time. Bits of lyrics were discernable from the grinding, heavy-metal din, sung by an electronically demonized voice: ". . . we gonna crucify . . . eat your eyes . . . drink your blood . . . ."

"Sure we have the right place?" Mitch asked, cuddling his briefcase.

"Lot six. That's what they said."

"What do you want?" a voice said from behind me.

Jon! He brandished a pipe wrench, either as a tool or a weapon, I couldn't tell, but it was Jon all right, especially in his quick, dark eyes.

"Jon, it's me, Brad."

"Holy shit! Brad! What are you doing here?" Jon shook my hand, squeezing hard, grinning hard. "What happened to your hair, dude?"

"Guess the last time we saw each other it was a bit longer, huh?"

We both laughed, for Jon's dark-brown hair was cropped short, and had thinned at the crown. The time-carved lines on his boyish face showed some age, but couldn't dim the glow of his mischievous smile. Jon tossed the pipe wrench onto a rock pile near the wooden steps and wiped his hands on his jeans.

"Helping out a neighbor," Jon said, checking out our pickup. "Isn't that Indian Charlie's wheels?"

"Bought it from him," Mitch said.

Jon turned to Mitch, dropping his smile. "You. Never thought I'd see you again. Ever." The air became tense, so I figured I'd better step between them.

"Something really big came up, we need to talk," I said.

Jon broke off his stare at Mitch and led us into his trailer. I ducked through the doorway and found myself in a small living room cluttered with modest furniture. An entertainment unit filled one wall. Nearby, sat a weight machine with laundry hanging from it. Sony TV. High-end stereo. Jon turned down the scrunching, growling music, then thought again and switched it off. I did a double take, still not accustomed to Jon being so much older than the last time I'd seen him. His compact body was in great shape, far more muscular than I remembered, but his mannerisms were still the same. It was the face where age revealed itself the most.

"That stuff's called 'death metal.' I'm researching it for the church, to better understand how the devil's music targets our youth, and encourages destructive habits," Jon said, speaking as a tour guide. Then he chuckled.

The phone rang.

"The machine will get it, grab a seat. Want anything? Coffee? Beer?"

"I'm starving," Mitch said. He plopped down next to me on a sofa of cowhide and brass buttons.

From a desk in the corner, next to a computer, an answering machine picked up: "Hi, honey, I see you got visitors, I don't want to bother you, but that leak—" Jon hurried over and turned off the machine.

"Just a friend— someone I was helping, a neighbor."

Mitch rubbed his belly. "My stomach needs some help, tell you what, I'm starving."

"I could throw together some sandwiches."

"Sandwiches? That's it?" Mitch said.

A disgusted look passed over Jon's face. "There's always bacon and eggs. That's about it, till I get to the store over in Callahan."

"Perfect," I said.

As the aroma of bacon, eggs, and brewing coffee filled the trailer, Mitch wandered the living room, examining things. An oddly shaped rock. A statuette of a warlord. A cigar humidor. He removed a cigar, sniffed it, and slipped it into his shirt pocket. Mitch wandered to the desk and paged through a handwritten journal. He opened a drawer and browsed.

"What are you doing?" I whispered. "Get over here!"

"So how did you guys find me?" Jon called from the kitchen, amid the sound of dishes. One step backwards and he would see Mitch snooping through his desk.

"Your mom gave me the monastery's address. They told us where you lived."

"Really? The monastery told you where I live? Idiots. What brings you guys out this way?"

"Something's come up," I said, "it's about the band."

Jon laughed. "What? Is Mitch going to pay back the money he stole from us? I'd like to see that."

"It's a long story, let's eat first," I said.

The breakfast nook had a cheery view of granite-clad mountains and blue sky. We dug into crisp bacon, eggs over easy and golden toast. Coffee steamed in our cups and the conversation surrendered to the clink of silverware and crunch of toast.

Mitch took a huge bite of bacon, chewing roundly, his eyelids drooping in ecstasy.

"Know why bacon tastes so good?" Mitch asked, his mouth paused in mid-chew.

We ignored him.

"Because pork is genetically identical to human flesh. No kidding, I read it somewhere. We love the flavor of bacon 'cause it tastes like us."

Jon gave me a look.

"You made that up," I said with a laugh.

Mitch slurped coffee and resumed chewing. "Had you guys going, didn't I? Huh?"

I gazed out the window and noticed two children walking a path along the edge of a pine grove. What a place to raise a kid. So different from Florida— clean, innocent, alive. I envied the parents of those children— living in this paradise, raising kids here. Maybe if my life had turned out differently, I'd be sitting with Gjerna, watching my own kids play in that field. Sorrow eclipsed my heart like death's shadow. I put down my fork.

"So, how long you been doing this missionary thing?" Mitch asked.

Jon shrugged. "Quite a while. It's mostly administrative work here. God's work, you know."

"You Catholic?" Mitch asked.

"Depends."

"Are Vituscans Catholic?"

"I'm a Vituscan, if that helps."

"What do Vituscans do?"

"The work of Vituscans."

"What's the point of being Vituscans?"

"We endeavor to be good Vituscans."

Mitch scowled. "How come I never heard of Vituscans?"

"Our legacy defines our work."

"Which is?"

"To be good Vituscans."

Mitch released a breath and looked at his plate.

Jon laughed. "We convert the generosity of others into aid for the needy. We call ourselves monks, but we're not into the denial thing, we don't starve just to prove a point. A lot of people around here don't trust Catholics, so we're officially non-denominational. As you can see, I don't live in a monastery. Now, why are you guys here?"

Mitch glanced at me.

"We need to find Danny," I said. "You seen him?"

"Yes, but, mentally, Danny's not— what do you want with him?"

I sat up straight. "We're putting the band back together."

Jon laughed out loud and covered his mouth with a napkin.

"The band? Ha! I should have known. It's Mitch, isn't it? He's got you dragged into some bullshit. I should've seen it coming. Mitch, you sorry bastard, ain't you heard? Frank's dead. There's no band. And if it weren't for Brad, I'd kick your sorry ass right now. You've got nerve coming up here."

Jon sat back, glaring at Mitch.

"We're being offered a lot of money if we put the band back together, even without Frank," I said.

"Absolutely not possible. Ain't happening. Danny's in no shape for anything like that. You don't know, or you wouldn't even ask. Besides, my work here's too important. Answer's no. Beyond consideration. Wouldn't do it for a million dollars."

Mitch cracked his knuckles. "That's what it pays. One million. Each. Cash."

Jon coughed in his coffee. "What did you say?"

"One million cash for each of us, for one week's work. Paid in advance to the bank of your choice." Mitch's chair creaked as he leaned back, his hands clasped behind his head.

"C'mon, a million dollars? For what? Who has that kind of money to— throw away on us?"

"His name is Pablo Lupa. He's—"

"Pablo Lupa!" Jon shot me a look.

"I heard he's a fan of ours," I said. "Grew up with our albums. Thinks we're like the Stones. Got tons of money and wants us to fly down to his ranch in South America. We play a few

53

songs, jam with him, go home rich. Guarantees that we get paid before we step on the plane."

Jon sat back, blinking his eyes. "Wait a minute. How did Lupa— let me guess: Mitch?"

I nodded. "Pablo Lupa saw that special about the Jammies last week on MV-1, one of those where-are-they-now things. His lawyers got ahold of Mitch through the MV-1 people, and, here we are."

Jon scowled. "Now that you mention it, somebody from MV-1 called me a while back, asked a few questions. I don't get MV-1 here. Did you see it?"

"Ran some old film footage, shots of our album covers, that sort of thing. Said you'd become a monk, Danny was a hermit, and I was a photographer in Lauderdale. Showed newspaper clippings about Frank and the way he died."

An awkward silence filled the room. Mitch stared at his lap.

"Pablo Lupa," Jon slowly said. "Interesting. Brad, how do you feel about taking money from a drug-dealer's son?"

My head jerked. "A drug-dealer's son?"

"You didn't know? Pablo Lupa is the playboy son of Carlos Lupa who ran the old Oro Cartel. Old man Lupa was a mean-assed son-of-a bitch. Got assassinated years ago when— the Oro Cartel was put out of business. Before he died, he stashed away a ton of loot where nobody could touch it. Most of his money was inherited by his favorite son, Pablo."

I glared at Mitch. "Lying bastard! You told me he wasn't a drug dealer!"

"I didn't lie! He isn't actually a dealer."

"Damn you!" I slammed my palms on the tabletop, rattling the plates. Mitch cowered, his arms upraised.

"Kick his ass, Brad, c'mon man, go for it!" Jon sat back with a malevolent grin.

"All right!" Mitch said. "Everybody! Cool it for a second. OK, Pablo's dad was a dealer. Big deal. He's dead and gone, and hey, Pablo's just a regular guy looking for a good time. He's not in the business, never has been. Brad, what are you going to do, weenie out on us? This Pablo Lupa's just another rich guy, and this is our chance to get ours."

"What else aren't you telling us?" I asked.

"I'm being straight with you guys, swear to God, man."

Mitch flinched as I pushed my plate away. "Jon, I was misled about Pablo Lupa. Didn't have time to properly check things out and I just didn't know. I'm sorry."

Jon leaned back. "OK, let's say that if we were to go, and that's one *big* if, how are we supposed to get down to South America and back? And I don't even own a bass guitar."

"Not a problem. I bought both you guys new axes, got 'em in the truck." Mitch glanced at me. "As for travel arrangements, nothing but the best: Pablo Lupa's personal jet. It's no big deal, this cat flies his friends all over the world. All I gotta do is give his attorneys the word, and we're on our way."

"You sure about that?" Jon asked.

Mitch held up his palms, exposing the faded exhaust imprint. "The fix is in. Not a problem."

"Brad?" Jon asked.

"A million dollars," Mitch murmured, gazing out the window.

As much as I despised Mitch and his lies, the thought of returning to my old life disgusted me even more. "Screw it. I'm in."

Jon seemed amused. "Pablo Lupa, huh? All right. Let me make a few calls, maybe there's a way. Be back in a minute." Jon went into his bedroom and shut the door.

I glared at Mitch.

"Brad, what are you so steamed about?"

"You lied to me, you bastard!"

"I never! He's not a drug dealer, he's not."

"This whole thing stinks of weirdness. Where the hell you dragging us off to?"

"Same place Iggy Krotch and all the others went— where everybody wants to go— *Moneyland.*"

Jon stuck his head out the bedroom door. "You guys sure we're actually supposed to stay at Pablo Lupa's ranch?"

"His ranch? Absolutely! Me and Brad here were just talking about how we can't wait to go to— Moneyland."

Jon returned the receiver to his ear and shut the door.

Mitch smiled. "Still have that cell phone?"

"What's it to you?"

"I'll need to call Lupa's lawyers when the time comes." Mitch glanced around and lowered his voice. "Know what's weird? Ain't no crosses around here. No bibles. No religious shit. This guy's no monk."

"Not everybody flaunts their religion."

"I gotta go flaunt my lizard. Where's the bathroom at around here?"

"Probably that door next to his bedroom."

Instead of entering the bathroom, Mitch paused in the hallway with an ear to Jon's bedroom door. Mitch's expression went through several changes, his eyes roaming back and forth as he listened. He then darted into the bathroom and shut the door.

Jon returned to his chair. "You're sure about this, and I mean all of this?"

"Here's one thing I'm sure of," I said, and opened Mitch's briefcase. The smell of freshly printed currency overpowered the remnants of breakfast.

"Christ, how much is in there?"

"One hundred thousand. It's a down payment from Pablo Lupa's lawyers. Fifty thousand of this is yours."

"Amazing," Jon said.

I turned a cash bundle over in my hand. "Of course, Mitch owes me a few thousand bucks for that pickup outside." I told him of the switch with Indian Charlie's truck, and the white-haired man who followed us from Florida.

Hardness crept over Jon's face. "Where are these two guys now?"

"They followed Indian Charlie. North of town, I suppose."

Jon pursed his lips. "Think they know anything about me?"

"How could they?"

"And they just appeared when Mitch showed up?"

I nodded.

"Get the Blazer's plates?"

"No, but it might be in some of the photos I shot. It's in the Nikon."

"Good. We can drop the film off at the— monastery. They can make us some prints."

A flushing toilet announced Mitch's return, and the dusty odor of cigarette smoke trailed him. His face brightened at the sight of money. "So, Jon, you in?" He began stacking Jon's share of the cash on the table.

Jon slowly nodded, his eyes on the money.

"Cool. Here's your fifty thousand. I'm gonna need your bank's wire number and your account number, so when the time comes, Pablo's people can wire nine hundred and fifty thousand to the financial institution of your choice, immediate confirmation. Same for Danny."

"I'll get all that information from the monastery. But Danny's not going. That would be way too dangerous— he's in no condition for something like this. I know another, uh, drummer we can use. He's close by."

"No dice," Mitch said. "They told me it's gotta be the original band. No Danny, no deal."

Jon closed his eyes as if conferring privately with someone, and then huffed out a heavy breath. "OK, leave Danny to me. Let's go do this thing."

"Great. So where is Danny?" Mitch asked.

"Thirty minutes from here, up near Deadwood Camp."

"How's he support himself?" I asked.

"His parents send a little money each month. I help out some."

"Can we go see him?"

Jon grabbed a green ski jacket from the back of his chair. "It's your funeral. We'll take my car, since your buddies in the Chevy Blazer have probably figured things out and will be watching for Indian Charlie's truck. We'll drop off your camera's film at the— uh, monastery and get prints made. I'd like to have a look at this white-haired guy."

Chad Peery

9

With Mitch stuffed in the back seat and our two guitars stowed in the trunk of Jon's yellow Mustang, we stopped at the Vituscan mission, dropping off the film and Jon's fifty thousand dollars for safekeeping. As Jon drove his aging muscle car I told him what I'd been up to all these years, all the while keeping an eye out for the Chevy Blazer.

" . . . After the band broke up and you went for that solo deal, I had to sell some of my amps and guitars. I got a little session work, but it was the same for all of us— when they found out we were with the Jammies, they'd just turn cold, wouldn't return calls. The damned record company put out the word on us. Couldn't steal a decent gig, and I wasn't going to go out and play nightclubs. So, I drifted back to San Jose and worked as a DJ. I met this model, Victoria, and she said that since I was interested in cameras, I ought to become a photographer. She had some friends in the business who helped me get started, and I've been doing that ever since. It's OK. Nothing's ever what you think it's going to be."

"I heard that," Jon said. "You still with Victoria?"

"No, now it's Carol."

Jon nodded, his lips a thin line. The Mustang's air conditioning didn't work, and Jon refused to lower the convertible top, so we rolled the windows down to let in cool air as we climbed higher. The highway cut through forested mountainsides peaked with jagged granite, jutting skyward in a gesture of defiance. The thin air was exhausting, but at the same time exhilarating, almost intoxicating with its heavy aroma of pine. It occurred to me that this was one of the finer moments of my life— I wished today's journey would never end. Jon lit a cigar, and assumed a manly grimace behind great swells of bluish smoke. Immediately, Mitch lit a cigarette, sighing deeply as he exhaled. I angled my face toward the open window, grateful for the pure air of the Rockies.

Jon began grilling Mitch, wanting to know all about Pablo Lupa, the names of his attorneys, the bank, and the method of payment.

"I ain't that stupid, guys," Mitch said. "I'm your only contact with Lupa's people. That's my guarantee that nobody's going to stiff me, know what I mean? Without me, you guys got squat." He sucked an emphatic drag from his cigarette, and I took comfort in the thought of another nail in his coffin.

Jon whipped his Mustang around an old pickup with its camper plastered with anti-government stickers, and then slowed to take an unmarked dirt road. The car bucked and rattled over ruts and potholes, while dust boiled in our wake. The switchback road ascended a steep mountainside, covered with stands of conifers broken only by the occasional rockslide. Looking down slope, the forest blurred off into the distance, becoming a soft, green carpet that climbed the haunches of snow-flecked mountains. Jon put the car in low gear, and rocks kicked up against the chassis as we climbed higher.

"Listen, guys, Danny's not well. Mentally, he's been through a lot, done a bunch of speed and acid years ago. Got a lot of demons. As long as you guys humor him and don't talk politics, we'll be OK."

"So what is he," Mitch asked, "Republican or Democrat?"

Jon laughed. "Danny's way out past the wing-nuts. Don't get me wrong, I love him like a brother." Jon twisted the wheel to avoid a basketball-sized rock. "He's just not comfortable with civilization, and if he's around people for very long, something could happen."

Instinctively, I grabbed for my camera as a jackrabbit ran up the road, zagging crazily till it escaped my view by jumping a downed tree. My ears popped from the altitude.

"How high up are we?" I asked.

"Eight, maybe nine thousand. Arapaho Peak, over there, is thirteen thousand. We're in the Front Range— it's where the Rockies first rise up from the plains. Beautiful, ain't it?" Jon flicked his cigar ash into the ashtray.

"Will we be going through snow? Don't you need a four-wheel drive up this high?" Mitch asked.

"The Mustang's fine in the summer. Other times, when you can get through, I take the mission's SUV. Either way, you gotta know how to drive."

In the crook of a hairpin turn Jon stopped the car, and the cloud of dust caught up to us. He killed the motor, and the drift of wind sighed through the trees, their broad boughs whispering to one another.

Jon opened his door. "Give me your briefcase."

"No," Mitch said, giving me a frightened look.

"Mitch, give it up. I gotta hide it. And use your damned ash tray for that cigarette."

Mumbling to himself, Mitch surrendered his briefcase. Jon popped the hood and stashed the case between the radiator and grill.

"Deadwood Camp's about ten miles," Jon said, as we resumed our journey. "We're close to the checkpoint— Danny has a place just past that."

"Checkpoint? Forest Service?" I asked.

Jon laughed. "Forest Service doesn't come up this far— no sheriff, no feds, nobody. From here on up, it's Deadwood, run by Patroticus Invictus, which is pig Latin for Shitheads-R-Us. The Trotts, as the locals call them, is an armed gang of anarchists and militia psychos, run by the granddaddy of 'em all, General Ray. They're hunkered down in some abandoned silver mines, near an old ghost town."

"How do you know so much about these Trotts?" I asked.

"Occasionally, we Vituscans drive up and bring supplies for the women and children who live up here with the men. General Ray's father owns the land and bankrolls the Trotts, but he only provides them with guns, food, and fatigues. Guess he figures that's all his son's whacko army needs. But some of the Trotts have wives and kids. General Ray doesn't allow anyone to leave the compound except on authorized supply runs, so sometimes we'll send a nurse up there to make sure the families are OK. The Trotts know that the IRS hassles us Vituscans, so they figure if the government's after us, we must be OK. Of course, we had to convince them we weren't Catholics, because General Ray says the Pope is Satan, and priests worship the devil."

"Has Danny become one of these Trotts?" I asked.

"Not really. Danny only lives out here because he feels safe. I convinced the Trotts to let Danny move into an abandoned miner's cabin, way off on his own. But he's definitely a believer, buys into whatever General Ray's selling, hook, line, and sinker. He was always kind of paranoid, even when we were kids, but lately, I don't know, sometimes I can't get through to him. Don't say I didn't warn you."

Jon stubbed out his cigar as we rounded a curve. The road ended in a broad clearing rutted with tire tracks, and across the clearing stood a metal gate. A hand-lettered "No Trespassing" sign hung from the metal bars. As we pulled to a stop, two bearded men with assault weapons sauntered toward the Mustang, one on each side. The older man spoke quietly into a handheld radio, and then returned it to his belt.

"Hi, guys," Jon said, stepping out of the car, "coming up to visit Danny."

"Hey, Jon," the older man said. "Bringin' some friends up today, are we? Let's everybody get out, pop the trunk."

We did as ordered. The Trotts opened our guitar cases. "You guys those musicians from Salt Lake them two cops are looking for?"

Jon and I exchanged glances. "Yeah, right," I said.

The guards' hardscrabble faces showed no reaction. The younger one shook the Crate practice amp. "You boys got any guns besides—"

"No," Jon said abruptly.

A problem arose with my camera. "No surveillance equipment allowed, them's the rules," the older one said. Jon walked with him, talking, and when they returned, the guard said, "You three are cleared only as far as Danny's place. Don't try goin' no farther. And no pictures." He gave me a hard look as he returned my camera bag.

As we left the checkpoint behind, the road became badly rutted, and the Mustang labored up a steep grade. The air hung sweet with the fragrance of plants that grow fast and wild in the summer months. Jagged rockslides had shoved trees aside, which became spindlier the higher we climbed.

"Those two guys knew we were coming," Mitch said.

"See that ridge, over on Gunsight Mountain? They have a spotter up there. Nobody gets in or out of Deadwood without being seen. At night they use infrared."

As we neared the mountaintop, broken-edged boulders dominated the landscape and the vegetation became scrubby and thin.

"End of the line," Jon said, parking in a small clearing alongside the road. "We walk the rest of the way."

At first, I didn't spot the side road, which took off straight over a rise, much too steep for our Mustang. As I got out of the car, the sun beat down from a deep blue sky, but the heat seemed transitory, as if the earth couldn't hold its warmth. I followed Jon up the rock-ribbed hillside, which descended from a stony, snow-covered peak much farther up to our left. Patches of tiny wildflowers, pools of blues and yellows, shimmered in the breeze. Clutching his briefcase, Mitch wheezed after a few steps and unbuttoned his shirt. Gasping for air, he spat upon a flat rock.

"What the hell— or who the hell— wants to live up here— for Chrissakes?"

I laughed, until I realized my lungs ached as well from fighting the thin air. Just ahead, hanging from a rope strung across our path, a hand-painted sign read: KEEP OUT— LAND MINES.

Jon waved at the sign. "See what I mean about Danny? There aren't any land mines up here, never have been."

"Hope you're right," Mitch said, as we stepped over the rope. As we crested the rise, a cabin came into view, partly obscured by scrub trees. Its exterior was clad in weather-beaten wood— old signs, boards, and irregular scraps formed its walls— while like a sagging hat, the cabin wore a rusty, corrugated roof. Wide-gapped boards served as a porch, with a stack of firewood strewn at one end. A dilapidated pickup sat nearby, its autumn-red paint mottled and sun faded. Not far beyond that lay the mouth of an old mineshaft with tailings heaped around the entrance, like an open wound that wouldn't heal.

"He should be home," Jon said, waiting for Mitch to catch up. "Stay here, let me go in first."

While Jon trudged ahead to the cabin, I was amazed how my lungs burned from laboring at this altitude— and my poor knees! All around, shattered rocks and sharp stones lay scattered in the short grass, while the tinkle of an unseen creek came from behind a thicket. How I craved a drink— I could actually smell the icy-cold water.

Jon rapped on the cabin door. After a moment, he swung it open and disappeared inside.

"You sure there aren't land mines up here?" Mitch asked, breathing hard, eyeing the hard ground. "What's that thing?"

Before I could tell Mitch it was just a rock and not a land mine, a bullet seared the air over our heads. It was followed by a sharp crack, and the gunshot's echoes whipped off the hillsides.

Chad Peery

10

As the gunshot's echoes faded, I fell into a crouch. Mitch let out a fearful howl and dropped to his knees, clutching his briefcase.

Someone yelled, "Down on the ground. Face down! Do it now or you're dead."

I dived onto the rocky soil, my face in the dirt and the sting of dust in my nostrils. A rock jabbed my ribs near my hammering heart, but I remained still. Jon yelled, and someone yelled back. Footsteps crunched over the ground. Oily boots came into view, coated with a velvety sheen of dust. Camouflage trousers. The slots of a flash-suppressing muzzle. I glanced up. A longhair greybeard stood over me, pointing a rifle at my head. Grizzled hair obscured the man's face, and his blue eyes were like a pair of uneven headlights glaring at me from the lonesome highway of some god-awful nightmare.

I recognized Danny's voice.

"Shit! Brad Wilson? I'll be damned. I always knew I'd see you again." Danny offered me a Roman handshake and pulled me to my feet.

As I dusted myself off, Danny noticed Mitch, who still had his hands over the back of his head, his face pressed to the ground. "You." Danny kicked him in the ribs.

Mitch groaned and rolled over.

Danny hissed through his teeth. "Never thought I'd see you again. Never."

Jon ran up to Danny's side, panting.

"Danny, Danny, hey man, whaddya know, Brad and Mitch came up here to see us. Got some good news, too. Let's just take a deep breath here, relax, and like we'll all go inside, and hey, we haven't seen each other in such a long time, right?"

Danny lowered his rifle, gazing at the cabin.

"Can't let no one in there. Can't compromise my last line of defense." He rubbed his gray beard. "Who sent you guys?"

"Come on, Danny, you know you're safe with me," Jon said.

Danny banged his forehead with the fore knuckles of his fist, the way he used to do as a kid when he was perplexed. "This is one bodacious-assed security breach. How did you all get past the checkpoint? No. Shouldn't have got in. Somebody sent you up here. Didn't they?"

With much effort, Jon calmed Danny and convinced him to let us into his cabin. I was shocked at how my old drummer lived. A sleeping bag crumpled in a corner. No electricity or running water. In the middle of the room sat a table fashioned from a wooden spool, with crates serving as chairs. Dingy light filtered through the warped panes of a single window. An unlit Coleman lantern hung from the ceiling. Guns, lots of guns, adorned the walls— pistols, rifles, a crossbow, with an assault rifle taking the place of honor over a small iron stove. In a kitchen area sat foodstuffs, a plastic water bottle, a basin, and a frying pan.

Posters and bumper stickers were plastered upon the walls, difficult to read in the dim light. Danny closed the rickety door and jammed his rifle against it. Seeing him now, I remembered him as a kid playing army in his make-believe fatigues that his mom made for him, with his dad's Army-surplus ammo belt hanging on his skinny waist. As Danny glanced about his cabin and then at each of us, one hand hovered near the leather holster on his hip.

"Danny, I brought Brad and Mitch up here. They came to see me, and I thought it would be kind of cool to get together, you know, visit a little bit."

Danny said nothing and sat on one of the crates, using the wall as a backrest. He seemed distant, but his mannerisms were so familiar. The way he sat on the makeshift chair reminded me of how he used to command a drum stool, and how his long arms and legs would pound out a drumbeat as solid as steel. He always had such good meter and sense of rhythm.

Danny exhaled loudly, and then began picking at the splintered table. "Sorry, you guys. I didn't mean nothing. I was on watch, that's all. Jon, when I saw you with a couple of strangers, I mean, how was I to know? They could've forced you to take them up here. Never know who you can trust. Government's sneaky as hell, ain't they?" He looked up at Jon. "Ain't they?"

"Oh yeah, yeah," Jon said. He muscled a tree stump over to the makeshift table and sat upon it, nodding to us. I followed his example, clearing splinters off a stump near the stove, which Danny must have used for chopping kindling. Mitch sat upon a crate, which groaned beneath his weight.

"What's in the briefcase?" Danny asked.

Jon looked at Mitch, warning him off. "We came up here with a wonderful— story."

"Story?" Danny's right leg began bouncing as if he were playing the kick drum. "You think life is a story? Tell you what, man, this ain't no dress rehearsal, this is the real thing. You seen the shit that's going on out there? Everybody knows these are the end times, ain't that right?" He pointed at Jon.

"Right," Jon murmured.

"General Ray's ready. He knows. That CIA, them one-world bankers, them politicians, they've been runnin' this show from the git-go. Ever hear of the Illuminati? No? Man, you people are gettin' played for suckers and you don't even know it."

Jon shifted on his stump. "Danny, like I was saying, the three of us were thinking how it would be—"

"The shit's gonna hit the fan, man, and when it does, General Ray's gonna be standing tall, leading us back to a free America. If the U.N. ever tries comin' up here, they'll find out why this place is called Deadwood. We're ready to rock 'n roll on them cockroaches, and that's why the government keeps trying to get rid of us." Danny flared his nostrils, looking from man to man.

I figured this wouldn't be a good time to remind Danny that he'd promised to kill Mitch on first sight.

"OK if I smoke?" Mitch asked

"No!" Danny and I said in unison.

"Camels," Danny said, eyeing Mitch's cigarette pack. "Know what's in them things? Camel dung. Remember that baseball field in North Carolina, the one in movies? Used to be a stockyard, owned by the tobacco companies, to keep 'em supplied with manure. That's why the sneaky bastards won't tell ya what's in them cigarettes. You guys are smoking shit, man! And Jon's cigars, those big fat turds he lights up and sucks on and blows smoke like he's king shit, know what's in 'em?"

Danny threw his head back and laughed and laughed. That was the old Danny, with a laugh that knew no reserve, a joyous roar of the heart. Abruptly, Danny's demeanor darkened and he stroked his beard.

"You don't know," Danny said. "They got you all strung out, you're eatin' their pills, watching their television, spending their money. Money, pills, and TV. Whoever controls the money controls the world and everybody in it, and you'll follow their fucked-up road all the way to hell. General Ray knows— money is the soap that brainwashes your minds, it's the opium of the heart."

"Yeah, well take a toke off this," Mitch said. He snapped open the briefcase and placed it on the table. "We're getting' the band back together, and gettin' paid one million dollars apiece to do one easy gig. Cash money. Here's your advance. Fifty thousand dollars. It's yours. We're going down to South America to do this one gig, then you can come back here and live like a hermit, or whatever. Give it all to this General Ray if you want to, I don't give a damn. What do you say?"

Danny sat with his mouth gaping, staring at the cash. Gingerly, holding it by the edges as if the ink were still wet, he withdrew a packet and set in on the table. With a smug grin, Mitch leaned back.

"The band? You want me to play in the band again?" He glanced about the cabin and rubbed his shirt. "Ain't got my drum kit. Sold it." His eyes returned to the cash. "Whose money is this?"

"Yours," Jon said.

"Where'd it come from?"

Jon gave Mitch a look that said shut up. "This money comes from a man who understands what it's like to fight for freedom, to always have to be on guard—"

"Cut the crap, man, I ain't no retard."

"OK. It's from Pablo Lupa. He has a place in South America, where we'll all be safe."

Danny's brow furrowed. "Safe? You're never safe. Don't ever forget that. Just when you think you're safe, you're dead."

Jon puffed his cheeks. "Pablo Lupa's got a lot of money and he loves the Jammies. He's a big fan."

"Jammies? Ha! What a dipshit name for a band."

"So, what's the word?" Mitch asked. "We're gonna do this thing, right?"

Danny got to his feet and moved his head in robotic motions, as if trying to get a thought unstuck. "Could be a trick, you know. They're clever bastards. Gotta think this out." He paced the cabin, tromping on old boards, talking in circles. " That's it, when you understand but you think you don't know, and when you do get it, it comes to you, and you understand everything, then

Smoking Jimi

they say, 'help me I'm falling.' Falling? Oh, sure, if they're falling, then they just don't get it— life sucks, and then you die."

As Danny paced the cabin, my legs ached with restlessness. Jon removed Danny's rifle from the door so the three of us could go outside. The setting sun hung beneath rows of thin clouds formed like neon-pink sand dunes. Jon parked Mitch on the cabin's porch with a cigarette, and then the two of us hiked down the steep hillside to get our guitars from the Mustang.

"Who's going to steal our guitars out here, squirrels?" I asked.

"When you see what I've seen, you get so you don't trust anybody."

"I used to trust Danny, I mean, he used t be rock solid. This isn't the Danny I remember."

"It's Danny all right, you just have to know where to look," Jon said, sliding on a slanted rock face. "Don't tell anybody this, but he's been talking about eating the barrel of that M-16."

"You're kidding."

"Wish I was. Just keep it quiet, don't get him started."

"I remember Danny was always a bit paranoid, even as a kid, but nothing like this. Is that why you two live close to each other?"

"Well, I helped him move from Montana when I got transferred— you know, when the Vituscans sent me here. I found that old miner's shack for him, helped him get set up. Back in Montana, he got mixed up with the Alpha Rangers, a really bad militia group that's now doing hard time, so I was glad to bring him down here. I tried to get him counseling but he won't have any part of it. Seems happy enough now. As long as the Trotts just leave him alone, I think he'll be OK. But taking him to South America?" Jon shook his head.

"There's a lot riding on this, for all of us,' I said.

"Don't worry, he's going."

My heart pounded from the altitude and I took short, quick breaths, even though the Jeep trail went downhill.

"Once we get to South America, are you sure you're going to be able to control Danny?"

"Brad, I'll take care of him, I'll have to."

"So, what happened, how'd he get this way?"

Jon stopped and hands on his hips, stared into the distance. "After the band broke up, he fell in with some bad dudes, doing a lot of speed and stuff. He was OK till he got high off something somebody made in a bathtub out of hardware-store chemicals. Pushed Danny off the deep end. Spent time in the psycho ward, but it didn't do any good. When they let him out he stopped taking his meds and went on the road with a club band. Almost killed some guy in a bar fight."

Breathing hard, we reached Jon's old yellow Mustang and grabbed our things.

"I heard that after the band you went off to college," I said.

Jon laughed as we began the trudge uphill.

"After the band, I went into the Marine Corps."

"You? The Marines?"

"Yeah, me. Wanted to straighten my head out. Got it shaved instead." Jon laughed.

"Looks like you've kept in shape. Saw your weight machine."

Jon's response was lost in his heavy breathing.

"Back in '79 somebody saw you at USC, said you were going for a law degree."

"Law degree?" Jon said. "Yeah, right. Now it's the law of the jungle."

"So, you've found what you're looking for, here with the Vituscans?"

Jon stopped and gave me a hard look. "At one time I thought— religion was the answer. I really believed that." He let out a deep breath. "Now, I don't know. I guess, in the end you've just got to believe in yourself."

"So, why are you still at the monastery?"

"I've got one important thing I have to help finish up here. After that, I'll think about where I'm going, and why. Julie and I have some things to talk over."

When we returned to the cabin, Danny sat at the table, wire-rimmed glasses perched low on his nose, and speaking softly to a hundred dollar bill. He held it up to the hissing lantern, rotating the currency, tilting his head as if trying to read invisible ink. Danny explained to the hundred-dollar bill how soon all of its little nephews and cousins would be worthless when the government recalled all currency in preparation for the New World Order.

I went outside and sat next to Mitch on one of the old loading platforms that served as a porch. I was tired, hungry, and thirsty, and it felt good just to sit, watching the red crescent notch into a distant mountain ridge. A cool breeze kicked up, playing over my face, reminding me it could chill quickly up here even in the summer months.

Jon emerged from the cabin, his expression tough. "Look, I think Danny's almost there, he's calmed down quite a bit. Still wants to talk to General Ray. But we don't need that. No General Ray. Understand?"

"I'm hungry," Mitch said, slouching against the wall, "let's go back to town and get some dinner."

Jon grimaced at the setting sun. "We stay here tonight. Danny has food."

Mitch snapped to. "Stay? Here? What the hell you talkin' about?"

"Danny's got a few blankets, we'll build a fire, no big deal."

While Mitch whined and Jon told him to shut up, I took my guitar from its case and plugged it into the Taxi amplifier. Mitch bellowed profanities. Jon screamed back. I strummed a power chord. The yelling stopped. Jon grinned and opened his guitar case.

"Hey, a P-bass, just like my old one," he said.

"We bought it for you and it's coming out of your share," Mitch said.

The sunburst design on the body of Jon's guitar was typical of the vintage Fender Precision Bass, with orange and yellow at the center exploding to black along the edges. Jon played a few notes on his bass, and then pressed the instrument's body against one ear while he twisted the tuning pegs.

I said, "Plug into my amp, let's try playing."

Jon did so and we noodled around, jamming on whatever riffs came to mind. After a few minutes we both stopped and waved our aching hands in the air, laughing at ourselves.

"Remember any of the old songs?" Jon asked.

I said, "I'm not sure if those particular brain cells are still in working order." I began playing the intro to our Top-10 hit, "Jammie Time." The Taxi amp's small speaker growled from the low frequencies when Jon's bass joined in, but the strains of the familiar tune began to jell.

"Oh, man, let's not play that turkey," Jon said. "How about 'Snakewalk,' remember?"

I played the slinky guitar line that began the best song from our second album. When Jon joined in with the bass, I switched to playing choppy, rhythmic chords. Both of our heads nodded to the beat, and even Mitch tapped his foot. Suddenly, the drums began. Danny, leaning by the doorway, slapped his thighs and thumped his boot on the cabin wall as if it were a bass drum. His face became soft and pliable, shaped not by fear and anger, but by the joy of music and the groove of a beat. Mitch stood to the side, the misfit, the castoff, the voyeur.

This was how it began so many years ago in my parents' garage, just some kids playing around with ideas that eventually became songs we would record on our second album, in defiance of the record company's demands. "Jammie Time," our teenybopper sweat anthem, as well as most of the first album's material, was written by staff writers at the record company— a cabal of cringing, anemic hacks. "Snakewalk" was a total departure, a sexual, sensual, riff-driven song that soared beyond the comprehension of sophomoric executives and boardroom lizards. And when we played live, we would stretch out the commercial songs with hip instrumental passages, reluctantly returning from free-form voyages to dutifully play the last insipid refrain.

Jon began humming the melody for "Snakewalk." I grinned, remembering how audiences would stare in disbelief when the band broke from the bubble-gum hits and did the hipper songs from our second album, like "Snakewalk." Before long, the crowd would end up dancing and rocking, mesmerized by the compelling lines and seductive lyrics.

The Stratocaster guitar felt like an old lover against my body— while my fingers, still struggling to keep pace with my thoughts, pressed the strings to the frets, forming chord patterns I knew so well. My right hand became stiff from strumming and gripping the pick too tight, but joy overruled my protesting muscles. Each crunch against the strings, each chord change brought me closer to who I used to be, and could be again.

The song's guitar solo was lyrical, brief, easy to play, and the passage soared, carrying my spirits with them. I almost expected the Taxi amp to be smoking from the effort, and as I played the closing cord I cranked the guitar's volume wide open. The amp roared, then released a tortured shriek and collapsed into silence. We looked at each other for a moment, and then broke out in laughter. As I wiped my eyes I spotted a small herd of deer, fifty yards up the hillside, staring at these noisy men and their bizarre antics. I shivered as I returned my guitar to its case. The sunlight had departed, the air held no warmth, and for now, the music was over.

Danny spoke first: "Anybody wants water, there's a spring up near those deer. There's a rock pool to wash in downstream, and you got your regulation outhouse out back."

Mitch scowled, glancing around for sympathy.

"Danny, I figured we could all crash here for the night," Jon said. "You got enough grub?"

"Got plenty of Jerky. Tack. Canned stuff. Yeah, we could do that. Like the old days, huh?"

Danny remained inside the cabin, while the three of us walked up to the spring and talked of money. What would it be like to have a million dollars? Where to keep it? What to spend it on? Jon's lack of excitement over the money puzzled me, especially his words, "I have tough choices, this isn't going to be simple." Did he mean his Vituscan vows, which he didn't seem to take too seriously? I stood at the spring's edge, my reflection dancing upon waters fed by melting snow.

Jon dipped one of the cups Danny had given us into the water, and I did the same with mine.

Mitch stared at the ground. "What the hell, who crapped all over around here?"

"That's either deer shit or chocolates," Jon said.

"You could make a cigar out of those big ones," I said.

Mitch pointed. "Deer lips! Don't drink that water, deer lips have been in there!"

I laughed and put the cup to my mouth. Cold. Clean. Sweet. How could water taste sweet? I drank so fast my teeth ached and I had to catch my breath. "Nothing like this in Florida," I said.

"It's the best," Jon said, dipping his cup again.

Water from the spring traveled down a rocky bed and into a small pool. Mitch knelt at the pool's edge, removed his shirt, and splashed water into his armpits. His reaction was immediate Mitch screamed and howled and flapped his elbows like a crazed fowl. Moaning, he put his shirt back on.

"Goddam freezing-assed place! Now I gotta go dump a load."

"Thar she be," Jon said, "ye old shithouse." He motioned toward the outhouse behind the cabin, a crude thing of weather-beaten wood and stained with age.

As the vanishing sun sucked light from the sky, Mitch wandered down to the outhouse with his odd, penguin-like gait. Jon and I sat near the spring and watched the sunset's glow burn away.

"Brad, do we really need Mitch? I mean, I don't trust the guy as far as I can spit."

"We need him, at least to get down there. He's got all the contacts, all the numbers." I kicked a loose rock and sent it tumbling down the hillside. "You gotta admit, this whole thing's strange. We really don't know what's going to happen once we get to South America. Sure, we'd have to be out of our minds to turn down that kind of money, but has anybody considered what could go wrong? Things can get real crazy real fast down there."

"I know," Jon said, squinting at the wounded sunset.

"According to Mitch, Pablo Lupa's done this before— he just flew Iggy Krotch and his band down there."

"Iggy Krotch? That guy with all the leather and spiked hair?"

"That's him." I wondered if Jon had been monitoring Iggy's albums for indecent lyrics.

Jon continued, "We're talking about the guy who holds his hand over his crotch when he's singing, like he's got crabs or something?"

I nodded.

Jon laughed. "This should be interesting."

"I imagine so," I said. "Still, doesn't it seem odd that anyone would spend that kind of money on— the three of us?"

Jon shrugged. "Pablo Lupa's one of the richest men in South America. Got more money than he could ever spend. Knows life's short. Look how young his father died, and the world this guy grew up in. He has a couple of brothers and word has it that those two might be trying to put the Oro Cartel back together. But I don't think the old cartel people and Pablo are close at all. He seems only to be interested in playing with his money. Like a kid in a toy store. But you're right, Brad, let's keep our eyes open and be ready—" His voice trailed off and he tossed a pebble down the hillside. "First, we gotta get there."

"How do you know so much about Pablo Lupa?"

"Asked around. Made a call or two."

As purple velvet drew across the mountains we gazed at the cabin below us, a sad shack of weirdness and shadows. In the

Smoking Jimi

silence of our thoughts we contemplated the spooky challenge of Danny, and the tense night ahead.

Chad Peery

11

Finishing the last slice of canned peach, I released a satisfied sigh. I found the deer jerky pleasantly chewy, the hard tack hopelessly hard, and the canned potatoes mushy but filling. Suppressing a shiver, I pulled on my new leather jacket.

"I bought that bomber jacket for Brad," Mitch bragged, chewing something that bulged his cheek.

Silence.

Mitch had already donned on his blond leather coat, and now Jon put on his ski jacket. Danny scoffed, shaking his head as if we were all sissies, and then went to the stove to start a fire.

"That was great beef jerky," Mitch said, spitting something into a corner when Danny turned his back.

"Venison. Deer meat. Here's how you shoot 'em." Danny whirled and pointed his finger at Mitch: "*Bang!*" He glared at Mitch while noisily breaking some kindling. As Danny tended the stove, he said, "I take the venison down to Deadwood Camp, they've got a jerky smoker. Remember how Frank's dad used to make jerky?"

Mitch shrank.

Danny said, "Frank's dad never wanted him to have a sports car, said it was too dangerous. Anybody remember why Frank totaled Brad's Porsche?"

Everyone murmured. Mitch's eyes shifted toward the door.

Danny cracked a thick branch against his knee. "Think again. He didn't do himself. They just want you to believe that."

"Let's not go there," Jon said, glancing at me.

"Why not, are you sissy boys afraid of the truth? They killed Frank because they thought he knew something. Made it look like an accident. Do it all the time."

Mitch closed his eyes and silently exhaled.

Danny stuffed more firewood into the stove. "Remember that fire in the MGM Grand? Wasn't no accident either. Or TWA? Or how about—"

"Enough!" Jon said. "Nobody wants to hear that crap."

"I do," Mitch said.

"No, you don't," Jon shot back.

Kindling snapped and flames sprouted as Danny closed the iron grate. The scent of smoke filled the room, a dreamy incense of campfires and mountain nights. I sat upon a stump by the wall opposite Danny, who seated himself across from Mitch at the table. Danny pulled what appeared to be an Army-issue Colt .45 automatic from his leather holster, and placed the heavy, angular weapon upon the table. I wasn't sure if he was just getting comfortable, or had some other purpose in mind for the gun, since its barrel was pointed at Mitch's midsection. Shadows cast by the Coleman lantern made the weapon appear twice its size. As I closed my eyes, I could still hear the report of Danny's rifle and the snake hiss of hot lead streaking over my head.

Jon parked himself near the stove which now held a roaring fire, its hot breath groaning and creaking through stovepipe hung by bailing wire. As our conversation turned to old days and stories of the road, Jon occasionally got up to toss another piece of wood into the fire. When talk got around to our band breaking up, silence crept over us and Mitch shrank another inch.

Danny hunched his shoulders and looked at me with watery eyes. "Why can't Frank be here with us, man? It was his band too." He wiped his eyes and turned toward Mitch. "You killed our band, man."

"I— don't do this to me man, that was a long time ago."

"I ain't forgotten," Danny said, straightening up. "You forgotten, Brad?"

"Nope."

"Look, you guys, I— put this deal together that would return us five hundred percent profit. Remember that record company advance for studio expenses, you know, for the third album? I was gonna turn that two hundred grand into one million bucks in three weeks. Bingo. Use that money to take the band to the top. Nobody was even supposed to know the money was gone. You guys don't realize how screwed up things were, the record company was only paying for a third album because the contract required it. They were gonna press a few albums, and then drop you guys like a rock. End of record deal, end of band, end of everything.

"So this opportunity came up. See, I knew this guy who knew a guy who won a DC-8 in a poker game. I checked it out, that plane was really there and it really belonged to this dude, I saw the papers. So, you got this big-assed jet plane just sitting in a government hangar in Thailand, and all this guy needed was some up-front cash to bribe Tai customs officials and buy enough fuel to get back here. This guy goes over there with some World War II fighter pilots who know how to fly the plane, but the crazy sons of bitches get their asses thrown in jail after they shot some guy in a whorehouse, and then the Tai government impounds the plane and the money disappears."

I had the urge to spit. "Are you trying to tell me our lives ended up in the toilet because you fell for some con job?"

"If I said I was sorry, would it help? Like, I had to leave town, man, the record company sent the cops after me, and let me tell you, my life ain't been too pretty since."

"Your life?" Danny toyed with his pistol. "How about Frank? Don't think I forgot. I made a promise at Frank's funeral. I'm keepin' it, too."

Jon said, "Danny, not now."

Danny rotated his face into the lantern, as if he were a moth, set on immolating himself. "After Mitchy Boy screwed us over, the only gig I could get was playing in nightclub bands. Ever tell you about the time I almost killed a guy? Son of a bitch had it coming, everybody said so."

"Let's not go there," Jon said.

Danny spit on the floor. "Why? Little Mitchy Boy gonna pass out? Big Brad Boy gonna pee his pants? In case you people ain't noticed I live in a shit box and I got no life, and you can't go back, there's no going back, never. Life sucks and then you die. Ain't that right?"

No one responded, and Danny reset himself. "So, it's Tulsa, dead of winter, at some rat-hole off the Interstate. We just finished our third set and we're taking our break. I sit down at the bar with a couple of waitresses, no big deal, we were just sittin' and talkin', when in comes these three guys, and right away the place gets real quiet. This one waitress gets real nervous when she sees the big guy— man, talk about a goon— buzz-cut, shotgun face, mean-assed ugly."

Danny took a swig from his plastic bottle, and then slapped the cap back on.

"In those days everybody in the band worked out, I mean, you had to or you'd get the crap beat out of you. I bench-pressed over three hundred pounds. Should have seen me. Sometimes, when I mixed it up with some dude, you know, and like I'd really connect, I'd lift 'em clean off the ground with one punch. Like *bam,* and it was over. Ha!"

Mitch sat stiffly, his mouth hanging open. I suppressed a grin.

"So, this big guy starts hassling some people at another table, talking real mean and loud, then comes over and wants a private conversation with the waitress I'd been talking to. She says no, but he won't leave her alone. He grabs the back of her neck and starts whispering shit in her ear. She's like gettin' all freaked and trying to squirm free, so I get up and tell him to leave her alone. 'Well, what do we have here, a sissy boy?' this guy says, trying to stare me down. His other two buddies are standing behind him, their arms folded like big, bad-assed weenies.

"Before the big one has time to get up his guard, I catch him square on the jaw, *bam!* and he like goes over backwards and smashes a table. He gets up and I freight train him, like *bam! bam! bam!* and he stumbles backwards, kind 'a bent over, so I knee him. Man, you could hear his ribs going in one big crunch, like stepping on chicken bones. Down he goes, and man, all this happens so fast that his buddies just stand there with stupid smeared all over their face. I tell the big guy to stay down, but no, he keeps trying to get up, so I heel stomps him. Son-of-a-bitch still won't stay down. *Again! Again! Again!*" Danny pounded the table to accent each kick. "Finally, he just lays there, not moving at all. His chicken-dick buddies book out the door, like they can't get out of that joint fast enough. Ha. Should'a seen it."

I glanced at Jon. With a wary look he shook his head at me.

"Man, talk about quiet, nobody says shit. You guys would've cracked up, I mean, there he is, all laid out on the dance floor like roadkill, and me and the band get back on stage and start playing our next set, just cool as can be, like it's all in a day's work. A few people start dancing, I mean, nobody steps on him or anything, then the bar manager comes and throws a glass of water on the guy. But he still don't move. I'm startin' to wonder if he's dead, I mean, maybe I killed this dude, and here I am in some dick-weed town with his buddies waiting for me in the parking lot.

"But you know what? This girl I never seen before, she comes up and thanks me, and some other people do too, saying the asshole had it coming. A couple of songs later, some ambulance guys show up and cart his ass off on a stretcher. Ha!"

Danny picked up his pistol, handling it as if it were made of the thinnest glass, and then placed it on the table with its barrel pointing at Mitch.

"Next day the cops said I shouldn't leave town— this guy was in a coma and they wanted to see if he died or not, so that way they could put the correct charges on my arrest warrant, since it's like a real hassle to fill out the forms twice. I told them how it went down, I had a bar full of witnesses, but they were cops, what did they care?

"A couple of days later, this guy came out of his coma and wanted to press charges. Had a busted jaw, crushed eye socket, broken ribs, stuff like that, no big deal. But then the cops found some out-of-state warrants on the bastard, he'd beat up some woman in Arizona, so they shipped his ass off to some jail in Tucson. His chicken-dick buddies drove by the motel that night and shot out our windows, damned near hit the lead singer. Next day I quit the band, sold my drums, and I ain't played since."

I took a breath, the first one in what seemed like an eternity. Mitch leaned away from the table, as if worried that Danny would pound him into a senseless pulp. Jon threw a log into the stove and slammed the door.

Danny slapped the table, making us jump. "So! At ten-percent interest per annum compounded annually, the interest due on two hundred thousand dollars over twenty-five years would be what? Anybody?" Danny glanced around, then pulled a tattered paper from his shirt pocket and scribbled. "Looks to me like over two million dollars."

"You just figured that out?" I asked.

"Come on, now, interest?" Mitch asked. "That's crazy talk."

"You saying I'm crazy?"

"No. No, I wouldn't say that."

Danny leaned over the table. "You sayin' you didn't just call me crazy?"

"I didn't— of course not, nobody here thinks that."

"Then you're calling me a liar. Gettin' called a liar pisses me off. You're either trying to piss me off, or you're calling me crazy. Which is it?"

"Not, no, me? I wouldn't do anything, no."

"Now you're jerkin' me around!"

"That's enough," Jon said, kicking the stove for effect.

I relished the moment. Mitch had it coming as much as that thug in the bar. This place, this moment, reminded me of long ago, in a cramped rehearsal room in Los Angeles, arguing over some long-forgotten musical triviality. The thought made me smile. A part of me missed it so much.

"Guess what, Mitch," I said, "if you fork over your entire share, you'll still owe us over a million dollars. Like you said, a million dollars is serious money."

"Brad, Jon, c'mon you guys, talk some sense here. Look, I'll pay you guys the two hundred thousand, alright, is that what you want? I took it, I'll pay it back. Satisfied? Look, I'm bringing you guys a gig what's worth three million dollars, and you're bringing up this interest thing?"

Danny slapped the scrap of paper. "Either you pay what this says or I don't go."

"Me too," I said, glancing at Jon, who stood quietly, like a smart student waiting his turn during a spelling bee.

"Right," Mitch said. "Here's what I'll do, I'll pay the three of you, let's say, an even two million dollars. But you've gotta let me work my share up first. Give me a couple of months."

Danny grabbed Mitch's collar and got in his face. "What are you trying to pull? I ought to throw your ass down that old mineshaft out back."

"Danny," I said "I'm gonna trust him. I know how to find his ass, he can't just vanish this time. I say we do it. Agreed?"

Jon quickly said yes. Danny scowled and released Mitch's collar. A long silence passed. A log popped in the fire.

"All right, I'll do it— I'll do it for the band." Danny spread his arms to the cabin. "I must be crazy to leave all this behind." He roared a laugh, but then cut it short.

"Right, then," Jon said, stretching.

"About goddam time," Mitch muttered, rubbing his neck. "Hand me the phone."

Danny laughed. "Ain't no phones out here, retard."

"I meant Brad's cell phone."

I reached for my camera bag. All the photos I could have taken, and my camera was still in the bag! What was wrong with me? All I had thought of was playing music again. I smiled at the notion as I handed Mitch my cell phone.

"May not work out here," I said.

"There's an old analog repeater on Gunsight Mountain," Jon said.

Mitch pulled a number from his wallet and dialed. "We're in, got their machine." Mitch put a hand over his other ear. "Hello, this is Mitch Damian, we're ready, it's on, we're coming, so make the arrangements. We're in Colorado." He put his hand over the mouthpiece. "Where is this place?"

"You're in sovereign Patroticus Invictus territory, as authorized by the United States Constitution," Danny said.

"Uh, Colorado," Mitch said, "I'll check in tomorrow." He handed back the phone. "Guys, we're on our way."

"On our way," Danny said, "and we're a band again. A band!"

I stepped outside and stood on the cabin's porch, leaving the others inside talking about old days and new money. I looked up at the stars and inhaled crisp air. So. It was done. We were really going, nothing could change that now. I zipped up my coat and found a rock to sit on.

I'd forgotten how the night sky looked away from the city. Thousands upon thousands of stars hung low, so bright and clear that I could almost make out the miniature disks of ancient suns. Looking at that incredible sight, I felt humbled by the universe, so full of life. And me, so far from home. What home? With Carol? No. I had no home, I was from among the stars. My mind whispered a familiar prayer: "Please God, help me . . . ." But I never finished the phrase— help me with what? Money? Love? If only I understood my own secret longings.

Later, on the cabin floor rolled up in my blanket, an alarm clock sounded in my mind— what about my vitamins, my melatonin, and my DHEA? I smiled. In place of supplements and herbs, I had tapped into the energy of the road, an amphetamine high that comes when the road cranks you up and sweeps you away like a twig on a raging river. A delicious wave of exhaustion brought me to the point of intoxication. Within that high I drifted into thoughts of Gjerna, wishing I could live forever in that night in Copenhagen, where it would always be just the two of us, wandering the gardens of her heart.

Chad Peery

12

I blessed morning's first glow— a kind of bloodshot dawn that seeped through the cabin's foggy window. My bones ached from sleeping on cold boards, and the pain behind my eyes reminded me that crashing on floors is for the stoned, young, and stupid. My leather jacket and thin blanket gave little relief from the cold. Mitch and Jon were engaged in a snoring contest. I sat up with a start.

"Danny! He's gone!"

Jon stirred. Mitch released a generous fart.

"I mean it, you guys! His guns are gone. Danny took off on us!" I scrambled to my feet and threw open the door. The mountainside greeted me, smeared by the surreal glow of dawn.

"His truck's still here," Jon said, pushing past me. He cupped his hands and yelled, "DANNY! DANNY!" Mocking echoes of Jon's cries cascaded from the rock-strewn hillside.

"He split on us," Mitch said, joining us on the porch, pulling up the collar on his buff leather jacket. "Crazy bastard took the money— we're screwed."

While Jon ducked back into the cabin, I began searching the stony earth for tracks. I noticed the old mineshaft that Danny had threatened to throw Mitch into— a sucking wound in the ground, wincing at the sight of dawn, inhaling its fill of last night's darkness.

"Could he be in there?" Mitch asked.

"That's why I got us this flashlight," Jon said, walking up behind us. "Somebody has to go in there."

"In there?" Mitch asked. "I ain't goin' in there. No telling what's in there. You guys ever heard of a cave-in?"

"We'll flip for it. Odd man goes," Jon said.

Mitch lost.

Mitch said, "Jesus, you guys, this is goddam insane."

"Fine," Jon said. "We'll just pack it in, go back home and forget it. End of problem."

Mitch spat a curse, snatched the flashlight from Jon, and trudged towards the cave.

"Don't touch the wooden beams," Jon shouted, "they're old as hell. Look for fresh tracks. Don't stay gone more than ten minutes." Mitch looked back, grimaced, and then was swallowed by the mouth of the tunnel.

"I should've known. This was all going too easy," Jon said, shaking his head.

"How deep is that mineshaft?"

"Who knows? Danny chased a bear out of there once, said the thing used to raid his cabin every night."

"A bear?" I whistled.

Jon stifled a smirk.

"I can't believe Danny just ran off," I said, as I picked up a stone and threw it up the mountainside. The rock cracked and ticked through shattered rock and scrub brush. Above that, a neighboring mountaintop and its jagged peak notched the upper atmosphere, blocking the young sun. The sky had turned steely gray above the mountain, transitioning to a faded blue toward the western horizon. This was a place of no equal—perhaps someday I would live somewhere like this, thin air and all. The light intrigued me, and I considered taking some shots while we waited. After all, if we couldn't find Danny there would be no trip to "moneyland," as Mitch called it, and wasn't I a photographer? Perhaps I could take some marketable shots. But I didn't feel inspired, it was too much like work. That was a sad thought.

"Hey, what're you guys doing out here?" Danny stood behind us, his floppy hat tilted on his head, the Colt .45 in its holster.

Jon did a double take. "Danny! Where the hell you been?"

"You guys were sleeping late, so I went out and stashed my guns and money and stuff. You don't think I'm going to leave my valuables just lying around while we go to South America, do ya? I ain't crazy, you know."

I grinned. "We thought you were hiding in the cave here, so we sent Mitch in to look for you."

"You sent Mitch into that old silver mine?" Danny roared with laughter, shaking his bearish head.

"Why, what's in there?" I asked.

"Sure as hell ain't silver."

At that moment, Mitch emerged from the mineshaft, his new leather jacket blotched and stained, his face muddied. Upon seeing Danny, Mitch threw up his hands, cursing the sky.

"What happened?" I asked. "You look like shit."

Mitch wiped a cheek. "The tunnel went down for a ways, then I took a branch that curved back around, then, I don't know, that cheap-assed flashlight started cutting out, and water was dripping down on me, and I slipped and fell in the mud. Man, that place stunk. Some animal must have died down there."

"It should stink," Danny said. "When they built that old outhouse, the idiots dug the pit directly over the mineshaft. That's not mud all over your ass, that's what's been going into that old latrine for the past sixty years."

Mitch's eyes became great white circles. Jon let out a snicker. Air squealed past my larynx. I couldn't hold back any longer, and a sick chuckle trickled out, which quickly exploded into a flood of hooting laughter. Jon doubled over, hysterical, holding his sides, while Danny danced about like a scarecrow on laughing gas. Mitch tried to sling the brown goo from his jacket, scraping at it with the flashlight. Dark ovals marked his knees, and his toupee was streaked.

"If you could fly," Danny said, "you'd be a shit bird!"

Roars of laughter echoed madly from the mountainside.

While Mitch hiked up to the springs to wash, the three of us made it back to the cabin, started a fire, and ripped open packages of strawberry toaster pastries. We wolfed them down between bouts of giggles, while the mountainside reverberated with Mitch's mournful yowls as he splashed in the icy water.

"Poor son of a bitch," I said.

A cry of agony echoed down the hillside.

"What do you guys think? Rescue party?" Jon asked.

"I ain't goin' up there," Danny said.

Jon and I took a blanket up the hill. We found Mitch squatting on a flat rock by the pool, shivering, hugging his stark-white body in a ridiculous effort to keep warm. I threw him the blanket. Mitch had draped his soaking-wet clothes over rocks, where they steamed in the morning sun. His new leather jacket was a mess, and his toupee lay nearby, a soggy ball of fur. From the rocks above squirrels gossiped and chattered.

"Dammit, you guys! What did I do to deserve this?"

I couldn't help but laugh— I almost pitied him. Almost.

"Come back to the cabin, you can warm up and dry your clothes," I said.

Wrapped in a blanket, his wet shoes squeaking, Mitch trundled back to the cabin and collapsed near the stove. I threw him a package of toaster pastries, hoping it would stop his moaning.

As I hung Mitch's clothes on a rope, I heard loud voices from outside the cabin. Instinctively, I grabbed my camera. Danny and Jon stood by the old red pickup, yelling.

"You gotta ask General Ray every time you want to wipe your ass?"

"I just wanna check in, I mean, he depends on me to be there—"

"The hell. That butt-head doesn't depend on anything except dumb-assed morons like you hanging around kissing his ass. He's a goddam egomaniac—"

"What you bad rapping General Ray for? I thought you were buddies, the other day you two were hanging out, drinking his brew, acting like you were friends. What happened to that?"

"Forget that. Never happened."

"Sometimes, you don't make a damn bit of sense."

"I'm sick of you. I'm sick of your craziness, I'm sick of this paranoid shit. I'm just sick of your ass and those goddam numb-nut Trotts."

"Don't you call them names. They gave me a place to live, what did you ever do for me?"

"Do for you? Dammit! I was the one who got you this place! Christ, I brought you here, I made things right with General Butt Head."

"Don't you call him that!"

"Don't *you* ever tell me what to say."

"Stupid monk."

"Whacko."

"Monkey monk! Monkey monk!"

I leveled my camera, focusing in on Danny, his eyes firing toward me as I snapped the shutter. I swung the lens toward Jon, capturing an expression of unrestrained malice.

"God dammit," Jon screamed, and kicked the truck's fender, scuffing the oxidized paint. Rust rained from the tire well.

"You're losing it man," Danny said, shaking his head. "See, Brad? He's out of control. I just wanted to take a run down to Deadwood."

"No! Goddamit, no, I'm telling you no. No means no!"

"Jon's lost it, man."

Smoking Jimi

    I lowered my Nikon. "Hey, it's all OK. Know why? We're a band again, and this whole thing is bigger than any of us. Someday, we're gonna look back and laugh, and know this was all meant to be— the sorry-assed time we spent apart was for a reason, and I love you guys, and even if there weren't any money, I wouldn't want to be anywhere else. I missed you guys so much."

    I wasn't the only one with tears, and I put my arms around Jon and Danny, hoping that my words weren't just feel-good bullshit.

    "Hey, you queers, I got good news." Mitch stood at the door, wrapped in his blanket, holding up my cell phone. "We leave for South America tonight. Badger Springs Airbase. It's a done deal."

Chad Peery

13

Jon's yellow Mustang bumped and rattled over the road that took us back down to the Trotts' checkpoint. Mitch sat in the backseat next to Danny, grumbling. I braced myself against the car's lurches, amazed at how easily Jon negotiated this rutted, backwoods road.

"How far is this airport?" I asked Jon.

"Badger Springs Air Force Base? Five, maybe six hours. Deserted. Shut down back in the 80's. Northwest of here, near the Utah border."

"Anybody got any cash?" I asked. "I've only got a twenty."

"Got a few thousand, kept it from what you gave me," Jon said, steering around a deep rut.

"Stashed all mine," Danny said.

"I'm flat broke," Mitch mumbled, reaching for a smoke.

"Smoke in here and I'll cut your lips off," Danny said. Blinking, Mitch put his cigarette back into the pack.

At least Jon had convinced Danny to hide his Colt .45 under a board behind his shack, in case he needed it for later when the government came to take over. But Danny was still armed with a knife, cunningly disguised as part of his belt buckle. I thought Mitch might faint when Danny showed him the blade's vicious saw-tooth design.

"Something stinks," I said. "I think we're getting a bit ripe."

"It's Mitch," Danny said, leaning toward the open window.

"What's got those two going?" Jon asked, as we approached the checkpoint. The pair of Trott guards waved furiously at us. The older one, his face tense, jogged to Jon's window.

"A couple'a hours ago, two men in a Chevy Blazer came up here, asking about them two musicians. One of these fellas was weird, had white hair and these really blue eyes, but he wasn't old or nothin' like that. Strange foreign accent. Wouldn't say who they was. Could have been some U.N. spies, you know, an advance scouting party. Had a picture of that one there," he said, jabbing a finger at me.

Heat went to my face. Those two bastards were back! With a photo of me! My stomach clenched into a knot.

"They had a picture of Brad? You sure?" Jon asked.

"Yup. Wanted to know if we'd seen him, what Danny did, and if you ever came up here. Got squat from me. I informed them they were trespassing on sovereign Patroticus Invictus territory, and they had ten seconds to vacate or they'd be placed under arrest and have their vehicle confiscated. Watch yer back. That driver was packing, saw his shoulder holster." He backed away from the window, waving at his nose. "What the hell? You guys been dipped in shit, or what?"

"Here, have a new jacket," Mitch said, thrusting it out the window.

As we drove away, the young guard began to try on Mitch's mottled leather coat, and then threw it down in disgust. I grabbed my camera and leaned out the window, taking a few shots of the Trotts' checkpoint, just for the hell of it.

"Not supposed to do that," Danny said.

"Why do you think I did?"

Mitch cackled and slapped the back of my seat. "Way to go, Brad!"

"Why are those two guys in a Chevy Blazer following you around?" Danny asked.

"Who knows how they got my photo, but I think they're loan shark enforcers after Mitch, not me. Somehow, they got me hooked up with him. Mitch is a goddam plague."

"Right, Brad, I bring you a million dollars and I get complaints."

"Could be feds, I.R.S. maybe," Danny said. "They do shit like that."

"No," I said, "it's Mitch. It's always Mitch. Everything he touches turns to crap."

"Calm down," Jon said. "I'll drop you guys off at my place— you can get cleaned up while I go to the monastery."

"What about that Chevy Blazer?" I asked.

"Don't sweat it. Vituscans know how to take care of our own."

I almost expected to see the gray Chevrolet waiting around each curve, but there was no trace of it until we got to Wort Rock. If I weren't so paranoid, I wouldn't have noticed the Blazer lurking

Smoking Jimi

in the gas station's parking lot, a patient spider. As we passed by, White Hair and his partner looked straight at me.

"Sons of bitches," I said.

"Nobody panic," Jon said. "This is my town, I'll have it taken care of."

The old Ford pickup still sat in front of Jon's trailer, leaning slightly on its bald tires, the battered shotgun resting in its rear window. As I stepped out of Jon's Mustang, the gray Chevy Blazer slowly cruised by on the highway.

"You see that?" I said. "Dammit!"

"They're chicken-dicks," Danny growled. "Ain't got the guts to come down here or they be here already."

Mitch lit up a smoke and stood on the trailer's porch, puffing madly, his damp toupee hanging from his belt like a fresh scalp.

Jon ripped a note from his trailer door and stuffed it into his pocket. "Everybody inside, I'll take care of everything." He immediately went into his bedroom, grabbed the telephone, and kicked the door shut. A few muffled words later, he returned, wearing the look of a soldier girding for battle.

"Be cleaned up and ready to go. Keep someone on watch at the window at all times. Give me one hour, max. If I'm not back by then or if anything happens, call this number." Jon scribbled on a note and handed it to me.

While Danny went for his shower, Mitch took the first watch at the window. He wiped his nose on a sleeve like a kid. "Ain't Danny weird? I mean, wow, how could anyone in their right mind live in a dump like that? He gives me the willies, that one, watch yourself."

"He may be weird, but he never ripped me off."

Mitch grunted. "I'm next for the shower."

"We flip for it," I said.

Mitch lost.

While I showered, a musical riff came to my head, perhaps something I could use in a new song. I thought of my guitar in the trunk of Jon's car, and wished I could spend hours with it every day, the way I used to. I smiled, thinking how long it had been since I'd had those kinds of notions. I found fresh underwear and a clean white T-shirt in Jon's bedroom, but all of Jon's pants were far too short, so I put on my khaki trousers.

When I took over Mitch's watch at the window, all was quiet except for a couple of kids playing at the far end of the driveway, shooting each other with toy guns. Danny had slicked back his wet hair and stood at the stereo, playing CD's, jumping from track to track and surfing one disk to another. From Cream's "Toad," into "Crossroads," into "Sunshine," Danny's head would nod dutifully to a few beats of each song, and then he'd pop out the CD.

"Will you just play something?" I asked, turning away from the window.

"Will if I find something." He put on "Machine Gun," by Jimi Hendrix, and let it play.

I remembered I should call Carol, and moved Jon's phone to the window. I hesitated, but then realized that White Hair already knew where I was, so what did it matter if a call got traced? My heart brightened at her voice, but fell quickly.

"You didn't call last night."

"Couldn't get to a phone. Did any other weird calls come in?"

Pause. "Calls? No calls. You must have been too busy to use the phone. Were you with someone?"

I let the moment hang in the air. "Actually, yes, I was with three guys, and they were all butt-ugly."

"Brad, I think you're lying to me."

"C'mon, I was freezing my ass off on the floor of a cabin."

"Really? Did she make you happy, the way I can?"

"This isn't the time, Carol."

"Is she one of those baby machines you've always wanted?"

"This isn't funny. I was sleeping on the stupid floor."

"You never called me stupid before. See? That's how it begins."

"Carol, right now, I need you to be strong."

"Haven't I always looked out for you? If it weren't for me, you wouldn't even have gone on this trip. Now I'm losing you. She's only after your money, you know that, don't you?"

Occasionally, Carol would call me on the way home from work and we would engage in this sort of fantasy, at least I thought it was fantasy. It had always played innocent and campy, usually ending with a make-believe apology for a make-believe affair, followed by incredibly wild lovemaking.

"Carol, please, stop playing this game."

"Me? Stop? Brad, you're the one who's unfaithful. I can almost see her."

"This is insane. I gotta go." I slammed down the phone. Why had she gone off on one of her perverse fantasies? Was she flipping out? This was the first time I'd been away from her this long, maybe that had triggered it. Perhaps that anonymous call yesterday asking if I chased around with other women set her off. Stale dread awakened at the thought of going back to that woman.

Someone pounded on the door, banging so hard the wall rattled. Danny killed the music and crouched behind the leather sofa, his eyes scary slits. I opened the door a crack, my weight set against it.

She was a cute forty, petite, short brown hair, and decidedly shapely beneath her T-shirt. "Oh, I'm sorry, is Jon here?"

"He's gone to the monastery, should be back soon," I said as I opened the door.

She looked past me, and then glanced at the driveway. "Just tell him Julie came by, the leak's started again, you know, my plumbing."

"Hey, Julie, I'll fix it," Danny said, emerging from behind the sofa.

Before I could say anything, Danny had picked up the pipe wrench by the porch and followed her to the next trailer. Jon wouldn't be pleased, but so what? He wasn't the boss. I stood in the doorway and took a breath of air perfumed with pine scent. The trailer park seemed so serene and peaceful— I inhaled deeply before I shut the door.

"That chick that was just here, I saw a picture of her in Jon's bedroom," Mitch said, a white towel wrapped around his waist. "Sure like to fix her plumbing, that's one righteous babe."

I drew back the curtains to check the driveway while Mitch plopped his toupee on a lampshade to dry. The computer made the stuttering squawk of an Internet connection.

"What are you doing?"

"Checking email." Mitch made a face. "Sons of bitches. Bastards." He rapped hard on a few keys and fingered the mouse. "Oh my. Look here, my, my, Jon, Jon, you naughty boy." He bit his lower lip, the screen's glow illuminating his leering gaze.

"What?"

"I checked out Jon's browser history. Guess what popped up? Little Susie's XXX Parlor." He clicked the mouse.

"Mitch, dammit, that's none of your business, shut that thing off."

"Wow, check this honey out. And look at this guy's schlong, how'd you like to see that gnarly thing coming at you in a dark alley? Ha!"

A gunshot exploded from near the trailer, the deep boom rattling my chest. I looked out the window. From up the driveway kids with toy guns stared in our direction. A few trailers down, an old man peered out his door, blinking in the sunlight. Julie came running into view.

"Help! Somebody! Danny shot himself!"

14

My heart pounded as I rushed into Julie's trailer. From somewhere a dog yapped and a teapot whistled. I followed Julie into the bathroom, steeling myself for the worst.

Danny sat on the toilet, looking up at me. A shotgun lay on the white linoleum next to a scattering of blood drops.

"What happened?"

"Shot myself." Danny grinned, holding up his left thumb, which was wrapped in a red-stained washcloth.

My photographer's eye appreciated the red color, so bright and pure, spreading upon the white cloth— the picture of my downfall, the way something always happens to screw things up. Now, there would be no band, no trip, nothing.

"Aw, Christ," Mitch said, standing behind me, naked except for his towel. "I can't believe this. You fucked up your hand, Jesus man, how the hell are you going to play drums? Of all the stupid, dumb-assed . . . ."

Mitch ranted on as I knelt and unwrapped Danny's washcloth. A dime-sized, metal shard protruded from Danny's thumb, and blood ran freely from the wound. I moved his hand so it would drip into the sink.

"That shotgun's not mine," Julie said, peeking around Mitch. "Danny must have brought it in from that old pickup while I was in the kitchen with Bosco. Is Danny OK?"

"Don't worry," I said. "Give me some room."

As he backed up, Mitch's towel slipped to the floor. While he scrambled to cover himself, Danny laughed, pointing with his good hand.

"Look at that little thing, will ya?"

While I rinsed Danny's thumb under cold running water his defiant grin never faltered, but his jaw muscles clenched. His blood drops painted angry red splotches on the sink's white porcelain.

Toenails clicked on the linoleum and something brushed my leg. A small dog sniffed at a drop of blood on the white floor. Its tongue flicked in a tentative lick. Mitch groaned.

"Bosco!" Julie snatched up the dog and carried it away, speaking quietly into its ear.

"We may need pliers to get this shrapnel out," I said, "could be lodged in the bone. How'd this happen?"

"Needed some leverage against the pipe wrench, so I got the shotgun out of the pickup. Went off by itself. Tore the drainpipe all to hell, and some of it ended up in my thumb."

"You shot the pipe?"

"Fixed its ass good, didn't I? Ha!"

Before I could react, Danny put his wounded thumb to his mouth, gripped the metal shard with his teeth, and spit it into the sink. The twisted metal glistened with blood and malice. Danny's thumb bled profusely, and I wrapped it in a fresh towel.

Danny pointed with his good thumb. "Don't run the water, you're gonna make a mess under the sink."

I opened the under-sink cabinet. The shotgun blast had demolished the drainpipe and blown a hole into the adjoining room. Bloody water pooled beneath the drain.

"Makes a big hole, don't it?" Danny said.

"Here," Julie said, "I brought bandages and antiseptic."

I poured hydrogen peroxide into the gash. Danny's eyes narrowed as the peroxide fizzed, but his grin widened.

"This ain't nothing, man."

After I wrapped the wound with bandage and gauze, Danny scrutinized the fat white thumb on his left hand.

"Keep it raised so it won't start bleeding. You'll need stitches."

"No. No doctors."

I looked to Mitch and Julie for help. They shrugged.

"Let's get him back to Jon's," I said.

"Sorry about the sink," Danny said to Julie, as I led him out of her trailer. "Wait. My shotgun."

"I'll get it," Mitch said.

In Jon's trailer, Danny went straight to the CD player and resumed playing a Hendrix CD, as if nothing had happened. Suddenly, he slapped his forehead, whirled, and glared at Mitch.

"Where's my goddam shotgun?"

"I unloaded it and threw the shells as far as I could. Told Julie to keep the damned thing." Mitch readjusted the towel around his waist.

"Son of a bitch!" Danny jabbed his bandaged thumb at Mitch. "You just compromised our security. How are we supposed to defend ourselves?"

Jon threw open the front door and strode in. "OK, you guys, ten minutes and we need to be—" He stared at Danny's left thumb. "What the hell happened here?"

Danny explained his predicament, stammering and shuffling his feet, gesturing with his fat white thumb. Enraged, Jon kicked over the coffee table, scattering magazines and unopened mail.

"Dammit! I thought you guys had more sense!" Jon paced in tight circles, and then stopped. "All right. Nothing changes. We're still going, we have to go now, everything's set."

"I can still play. Done it before. Got stabbed once and played five sets the same night." Danny raised his shirt to show us the scar. "This ain't shit."

Jon smacked his palm with a fist. "Time. No time. Ten minutes and we're out of here."

"What about the Blazer?" I asked.

"They'll be taken care of, if we're on schedule. We can't stop for food, we don't know how big this thing is, somebody may be watching. Mitch, there's stuff in the fridge, throw some sandwiches together. Brad, give me the keys to the truck and grab some sodas from the pantry. Danny, just— stay there."

"Mitch should probably wear some clothes," I said.

Jon tossed a duffel bag at Mitch's feet. "Throwaways for the thrift store. Help yourself."

Danny fiddled with the stereo while Mitch picked through the wrinkled clothing. He selected a faded orange T-shirt that read: "Steamboat Springs, Honey Bunny Run, 1991." All the pants were far too short.

"I could cut the legs off this one, make Bermuda shorts or something," Mitch said, holding up a beige Sans-a-Belt. Danny reached in his boot and withdrew a sheathed hunting knife with an elaborately carved bone handle. He offered it to Mitch.

"Man, what else you carrying?" Mitch asked, as he sliced through the pants leg with the thick blade.

"That's for me to know and you to find out," Danny said, patting his belt buckle.

Five minutes later, I strapped myself into the passenger seat of Jon's Mustang as we pulled onto the highway. Alongside the guitars and practice amp in the trunk, Jon had stowed a gym bag that contained a few spare shirts and underwear for all of us, along with the guitars and practice amp.

From the backseat, Danny pointed with his bandaged thumb and said, "Look, up that road!"

My heart jumped. The Chevy Blazer was abandoned by the side of a dirt road, the driver's door ajar.

"What happened?" I asked.

"White Hair and his friend are doing the Vituscan Polka," Jon said with a smile. "By the time they walk back to their car, they'll think we're going south, because our Vituscan friends will make sure they see Indian Charlie's pickup heading toward Denver. Meanwhile, we'll be long gone in the opposite direction."

As we passed the outskirts of town, I suddenly realized I was famished. It was almost one in the afternoon, and we hadn't eaten anything since the snacks at Danny's cabin. I handed out the diet sodas I had packed. Mitch took a sip and crinkled his nose. Then, I passed around the ham-on-white sandwiches Mitch had made.

"What's in this stuff?" I asked, after the first bite.

"Something wrong?" Mitch asked.

"No, it's great. It's amazing."

"Just a few things I threw together."

As we feasted on Mitch's delicious sandwiches, the main highway took us north past the turnoff to Danny's cabin. With Wort Rock now behind us, the thought of a long road trip filled me with a satisfaction that food could not. It thrilled a part of me that had been dormant far too long.

"Mitch," Jon said, handing a slip of paper over his shoulder, "here's my bank's wire and account information. Have Pablo Lupa's people send the balance of Danny's share there too."

"And here's my bank numbers," I said, fishing a deposit slip from my wallet.

Jon adjusted his mirror to see Mitch. "No hang-ups with our money? We get confirmation of payment. Right?"

"Absolutely. No sweat. I call 'em right now."

"No service out here," I said, checking my cell phone.

"We'll find a pay phone," Jon said, adjusting his mirror.

"Ever get the car radio working?" Danny asked. "I want music."

"No." Jon looked out his window, as if concealing anger.

"So, you guys ready to play the old songs?" Mitch asked.

Smoking Jimi

"That's the least of our worries," Jon said. "We've got a whole week and we're getting paid in advance. We'll work up the songs once we get down there."

"Works for me," Mitch said.

Gazing out my open window, I wondered what the first explorers must have thought when they encountered the grandeur of these rugged forests. And today, how could anyone think of mowing down these magnificent trees, as if they were just so much corn in a field? Grasses filled the spaces between jagged rocks, as if the whole place had been thrust up in some geologic cataclysm, and then hastily seeded to hide its nakedness. Leading us on, white lines faded into the weathered asphalt. The rumble of the engine, the pop and thump of tires over pavement cracks, the sway of each corner, the car's shadow flirting with the road's crumbling edge—I loved it all. The warm air carried the sweetness of earth, trees, and moss baking in the summer sun. I let it all flow over me, wishing this trip would never end.

"Hey, you guys, next stop it's my turn to sit up front," Mitch demanded.

Danny grunted and pulled at his floppy hat. "Next time we stop, we put what's left of you in the trunk."

The longer Jon drove, the harder it was for me to shake the feeling that White Hair followed in the Chevy Blazer, squealing around the corners, gaining ground. Could we outrun them if it came to that? Jon's Mustang had a large V-8, with a fading MACH I emblazoned on the hood. The once-hot muscle car now blew a hint of smoke, and its front end had a slight shimmy. I laughed at myself as a herd of deer flowed across the road ahead of us. Those two men in the Chevy Blazer could no more catch us than we could capture that deer herd, melting into the brush. I cursed myself for not having my camera ready.

"Any sandwiches left?" Jon asked.

"Nope," I answered, sighting through my camera. "They were so good, we ate 'em all."

Jon wrinkled his face as only he could do. "We'll stop and grab a bite after a while, besides, Mitch needs to use the phone, right?"

"Right-o," Mitch said.

"Why do you wear that stupid wig?" Danny asked. "You think that road kill on your noggin looks cool or something?"

I focused my camera on Mitch, who primped the dirty blond thing on his head.

Click.

Mitch glared at Danny. "Yeah?" How much hair you got left under that Beverly Hillbillies' dunce cap you're wearing?"

Danny snatched Mitch's wig and flung it out the window. "Road kill belongs on the road."

Mitch's wig tumbled along the pavement, coming to rest like an upside-down turtle. Mitch's face froze in open-mouthed disbelief.

Danny laughed. "I'll bet one of them horny-assed, Colorado jackrabbits is humping the damned thing right now."

In a quick motion, Mitch pulled Danny's hat from his head and cast it out the window. Danny snarled and grabbed Mitch's throat with his one good hand. Mitch struggled, his eyes wild, his feet kicking the back of my seat.

Jon slammed on the brakes, and we slid to a stop. "All right, both of you, out. Now!"

Danny released Mitch, and they retreated to their corners of the backseat, like two wrestlers at a match, glaring at each other and waiting for the next round.

Jon smirked, shook his head, and our journey resumed. The steam of anger took a while to evaporate, even at that altitude.

The road reached a summit cut between two peaks, separated by massive rockslides and stubborn trees. The downgrade curved wildly, doubling back on itself. My ears popped. Everything here was so big, rugged, and inhospitable, what would it have been like in those early winters? I pictured foot-weary miners with their grubstakes and dreams of shiny metal, laboring till their hearts were broken by the sad, empty delusion of it all. Maybe that's who we were now, rushing along these same roads where old spirits roamed, four fools chasing riches, destined for the same fate as these miners' ghosts. A gust of wind whipped my face, a cool sigh from the past.

As the road flattened along a wooded plateau a small settlement came into view. Jon pulled into an old gas station that was attached to a dank little store. An old dog raised its head as we pulled up to the pumps, and I snapped a photo of a boy playing in the dirt near the entrance.

Jon switched off the ignition. "Mitch, use that phone booth. It'll take three hours to reach Badger Springs Airbase, plenty of time to arrange our money transfer. If anybody's hungry, grab something to go."

"C'mon," Mitch whined, "I need some walking-around money."

Jon grimaced and tossed a hundred over his shoulder.

Squeezing out of the back seat, Mitch said, "Can't believe people live like this, there's nothing here, nothing." Looking ridiculous in his ragged cutoffs and orange T-shirt, Mitch puffed a cigarette while flapping his arms in a gesture of exercise. Near the store entrance, a small boy made zooming sounds as he drove toy cars around an imaginary track. While Jon gassed up, Danny and I walked past the boy's make-believe racetrack and headed towards the restrooms. I gave up trying to hold my breath, I'd been in worse.

"How's your thumb?" I asked, zipping up.

"Never felt better. Wish asshole Mitch hadn't ditched the shotgun. Watch out for that bastard, he's out to rip us off again. Mark my words."

Inside the store, we found fried chicken and quarter-cut potatoes displayed under a heat lamp. In the shadows, an old man wearing a cowboy hat sat hunched over a newspaper bearing the headline, "John F. Kenney Jr. Dies in Plane Crash." The reader raised his hard-blue eyes from the paper to me. From his expression, I couldn't tell if he had been reading good news or bad. A heavyset man in a black T-shirt stepped behind the counter to wait on me, his boots clumping on oily boards.

As he prepared my bucket of chicken and potatoes, I picked up a crudely printed Patroticus Invictus leaflet. It warned all residents that the United Nations had taken control of the Condry County Deeds and Records Department with the intention of erasing everyone's family history, after which they would use environmental treaties to confiscate everyone's land, and Washington and the Jew bankers were in on this conspiracy, and at the next county commissioner's meeting Patroticus Invictus would demand that the Condry County Commissioners stand tall and pass a resolution requiring Sheriff Hardy to deputize all members of Patroticus Invictus, who would then search door to door, arrest the foreign devils, and put a stop to this ungodly conspiracy for once and for all, and all patriotic citizens were expected to attend. On the back was a coupon for ten percent off hollow points at The Gun

Shack, and below that, an official list of unpatriotic merchants who refused to distribute Patroticus Invictus leaflets.

"Good outfit, them guys," Jon said, rapping a knuckle on the leaflets as he paid for the gas. The man behind the counter grunted as if he knew it was bull.

Outside, I knelt down next to the boy as he raced his fleet of matchbox-sized cars in the dirt.

"Hi there. Hungry?" I offered the bucket of chicken.

"No thanks, just had something," the boy said, keeping his eyes on the cars so they wouldn't crash.

"Which one is fastest?"

He thought for a moment. "The Mustang, everybody knows that." He offered me a dusty red car. "This is the fastest one— it'll help you get away from the bad guys."

I stammered, "No— well, thanks." I took the tiny red car and handed the boy my last five. "Here. Get yourself a candy bar or something."

Mitch stepped out of the battered phone booth and gave me a thumbs-up. As he walked away in a cloud of cigarette smoke, I stepped into the booth to call Carol collect. We had unfinished business. She spoke first, her voice sounding far away in the receiver.

"I can't believe this. Brad, you've never hurt me like this before."

My stomach gripped itself. "Carol, I need you to be strong right now, and this game isn't helping."

"Don't be coy, Brad. She's young, isn't she? Are you planning to see her again?"

A wave of anger passed through me. I cursed Carol's twisted imagination.

"This is stupid. How about I just move out when I get back, and we'll call it even?"

Pause. "You never understood me, not the way I understand you. You've put a dagger in my heart. Do you love her, I mean, really love her, the way that I've loved you?"

I wanted to flee from Carol's madness, but my ear remained pressed to the receiver.

"Carol, you're playing a game with us, and it's just a game. You know there's nobody else."

"See, you can't even be honest. Brad, why do you want to hurt me? Is it something I did?"

A strange part of me had the urge to give in, throw her an apology and finish her perverse little game. Maybe this was her twisted, selfish way of manipulating me into making a commitment to her. A soft zone in my heart felt her need, and a dark part of me still found her weirdness attractive. All I had to do was utter one simple phrase, and it would be the end of the game, I would be her hero.

I hung up the phone, silencing her voice. As I walked away, the troubled ghost of my shadow spread over the gravel and I wanted to grind it into the dirt. Today's journey was about more than money. If the plane didn't show or the deal fell apart, then my old life would lure me back into Carol's comfortable web of perversion and creeping sorrow. If not her, then another like her. My only escape was going on the road with the band. So it was now, so it had always been. Such is life without Gjerna.

A thought occurred— perhaps something had been feeding Carol's paranoia. She would have been on the Internet reading up on Pablo Lupa, which would be rich with gossip about his parties and tastes in women. Carol was worried about losing control of her newly minted millionaire, wasn't she? That thought brought a smile to my lips.

While we sat in the car waiting for Jon to make his phone call, I passed around the bucket of chicken while Danny handed out cans of Pepsi.

"So, what's the word, Mitchy boy?" Danny asked, biting into a chicken leg. "We gettin' our money or what?"

"Everything's happening, we're cool," Mitch said, grabbing a fat breast, like a prison con snatching food from a neighbor's tray.

"Problem," Jon said, returning to the car and cranking up the engine. "Just called the monastery. After White Hair and his buddy walked back to their Chevy Blazer, they didn't go for the decoy— they were supposed to follow Indian Charlie's pickup. Instead, they drove straight to Julie's place, asked a bunch of questions about us and then headed north. They're on our tail, maybe thirty minutes behind us. Danny, did you tell Julie where we were going?"

"She won't say nothing, man, Julie's cool. Besides, if Mitch the Bitch hadn't dumped our shotgun, we could just wait for them suckers to come around the bend, know what I mean? *Bam.* End of story."

I had a mental flash of Danny, all crazy eyes and shotgun, springing from the bushes like a stagecoach bandit. "How did your Vituscan friends get those guys out of their Chevy Blazer?" I asked.

Jon laughed as he pulled the Mustang back onto the highway. "Unmitigated cleverness."

"Did my photos ever get developed?"

Jon pulled an envelope from the console. "Almost forgot. We don't know who these guys are. Definitely not feds."

"How do you know they're not feds?" Mitch asked.

Jon ignored Mitch's question. "Interesting thing about White Hair, he doesn't appear to be a true albino, just a young guy with white hair."

I studied the shot of the Chevy Blazer passing us at the gas station. From behind the wheel, White Hair stared directly at me. I had the awful feeling of looking at my own face, my death mask, and this man hunted me, only me. How absurd. I handed the photo to Mitch, and said:

"Wish you'd pay your bills, man. Recognize this guy?"

Mitch shook his head no.

As we passed the photos around, everyone talked at once. Who the hell were these guys and did they know we were going to Badger Springs Airbase? What did they want? Money? Mitch's ass?

Thinly forested, rock-cluttered hillsides rushed past as we climbed higher, and everyone fell silent. Jon squinted against the sun and lowered his visor. I found two pairs of sunglasses in the glove box, put on a pair, and handed the other to Jon. Danny had bought a pair at the store.

"Hey," Mitch said, "I want sunglasses too. How come I'm the only one without sunglasses?"

"Because you're wearing cutoff shorts with black socks," I said.

Mitch leaned forward. "Know what, guys? I may have black socks, but I'm making all you dudes millionaires. Hey, look at us here, four millionaires, running around in this beat-up, piece-of-shit car in the middle of nowhere! How about that? All because of me. Don't any of you millionaires ever forget that."

"So, the deal is, we're supposed to jam with Pablo Lupa?" Jon asked, sunlight glinting off his dark glasses.

I chuckled. "Think this dude can actually play keyboards?"

"Who cares?" Mitch said, munching a potato skin.

Jon massaged his neck. "Remember the changes to any of the songs? You should, Brad, you wrote most of them."

"I didn't write anything on that first album. Once we get there, I say we don't play any of that crap."

"What, no 'Jammie Time' for Pablo's teenybopper fantasy?" Jon started to sing the chorus of our old hit song.

"Shut up before I puke down your neck," Danny said, passing us the bucket of chicken.

The road curved upward again, and Jon slowed as he approached a tractor-trailer laboring through the curves. Metallic steer skulls glistened on the mud flaps. Behind us, a black pickup truck bore down, flashing its lights as if that would make Jon's Mustang and the big rig disappear. The black pickup was so high off the ground that only its massive grill and bumper appeared through the Mustang's rear window. The pitch of its howling tires fell as it slowed to avoid ramming us. The winding road made passing impossible.

"So, Brad, what are you going to do with your share of the money?" Jon asked, as he took a quick glance over his shoulder at the truck.

"Get my life back. Maybe play music again, start an art studio, I don't know. I couldn't see how trapped I'd become until I got away from my old life. It's a rut that eats you up till there's nothing left, and then you die."

"Life sucks and then you die," Danny said, taking a hard look at the pickup truck, which was still riding our bumper.

"You had it pretty good there in Florida," Mitch said.

I shook my head. "It's a comfortable prison with locked doors, quiet nights, and losing your life one day at a time. Nobody gets out alive. I just want to live, really live, maybe travel. What are you going to do with your share?" I asked Jon.

He shrugged.

"I'm getting a boat," Danny said. "I'll be the first to sail across the Atlantic inside the eye of a hurricane. I got it all figured out— since it's totally calm in the eye, all I gotta do is cruise at the speed of the hurricane, and I'll have a smooth ride with all this wind and shit going on around me. I'll be famous."

The highway curved upward following the contours of the mountainside, while below us stretched a vista of stunted valleys guarded by peaks flecked with snowy notches and clefts. In the deep-blue sky an eagle soared on invisible currents, all sharp talons and powerful wings. The black pickup behind us flashed its lights again.

A short straightaway opened up and Jon punched it, trying to pass the semi. Abruptly, he cursed and slammed on the brakes, nearly hitting the back of the trailer. The black pickup had cut us off and screamed past us, its oversized tires moaning on the pavement.

"Hey, god-dammit!" Danny shouted. "Who the hell do they think they are? Sons of bitches!"

Jon passed the semi and cut in behind the black pickup. Danny stuck his head and shoulders out the window, shouting obscenities, gesturing wildly at the black pickup. It slowed. Danny motioned for them to pull over while we all yelled at him to get back in the damned car. Mitch grabbed Danny's shirt, pulling him down into the seat.

"HEY! Don't you ever, *EVER* touch me again," Danny hissed, his face twisted beyond recognition.

"Shit, just what we need," Jon said, as the black pickup pulled off the road to let us pass. It loomed quickly behind us, blaring its horn.

"Time to kick some girly-boy butt," Danny shouted. "You gotta be a wuss to drive a sissy rig like that."

"Keep him quiet," Jon yelled. The Mustang's engine roared and the tires squealed around a tight turn. The black pickup leaned heavily around the curves, but stayed with us, blowing its horn. Danny screamed obscenities at the rear window.

I sank into the seat, cursing. Great. What now, a stupid fistfight? I remembered Danny's barroom-brawl story. Cops. Trouble. Moronic stupidity. What if the idiot behind us had a gun? Adrenaline soiled my stomach. To come this far, and end up dead by the side of the road. I opened the glove box. Maybe I could find a screwdriver, something. I moved an envelope. A black-leather holster. A gun!

"Close that," Jon said, pointing at the glove box. "Close the door, right god damn now."

I obeyed. Jon, the monk, with a gun in his car? Maybe everybody out here was armed, even the Vituscans. At least we had something.

A commotion in the back seat caught my attention. Mitch had taken out his hundred-dollar bill, and hung it out the window for the pickup's driver to see. He then released it. The bill fluttered past the black truck. The driver didn't stop.

"Give me another hundred, quick."

Jon cursed and tossed him a hundred-dollar bill. Again, Mitch held it out with both hands for the truck's driver to see. The hundred fluttered in the air like a fat, green butterfly as he let it go. This time, the truck screeched to a stop and backed up. The driver rushed out to fetch the bill, while Danny hung out the window calling him a chicken shit. The scene disappeared around a corner. Mitch sat back, laughing devilishly, his hands spread before him like a magician.

"See? Hicks are so predictable. Aw, my shoes! Dammit! Danny spilled soda all over the place back here."

"Did not. You spilled it yourself."

"Shut up you two," Jon shouted. The Mustang's tires howled as we veered onto a poorly marked turnoff.

"Goddamit, stop right here," Danny said. "I want that chicken dick in the pickup. I'll teach his ass. No goddam sweat."

"Danny, cool it," Jon said. "Nobody's following us now. Take it easy, man."

As my heartbeat relaxed and we settled into the winding road, anger radiated from Danny like heat from a stove. Now I understood what Jon meant about keeping Danny away from civilization. And we were taking him to South America? In the old days, Danny was the spark plug, the band's instigator, its cheerleader, its conscience— but now he was a hormone-drunk adolescent in a grown man's body.

I pulled the red toy car from my shirt pocket and twirled a wheel. What a cute kid, back there at the store. His parents were lucky to have a son like that, and probably didn't realize it. Did he even have parents? My mind wandered back to the kid and his cars. Finally, Danny broke the silence:

"You guys fly into the Denver airport?" Danny asked.

"What of it?" Mitch folded his arms.

"Bet you don't know what's beneath that sucker. The government built this huge underground complex. When the shit hits the fan, that's going to be UN headquarters for the west coast. But we're on to their little game. They ain't foolin' us."

Jon ran a hand through where his hair used to be. "Danny, do you have any ID?"

"No."

Jon grimaced. "What did you do with your driver's license?"

"General Ray said we should burn all our ID's, so the satellites can't locate us. No government's keepin' tabs on me. Don't worry about a stinkin' license. Worry about what's happening to your country."

"I'm more worried about what's going to happen in the backseat if I don't get to drain my lizard," Mitch said.

Jon pulled over, and the four of us stood at the road's edge, pissing onto the rocks below. Danny drew lazy circles in the air with his stream, like a kid playing with a garden hose. The late-afternoon sun was trapped in high clouds, and dusty warmth cooked up from the ground.

"Mitch never did tell us what he does for a living," Jon said, as we zipped up.

"He's a professional pickpocket," I said.

"I create things," Mitch said, taking a proud drag on a cigarette he had just lit.

"All you create is trouble," Jon said, kicking a rock over the edge.

"I just happen to be a gourmet chef," he said, pulling at a dangling thread on his cutoffs.

I laughed so hard I bent over. "You? A Chef? Ha! And I'm Jimi Hendrix."

Mitch didn't smile. "I just got hired at the Excelsior. Then that damned Bernie got me fired. It's all politics. What do you guys know? Why couldn't I be a chef?"

"Because," Jon said, laughing, "you're too good of a con artist."

Mitch trudged back to the car, ignoring our taunts.

"But you eat garbage," I called after Mitch, as flipped his cigarette onto the road and climbed into the back seat. "Your idea of living large is burgers and fries! C'mon!"

Mitch gazed out the window, nose held high.

Back on the road, Jon slapped the wheel. "A gourmet chef?" He burst out laughing.

Mitch cocked his head. "Fine. What's the recipe for Veal Cantonese Normandy?"

"Civilized people don't eat veal," I said.

Mitch recited the recipe, line by line, while Jon made an expression of exasperated amusement. After that, everyone became quiet, and a delicious fatigue settled in. I rested my burning eyes for a moment.

I awoke to an aching neck. The sun had become a glowing cinder beyond a range of huddled mountains, and a blanket of dirty-pink clouds covered the sky. Weeds grew from cracks that snaked across the pavement, and Jon slowed to avoid a three-foot pothole. The road continued across a windswept plateau, then wandered up a short hill where it ended abruptly at a chain-link fence. A padlocked gate crowned with coils of rusty wire blocked our path. On the other side of the fence sat two corroded buildings, probably old hangars.

"This doesn't look right," Jon said, opening his door.

I got out and followed Jon to the two-piece gate. A faded no-trespassing sign hung beneath coils of sagging barbed wire, which spilled over the fence in both directions. A guardhouse, its windows broken out, stood beyond the fence, and past that cement foundations lined a wide boulevard. It wasn't hard to imagine the bustle of jeeps and roar of jets at this once-bustling airbase. In the distance, a grid of runways spread at sharp angles, and despite a few tumbleweeds, they appeared serviceable. A few dead trees stood near the gate, and the sparse vegetation seemed scraggly, as if the ground were sick. I tugged at the age-crusted lock and chain.

"Wonder if there's another way in?" I asked.

"Stand clear," Jon said.

I took Jon's advice as he got behind the wheel and nudged the Mustang's bumper up to where the gate halves joined. The engine growled and the gates groaned, but the rear tires broke loose, spinning madly on the pavement. Mitch looked as if he wanted to crawl out the window, while Danny gleefully bobbed and howled. Jon mouthed a curse, backed up the car, and then roared forward crashing into the gates. One half of the gate wrenched violently sideways, while the other snapped loose and skidded across the ground. Jon slid to a stop in a cloud of dust and exhaust fumes.

Danny hooted and yelled in the back seat. A mangled headlight dangled from the Mustang's fender.

I jumped into the car. "Wow, Vituscan monks don't mess around."

"Monkey monk," Danny said, laughing.

I turned to Mitch. "So, now what? Where's the plane?"

Mitch checked his watch. "Not due for another thirty minutes."

Jon drove the Mustang down a boulevard, and then parked in the valley between the two hangars. From the shadows we had a panoramic view of both the runway and the crashed gates. Danny wanted to lower the convertible's top, so Jon and I worked the reluctant canvas down, exposing the deepening sky. I leaned back against the headrest. Clouds patterned with striations of marble floated above us, tinged pink from the remnants of sun.

"What about the money?" Jon asked.

"Don't sweat it," Mitch said, brushing imaginary crumbs from his orange T-shirt. He clambered out of the car to have a smoke.

Where Mitch stood, someone had once patched the pavement cracks with tar, which had long ago seeped into the ground. Just like me— I hadn't fallen through life's cracks, just seeped slowly through. But I was back. And so was the band!

"We're really doing it," Jon said, knocking me in the arm. "Your cell work out here?"

I pulled the cell phone from my camera bag, but couldn't get a connection.

"Looks like we'll have to use the phone on the plane to verify our bank transfers. Right?" Jon asked.

"No problem," Mitch said. "All taken care of."

As we sat in uneasy silence, I kept an eye out for the Chevy Blazer's headlights, certain that I would soon see its twin beams spike the dusk as it climbed toward the front gate. Mitch stood by the car in the deepening shadows, smoking and talking to himself, which made me even more uncomfortable.

"Look!" Jon said, pointing toward the entrance. My heart pounded as headlights slashed the air.

"White Hair?" I asked.

"Time to party," Danny growled, standing up in the rear of the convertible. "I still got my knife. I'll wait over there, and when they drive by—"

"No! Everybody stay cool," Jon said.

I put a long lens on my camera and peered through the viewfinder, locating the headlights. I twisted the focus ring. The blur became a white sport-utility vehicle, a Tahoe, with a row of lights and several antennae on the roof. The driver approached slowly, checking out the damaged gate.

"Let me have a look," Jon said.

I handed him the camera. The Tahoe sped toward the far end of the runway, stopped, dropped a burning road flare, and then parked at the opposite end of the tarmac with its headlights shooting down the landing strip. The floodlights on the Tahoe's roof lit up.

"Who are those guys?" I asked.

"Damned if I know," Jon said, handing the camera back.

Danny leaned forward. "Range, one hundred meters. I could pop their caps from here before they knew what hit 'em. If I had my '47."

Before Jon could tell Danny to shut up, a rumbling echo approached like the swell of thunder, which grew to the deep roar of jet engines. Red lights moved in low on the horizon, and then landing lights switched on, splashing the runway in white. A sleek jet touched down just beyond the flare, its tires barking. With a murderous roar, it reversed its engines, slowing as it approached the Tahoe. The plane's wingtips were of a modern design, bent upward at right angles, and it had twin engines mounted beneath the tail. As it taxied toward the Tahoe, its landing lights cast long shadows from the vehicle's two passengers, who now stood alongside the truck. One man held a scope-equipped rifle, while the other shined a flashlight toward us. Dust swirled as the plane swung its nose in our direction and lurched forward. Its landing lights became dazzling suns as the jet rolled closer. Suddenly, the glaring lights died out and the plane's white nose bobbed to a stop, pointing at us from fifty feet away, the pilots' silhouettes lit by the instrument panel. As the twin engines whined down, a side door opened. A ladder unfolded and touched the ground.

No one came out.

"Showtime," Jon said.

"Wait. Let me go first," Mitch said. His shoulders sloped submissively, and he approached the plane with his trademark penguin waddle. Standing at the foot of the stairs, he ran his hand over his face while peering at the five porthole-shaped windows. He then climbed into the cabin's yellow glow. During this time, the two men remained alongside their Tahoe, and the rifleman had his gun sighted in our direction.

"I smell weirdness," Danny said. "Could use that shotgun, dammit."

Mitch emerged from the plane and ambled toward the Mustang, his eyes to the ground like a beaten dog. He approached my side of the car.

"I, there's been some changes, we, I guess, look, the money's not here, it's somewhere else."

"What?" Jon shouted.

I shoved open my door and Mitch held up his hands, stumbling backward.

"C'mon, you guys—"

"Payback time," Danny growled, and leaped out of the car.

I planted myself in front of Mitch, blocking Danny.

"Dammit, Mitch!" I shouted. "You said the money would be wired to our banks before we got on that plane."

"I'll straighten this out," Jon said. "Who's on that aircraft?"

"Just the pilots," Mitch said. "They don't know anything. Listen—"

Danny shoved past me and seized Mitch by the throat, shaking him like a hound with a rabbit. Mitch collapsed with Danny on top of him. We yelled and tussled with Danny, grabbing his arms and trying to pull him back. Freed from his attacker, Mitch remained on the pavement, blinking at the sky, just like at the Wendy's restaurant.

With a screech of tires the Tahoe pulled along side the plane, its headlights glaring at us. The gunman hopped out and took a shooter's stance over the hood, sighting us through his scope. Danny held his hands aloft, flipping them two birds and one bandaged thumb, so I grabbed Danny from behind, trying to pull his arms down. I hoped that the man with the gun could see that we had a lunatic on our hands, and please don't shoot us.

Jon raised his palms toward the Tahoe in a calming motion. "Jesus fucking Christ, god dammit! Brad, stay here and watch Danny, I'm going to go talk to the goddam pilots, straighten this shit out."

"No," Mitch croaked, "you'll mess it all up."

Jon turned to Mitch. "You bastard! You blew it again, didn't you?"

Mitch shook his head. "This is just a minor problem, that's all."

"No goddam money? Pretty damned minor, huh?"

"No," Mitch said, sitting up, "the money never was supposed to be here. That wasn't the real deal. I lied."

Jon's face blushed crimson.

"What are you saying?" I asked. "Where's our million dollars?"

"You'll all get your money, but it's in South America, not here."

"Rat bastard!" Jon screamed. "Do you have any idea what I went through to get us here, huh? Damn you!" Jon kicked Mitch in the ribs, which made a thudding sound like a wet drum. Mitch fell over, groaning and gasping, clutching his side. As Jon drew his leg back for another kick, I let go of Danny to restrain Jon.

"You're gonna break his ribs."

Jon shuddered and growled, but I held firm.

"Please, look," Mitch said, cradling his side, "the money's there. Honest to God. In South America." He puffed his cheeks. "We'll get it— when we— arrive."

"Damn your ass," I said, "why did you tell us we were getting paid before we left?"

"Because. You wouldn't have gone. I know. You wouldn't have trusted me."

While Jon paced, the sniper near the Tahoe kept his rifle trained on us. Preferably, he'd shoot Mitch first, then Jon, then Danny. That would be the fairest order of execution. I visualized the gun in Jon's glove box. I'd be dead before I got halfway there.

"Why is this happening?" I asked no one.

"I say we leave his butt here," Jon said. "We can still put this thing together, and we'll split his share."

"Sounds good to me," Danny said, kicking the sole of Mitch's shoe for emphasis.

Mitch struggled to his knees. "No. Don't leave me. I'm the connection."

"Connection?" Jon yelled. "You're a washed-up, has-been, two-bit, scum piece of shit. We know it, Pablo Lupa knows it, the whole world knows it. Nobody needs your sorry ass."

Jon and I went to get our stuff out of the Mustang, while Mitch remained on his hands and knees, wailing, his words lost in the whine of the jet engines. How could Jon the monk have kicked Mitch in the ribs with such viciousness, even though he deserved it?

What now? We couldn't just leave Mitch on the tarmac. As I reached into the car for my camera bag, I remembered Jon's gun and pointed at the glove box. "No," Jon said quietly, and gave me a look. As we turned away from the car I felt the sniper's

115

crosshairs on my neck. I cursed Mitch again. What had the idiot dragged us into? As the three of us strode toward the plane, an older, uniformed woman appeared at the top of the stairs.

"You guys all right?"

"We're fine," Jon said. He led the way up the stairs, motioning for Danny and me to follow him. As I carried my equipment on board, I took one last glance at Mitch, who was kneeling on the asphalt, spitting and holding his side.

The captain, a gray-haired woman in a white shirt with gold-and-black-striped epaulets, had the creased face of someone who has seen much but says little. She motioned to the rear of the plane.

"You can stow your gear back there."

I carried my guitar and amp down the aisle between reclining, black-suede seats. Lush carpeting cushioned my steps. The plane's engines gave off a muted drone, and the air smelled of jet exhaust and travel. At the rear of the passenger cabin, a leather sofa faced a wide-screen television beneath a hardwood bar. Everything looked new. I stowed my guitar and amp behind the sofa, next to Jon's Fender case and gym bag.

The captain extended her hand. "I'm Captain Hobbs. That's Peterson." She motioned toward a stocky young man in the cockpit.

"Uh, hi, I'm Brad Wilson. Listen, there was this misunderstanding, our manager said we were supposed to get paid before we got on the plane."

"Don't know a thing about it. I'm just supposed to pick up four guys and take them down there. The one out there on the tarmac, is he coming or not?" The pilot looked to Jon, one eyebrow raised.

"No," Jon said, "he's nobody. Let's just go." Jon dropped into a seat that seemed too big for him, and stared straight ahead.

"You're the boss," the captain said, and returned to the cockpit.

"What about the money?" I asked Jon.

"I'll take care of it," Jon said, looking out the window. "Sit down. Let's go."

I stowed my leather jacket and sat behind Jon. Adrenaline swirled. Wouldn't we need Mitch? We couldn't just leave him behind. What if there was no money? What if Mitch had invented the whole million-dollar thing, and fifty thousand was all we were going to get? This was all going wrong and why didn't Jon seem to care? The copilot pulled up the stairs and slammed the door, securing it with a red latch. The engines revved as he returned to the cockpit, which was partly visible from my seat. Danny buckled himself into the seat across from me, his eyes alive.

"Wow. Here we go," Danny said.

I raised my window shade. As we taxied, Mitch jogged alongside the plane, waving his hands. In the flash of the running lights, he looked like a slow hobo chasing a fast freight train. He broke into an ungainly run, ducking beneath the wing as it passed over him.

"Mitch is out there," I said to Jon.

"Look at the dude run," Danny said.

I stood up. "We can't do this."

"Sit down," Jon snapped. "I mean it. He brought this on himself. He shouldn't have lied."

"What if Lupa won't pay us without Mitch?" I asked, leaning over to see out the window.

"Lupa doesn't want Mitch, he wants us." Jon returned his gaze to the window.

"Those guys in the truck might shoot him after we take off."

"You don't know that," Jon said to the window.

I craned my neck to see behind us. Mitch trailed doggedly after the plane, the jet engines' blast pinning his clothes back, a pitiful expression on his face. I gripped the armrests as the jet turned at the end of the runway and braked. The engines revved for takeoff.

"No! Stop," I yelled toward the open cockpit door. "Let Mitch on board. Open the door."

Jon's head jerked around. "Brad, what the hell—"

"Shut up," I shot back. "Let Mitch on the plane. Now!"

Exasperation flashed over the copilot's face as he glanced back at me. The captain powered down the engines while the copilot, grumbling to himself, opened the door and lowered the ladder. Mitch scrambled on board, gasping, trembling inside his sweat-ringed T-shirt. He sank into the first seat, then looked back at me and weakly nodded his head.

"Don't thank me, it was Jon's idea. He said it was the Christian thing to do."

Jon's face remained angled towards the window.

Chad Peery

As I tightened my seatbelt I was taken by a sense of foreboding, like years ago when I first discovered that Mitch had disappeared with our money. My stomach tensed as the jet leaped forward, engines roaring, and I leaned into the aisle to see out the front windshield. Ghostly white lines rushed to meet us, and the twin engines had so much thrust that the plane veered from side to side.

We arched into the air, rocketing upward at a steep angle. I looked out my window, and on the service road near the smashed front gates, a vehicle sat parked askew with its lights on, as if it had just slid to a halt. The Chevy Blazer! White Hair stood by the headlights, his face turned skyward, binoculars held to his eyes.

"Goodbye, you white-haired bastard, and may I never, ever, see your ass again," I said, as our jet powered into the darkness.

15

I sat back in the plush airplane seat, and cool air blew from the nozzle while my ears popped. We made it! The plane quickly reached cruising altitude and I unlatched my seat belt as we leveled off. Mitch peeked around the corner of his seat like a kid anticipating a spanking.

"You! Get your ass to the back of the plane, we're having this out," I said.

"What?" Jon asked.

"You heard me."

"About damned time," Danny growled.

Mitch rose slowly and followed the three of us to the rear of the plane. "I need a drink" he mumbled, and broke the seal on an expensive bottle of Scotch he took from a liquor cabinet. He filled a tumbler, and eyes closed, took a long sip, his gold chains flashing outside his sweat-stained T-shirt. Mitch collapsed on the sofa, cooling his forehead with the glass. "All right, I lied to you guys. Had to."

"Is the million dollars for real?" I asked.

"Don't bullshit us, man," Danny said, hovering over him.

"One million apiece, you guys. Pablo Lupa's got more cash than he knows what to do with. You'll get paid down there, that's the way the deal was cut. If I didn't tell you the truth, then you couldn't say no. See?" Mitch took another swallow, blinking heavily to avoid Danny's glare.

"All I see is one sneaky bastard," Jon said, grabbing a Diet Pepsi from the fridge.

"If the money ain't there, you ain't there, you ain't nowhere, cause you're dead," Danny said, brandishing his boot.

"What's supposed to happen next?" I asked.

Mitch gulped more Scotch. "Pablo Lupa's sending someone to meet us at the Maserta airport, and you'll all get paid in cash upon arrival at the ranch."

"You and your goddam lies." Jon chased his words with a slug of Pepsi, grimacing as if it were whiskey.

"This sucks," I said. "How do we know he's going to pay us at all? Once we're down there anything could happen. And how are we supposed to get that much currency back up here? You ever try bringing that much cash across the border?"

"See? The way you're talking? That's why I did what I did. You guys would still be back there, flapping your gums instead of flying. You gotta think big. Pablo Lupa has all kinds of cats coming down there to sell him stuff and do business and party. He'll pay and you'll all get back safe and sound. You'll see."

"So," the Captain said, walking her hands along the empty seats, "everybody OK back here? I see you found the bar."

After a moment's silence, Jon said, "No problems."

"You guys a rock band?"

"Yeah," Danny said, his eyes brightening, "we're the Jamrods."

The captain nodded. "Jamrods. Sure. My nephews probably downloaded some of your stuff. Anyway, we're scheduled to refuel in Mexico and touch down in Maserta around dawn. Your seats fully recline, the sofa makes into a bed, and there's food in the fridge."

"What about immigration?" I asked.

The pilot laughed. "At Maserta, you'll get the red carpet, believe me." She twisted off the cap of a mini bottle of Drambuie, poured it into a glass, and took a sip.

"Anybody got any smokes? I lost mine," Mitch said.

"Sorry, Mr. Lupa doesn't allow smoking in his personal plane," the Captain said. "Just about the only thing he doesn't allow."

"What kind of plane is this?" I asked.

"Gulfstream Five. Those two Rolls-Royce engines could push a plane twice this size and not break a sweat." The captain downed her Drambuie and picked up two small bottles from the bar. "I'll be up front if you need anything. By the way, another rule, a big one— no pictures." She turned toward me. "Did any of you bring a camera on board?"

I shook my head no and remained silent till the Captain had returned to the cockpit. "So what now?" I asked.

Jon combed his fingers through his bristly hair. "Play it by ear. We don't do anything till we get paid and we feel good about it. OK?"

Danny waited for me to nod and then did the same.

Smoking Jimi

    I found a fresh fruit plate in the refrigerator, along with roast beef, ham, duck, and caviar. After we feasted, Mitch sprawled on the sofa, while the rest of us stretched out in our leather seats.

    I thought of Frank and wished he could have been here—he would have loved every minute. What a sad, strange bunch: the grizzly mountain man on drums, his injured thumb in a fat bandage; the gourmet-chef street-hustler manager, sleazy as ever; the disillusioned monk with all his secrets on bass and vocals; and me, the man who lost his soul when he lost his band, wandering through life with a camera and a guitar he didn't play anymore.

    I smiled. I could feel it coming on, a centrifugal force pulling us headlong into places where adventures come true. On the road! At one time, my road led inevitably to Denmark, like every river must flow to the sea. Gjerna, had she lived, would have been incredibly beautiful. Age could never have clouded the life in her eyes or dulled her diamond light. Sometimes I wonder what our children would have looked like and how our love would have evolved after all these years. I held those thoughts like a pillow and escaped into restless dreams.

Chad Peery

16

I woke as we touched down in Mexico to refuel. Loosely uniformed men carrying machine guns milled around outside the plane, smoking drowsily, while the pilots stayed on board. As soon as the plane was refueled we took off, angling sharply into the sky like a rocket, the engine's muted roar powering us into the night. I returned to shallow sleep.

* * *

Tires squealed and the plane shuddered. We had landed again, and my body hummed with sleep, slow to waken. Yawning and stretching I blinked away the fog of senseless dreams. This must be Maserta. The gray sky hung low, pressing against steep hills dotted with stilted homes and clay-tiled roofs. As we taxied past small planes parked on the tarmac, the Maserta air terminal came into view. Painted in tropical pastels the building had a turboprop docked at its terminal taking on baggage. All around us verdant mountains rose to meet low clouds. Puddles glistened on the tarmac and everything seemed freshly washed by rain. Our Gulfstream continued past the terminal to an unmarked hangar, where it swung to a stop.

"That's it for us," the captain said, opening the exit door. "Hang loose, Mr. Lupa will send someone for you." The copilot barely acknowledged us as they hurried off the plane. Cold air invaded the cabin through the open door and I put on my leather jacket. Danny had his denim jacket, and Mitch wrapped himself in a red-and-black blanket he'd found under the seat.

"Here we are," Danny said, glancing around.

Jon stood up and donned his green ski jacket while frowning at Danny. "Look, everybody be cool, OK? We're in someone else's country now and the rules are different."

Mitch pulled his blanket closer. "Money's money, and money talks."

"And bullshit walks," Jon said, "so why are you still here?"

A brown-skinned man wearing coveralls entered the plane, ignoring us. He went into the cockpit and jotted on a clipboard.

Seconds later, a broad-faced man with copper skin and short black hair poked his head through the doorway. He touched the bill of his Yankees' baseball cap.

"You guys the band?"

I said yes. Jon seemed puzzled.

"Good," the man said, in an odd accent, his expression that of a child holding back a laugh. "You have bags?"

"Just our guitars," I said, motioning toward the back.

The man nodded humbly and went to fetch our guitars.

"Is Mr. Lupa here?" I asked, as the man lugged the guitars and amplifier down the aisle.

"He is very busy, *Senior,* but I will be most happy to take you all to Rancho Vizcaya. This way, *por favor.*"

Jon scowled, looking as if he wanted to say something but couldn't. I was first down the stairs and stood before a huge, black SUV with oversize tires and chrome rims. A gold, metallic Cadillac symbol gleamed on the front fender. I opened the passenger's door. The interior smelled of new car and fresh leather, and the Escalade nameplate was inscribed on the hardwood trim of the dash. Since I was first out of the plane, I hopped in the leather seat up front, while Jon and Danny climbed in the back. Mitch sat alone with the guitars in the last seat, facing the rear window. I rubbed my hands and zipped up my jacket against the chill. Mitch, wrapped in a blanket, complained about the cold.

The man wearing the Yankees' cap slid into the driver's seat, which almost seemed too big for him. Smiling, he turned the key and raised his hands when the engine roared to life, as if starting a vehicle on the first try were a miracle. As the Cadillac SUV lumbered forward I glanced in the side mirror. A white van with smoked windows followed us towards the gate, where a uniformed guard gave a bored wave. Both vehicles turned left on a two-lane highway, which according to the road sign, took us away from the town of Maserta.

The Escalade's driver wore ordinary jeans and a brown jacket, but there was nothing ordinary about his eyes, they were sharp and perceptive. He seemed to take in everything about me in one glance. He had a face made for mischief, and carried an impish expression. His cheekbones were set high and wide above thick, proud lips, while his eyes sparkled with pent-up glee. I wondered if he were full Incan, or perhaps mestizo, a mix of European and Indian. Other than his eyes, he seemed like any of the immigrants who venture north to the Land of Plenty. I almost laughed. Now, I was the odd-hued foreigner, coming to work in a strange land, dreaming of a fantastic wage.

The two-lane road seemed well maintained but sparsely traveled, only one truck passed us heading back towards Maserta. Why wasn't there more traffic on this main highway? Surely, this region couldn't be that impoverished. All around us, cattle ranches and farms were scattered on green hillsides huddled beneath low clouds. Up a dirt driveway, I glimpsed a cozy home with smoke curling from the chimney and a yellow dog snoozing on the porch.

This place— with its barbed wire fences relaxed with age, green fields, and thick stands of healthy trees— could have been anywhere in the world blessed by plentiful rainfall. They also had graffiti problems— scrawls of red paint covered every road sign.

I put on my sunglasses to shield my bleary eyes. "Whose initials are those?" I asked, pointing to another defaced sign.

The driver laughed in a short pent-up burst, and resolutely pulled his Yankees' cap around backwards. "Golden Path. If we have to stop for them, let me do the talking."

"Stop? Why would we have to stop?" Jon asked.

"Oh, the Golden Path sometimes likes to play games. They call themselves revolutionaries. I call them something else." He laughed, his eyes flashing wide as he shot a glance into the back seat. "It's OK, they know who we are, and they would never mess with a car from Rancho Vizcaya."

"Is that why that van's following us?" I asked.

"The van? Friends of mine. Yes. *Amigos,* you know?" He laughed again.

I couldn't figure the driver, he acted as if the world were one big joke. I tried to form a picture of Pablo Lupa— slick playboy, well heeled, jewelry, expensive cologne, Italian suits. Our driver was most likely one of his henchmen, a street-savvy thug who could snap your neck in a second, laughing all the while.

"What is Pablo Lupa like?" I asked.

The driver grinned and gave me a sideways glance. "Mr. Lupa is a god among men. A true saint."

I sensed a wave of anger from the back seat.

"He has been very generous, he has helped the poor, the sick, the schools, even built the soccer stadium in town. People here would die for him." The driver nodded, as if agreeing with his own thoughts.

"Why's this place we're going called Rancho Vizcaya?" Mitch asked from the rear.

"If you have ever been to Miami and seen Vizcaya, then you will know."

I had once taken a tour of Vizcaya, a garish castle built on Miami's Biscayne Bay by a rich eccentric. Pablo Lupa's ranch should be very interesting.

"What do people around here do, anyway?" Danny asked.

"Mostly, they are farmers, mestizos, poor but hardworking people. Some here still speak Quechuan, the language of my ancestors, the Incas. We were once the center of the earth, the greatest of all civilizations." He waved his hand at the road, as if scattering corn to chickens.

"Why is it so damned cold here? I thought this was South America," Mitch said from the rear.

The driver laughed and adjusted the heat controls. "It is winter here and we are very high up, this is the Sierra, our valley is two thousand meters high. Over there, Paxicoto, which you cannot see because of the clouds, is always with snow. Down near the coast, in the *Oriente,* it is very hot, and there is jungle. The *Coasta* is always nice, if you like the ocean. Me, I hate fish." He screwed up his face and laughed again.

I unzipped my coat. The terrain reminded me of the high plateaus of Colorado, except with more greenery and thicker vegetation. I wished the clouds would lift and reveal the mountains that must ring this beautiful valley.

"I'm starving," Mitch grumbled.

"Where did you learn such good English?" Jon asked, leaning forward.

"Doesn't everyone speak English?" The driver said with a laugh. "Any of you dudes speak Spanish?" He looked at me, his eyes bright and sharp.

We all said no.

"Ever been to South America?"

"No," I said, "we toured Europe once. First time here. It's beautiful."

"Wait till you see Rancho Vizcaya." The driver glanced back at Danny. "What happened to your hand?"

"Nothing," Danny mumbled, sticking his injured thumb under an armpit.

Smoking Jimi

    I suddenly realized I was missing some great shots, even in this limited light. I reached into the camera bag at my feet and felt the cell phone, the lenses, but no camera. My hand came across something weird. A gun! Jesus Christ, someone had put a pistol in my camera bag! Who the hell? Danny? Jon? I could clearly feel the flat-sided weapon's rough-textured grip, the hammer, and the trigger. And what happened to my Nikon? I searched the carpeted floor and felt under the seat. An ugly mix of anger and outrage flushed through me. I turned to Jon.
    "My camera's gone," I murmured through clenched teeth.
    "You sure?" Jon said, glancing at the back of the driver's head.
    "You like to take pictures?" the driver asked.
    "I had the Nikon in my bag, I know I did. Somebody stole it."
    The driver shrugged. "Perhaps you left it on the plane. Don't you have other cameras?"
    I suppressed the urge to tell the driver to go to hell. What did this oxcart jockey know, anyway? It wasn't like losing a disposable camera. And what was I supposed to do with a gun? What if they searched us at Pablo Lupa's ranch? Sweat prickled my brow. Should I ditch the gun under the seat? They'd probably find it and blame me. I felt sick. It couldn't be the gun from Jon's car, I was certain we had left it in the glove box. Perhaps whoever stole my camera had thrown this automatic in the bag so I wouldn't notice the difference in weight. Or maybe someone wanted to sabotage our visit.
    "That pilot warned us about not taking a camera on board," Jon said. "Might have taken it from you while we were sleeping."
    "Dammit. That was my Nikon. You know what that camera costs? Stinking thief!"
    The driver struck the steering wheel with the edge of a palm and sliced the air in a karate chop, repeating the motion with each phrase: "It is not important. Your camera is on the plane and will be there for your trip back. Mr. Lupa will see to it. Do not worry. In a few minutes you will see for yourselves the most beautiful *hacienda* in the world. This is a time to be happy."
    The driver scowled and let off the gas. Up ahead, a group of soldiers toting assault rifles milled around a truck that partly blocked the highway. A second vehicle, a delivery van, blocked the remainder of the road. Deep gullies on both sides of the highway

made passing impossible. What if they searched us and found the gun in my bag? A roadside execution? I closed my eyes a moment, trying to ease the panic in my chest.

"Let me do the talking," our driver said, as he slowed to a stop.

"They're just kids," Jon said.

One soldier, sitting on a thick rock, couldn't have been more than twelve years old. She stared at the dirt near her feet, ignoring us. Her new camouflage fatigues looked too large, as if she had stolen her parent's clothes. Three other teens dressed in olive-drab uniforms approached our Cadillac. Two stood by the driver's side, while the other parked himself near my door. They all held automatic weapons with worn wooden stocks. Of the dozen soldiers at the roadblock, only one appeared to be over twenty, and he dismissed the scene with a wave of his hand. Our driver nodded to an unheard beat while he powered down his window.

"Hey, *muchachos!*" he sang out. He and the soldiers spoke in a strange language, rhythmic and musical, but not Spanish. Probably Quechuan, I thought. The kid nearest me peered into my window, his gaunt face hovering like a snake's, drifting along as he inspected each row of seats. How could someone so young have such a hard face? I glanced into the side mirror. The white van had stopped snug against our Cadillac, and two men stared intently through its windshield. They were probably armed and ready to shoot if things got ugly. I mentally rehearsed ducking and grabbing the gun in my bag. Then what? Dying in a hail of bullets?

After a long moment, one of the teen soldiers moved the delivery van, opening a path for us. I closed my eyes in relief. Our driver shouted out the window and drove the Cadillac Escalade past the truck, accelerating onto open highway. Our bodyguard's van followed close behind, while the soldiers restored the blockade. I clasped my hands to steady them.

"What the hell was that all about," Jon asked.

"The Golden Path, they call themselves. This gives them something to do, since they are too lazy to work. Ha! It is nothing. They have been doing this for years. They would not mess with a car from Rancho Vizcaya, we pay them plenty, believe me. They are our protectors."

"What are they looking for?" I asked.

"Government spies, tourists, city people, anyone they can kidnap for ransom. People like you." He laughed and slapped the wheel. "Do not worry, you are perfectly safe. They know who is who around here."

"Can't the police or the army do something?" I asked.

"Soldiers, police? Ha! Gone. This is all Golden Path. Government soldiers never come here. Those young ones, they are just doing work the older ones are too lazy to do. If the government tried to send someone out here—" he drew a finger across his throat and grinned.

"That bunch back there, you don't have to worry about them. Besides, the Golden Path protects our people from government death squads. They are the murderers. They kill people, poor people, all for nothing. But still," he said, pointing a finger upwards, "even these death squads know better than to mess with the Lupas or their friends. If they did it would be the end of them, that's for sure." He laughed and then fell silent.

Jon leaned forward. "What about the SLA?"

The driver turned his head slowly, glared at Jon, and then laughed abruptly.

"The SLA? Ha! Cowards, bandits, Communists! They hide in the hills like rabbits and come out at night to steal. They're afraid, chicken!" He turned toward me and laughed, but there was no smile on his face.

"Do the SLA and the Golden Path get along?" I asked.

"Get along? They enjoy killing each other, so yes you could say they get along." The driver laughed again.

After a few more miles of green, rolling hills, the driver pushed a button beneath the dash, and slowed to turn onto a freshly paved road. I blinked my burning eyes and adjusted my sunglasses. Up the hill, an iron gate rolled open for us. The road skirted along a creek bed with steep slopes ranging up the hillsides. Densely packed trees, an odd mixture of pines, grew amidst thick underbrush. Low clouds blanketed the hilltops, and a light rain fell, speckling the windshield. Around one corner a man appeared, wearing a colored poncho with a rifle slung over his shoulder. He spoke into a hand-held radio as we passed.

"More Golden Path?" I asked.

The driver laughed. "No— security."

The road curved and then opened into a small valley where a heavy gate stood across the roadway. RANCHO VIZCAYA, monogrammed in gold letters, hung on its wrought-iron grating, and both halves swung inward as we approached.

"Hello, Moneyland!" Mitch sang out from the backseat.

"Wait till you see Rancho Vizcaya," the driver said with a laugh.

To my right I noticed an empty heliport with its concentric circles. Over a gentle rise a large, cube-shaped building came into view. Colonnades three-stories tall spanned the face of the stone mansion. A massive fountain anchored the end of the cobblestone driveway, and rows of nude statues lined both sides of the road, a mute testament to the unbridled extravagance of the place. I took off my sunglasses and did a double take. Someone had painted the statues' genitals bright red! A joke? A warning? Art? I wanted my camera!

"Wow, man, check out those statues," Mitch called out, "I can't wait to meet this dude."

The driver chuckled and shook his head. He wheeled the Cadillac around the fountain to the front of the mansion and squealed to a stop behind a red sports car. The white van pulled up behind us and a bald man with a brick-red moustache emerged. He could have been a professional wrestler. As he strode toward the Cadillac his impressive biceps bulged through a black muscle shirt. He bent his well-formed body to peer into my window, exchanged glances with the driver, and then opened my door. I gripped my camera bag, feeling the weight of the gun, praying there wouldn't be a security search.

"I am Rudy Umber," he said with a German accent. "Welcome to Rancho Vizcaya. Your luggage?" He stared at my camera bag.

"No, not, just our guitars, and my practice amp's in the back with Mitch. In the back, over there."

Rudy's blue eyes glared for a cold moment, and then he went to the rear of the Escalade. Our driver had vanished, which disappointed me because I wanted Jon to give him some money for a tip. The guy didn't look like he made much.

Rudy led us into the mansion through a set of large wooden doors, imposing enough to have been stolen from a church. As we trooped past the threshold, an alarm screeched. A metal detector! Christ! I had just set off a goddam metal detector! I closed my eyes, frozen in place, my mind racing through all the possible excuses for carrying a gun into Pablo Lupa's mansion. Danny bumped into me. Jon, carrying his gym bag, looked back at the detector's framework which circled the large doorway.

"Halt! Everyone!" Rudy shouted.

He approached, tapping the blade of a metal-detection wand against his left palm. My heart rattled against my chest and my camera bag seemed to weigh a ton. I flushed with heat and fear.

"Hands out," Rudy commanded. He scanned Jon first. Nothing. Then Danny. When the detector reached his boot, the wand's piercing squeal echoed through the foyer. Grinning, Danny bent down and pulled out his hunting knife.

"This little thing what you're looking for?"

Rudy turned the knife over in his hands, his sharp-blue eyes admiring the bone-handled weapon. "So. Very nice. This will be returned to you when you leave. Now. Does anyone else have weapons? *Cameras?*"

I didn't even breathe, avoiding his piercing gaze as he looked us over. He scanned Jon's gym bag, but for some reason ignored mine. As he put the detection wand away a cool mist of sweat settled over my forehead. I forced myself to take a breath. I vowed before every god that has ever been and ever will be that I would ditch that damned gun at the first opportunity.

"Are there any cell phones?" Rudy demanded.

I noticed that Jon's mouth had opened and he appeared tense. He must be thinking of the cell phone in my bag. I reached inside it and handed the phone to Rudy. He turned it over in his hand, scoffed, and returned it to me.

"Any other cell phones, *radios?*"

We remained silent. Satisfied, Rudy led us into a reception room, past antique furniture built for the short-statured people of bygone centuries. Houseplants sprouted from an ancient marble bathtub upon a stone pedestal. Oil paintings and tapestries crowded the walls, and the latticed windows had the watery appearance of antique glass. Romanesque statues of nudes in obscene poses stood motionless, frozen in mid-perversion. I chuckled. At least their genitals weren't painted red. Centuries-old chandeliers fitted with electric lights dangled from the reception room's ceiling. Rough-hewn stone blocks formed the inner walls, making me think of the inside of a castle. I glimpsed a cavernous inner chamber through gaps between columns and draped silk.

A bust of Napoleon, sitting atop a headless nude statue, stood guard near two heavy wooden doors. Rudy opened one of the doors and took us up a flight of marble stairs, never once glancing back, as if he had no doubts about his ability to lead. A gun butt peeked from a black holster on his hip. Why wouldn't there be tight security here? This house was probably the safest place in all of South America. And me, carrying a gun into Pablo Lupa's house. More sweat formed upon my brow.

At the second-floor landing Rudy led us into an open hallway. "These are your rooms," he said, indicating four, evenly spaced doors. "You will find your names on each door. Each of you has a private bath, and if you need anything use your telephone. Mr. Lupa asks that you join him for lunch, which will be served downstairs, on the main floor, at noon. Until then, for your comfort and safety, he asks that you remain in your rooms. Rest, relax, refresh yourselves." Rudy stood for a moment as if waiting for a challenge, and then disappeared down the stairs.

"Man, can you believe this place?" Danny asked.

Mitch wandered down the hall. "Oh, man, check this out."

I carried my camera bag to where the hallway opened into a vast chamber. The four of us stood at a wide stone railing, looking into the mansion's hollow interior. Below us lay a giant garden patio, while encircling the chamber were open hallways like our own that faced inwards and were divided by colonnades every few yards. Tropical foliage with impossibly large leaves spread across the ground floor, while fountains, benches, and stone pathways wound through the vast indoor garden. Life-sized statues stood frozen in timeless, erotic poses, depicting a creative variety of sexual positions.

A gardener wearing a jungle hat waded amongst the plants with spray bottle in hand. Black-and-white tiles covered an open area, where a man in a white apron busied himself setting a large table. Toward the far wall an Olympic-sized swimming pool seemed dwarfed by the enormous chamber. The agitated water and wet footprints meant someone had just been in the pool.

The second-floor walkway, upon which we stood, completely encircled the cavernous chamber. Above the third-floor hallway towered a domed glass ceiling that let in outside light. The place reminded me of a museum or perhaps a centuries-old palace. Who would build a mansion like this? Someone with an ego the size of a 747. Someone who could have had me shot for smuggling a gun in here. I'd better find a way to ditch the damned thing, fast.

"Not too shabby," Jon said.

Mitch smacked his lips. "Wow, check out that statue! Man, I didn't know two people could do that! Tell me this guy don't know how to live large. Moneyland, here we are! Didn't I tell ya? Huh?"

"Maybe so, but we still haven't been paid, have we Mitch?" I said.

"Gimme a break. It'll be taken care of."

Danny fiddled with the bandage on his thumb. "That Rudy dude's packing a piece. You guys see that?"

Jon said, "What'd you expect, an English butler? C'mon, let's check out our rooms."

I found my guitar case leaning against a door emblazoned with BRAD WILSON in gold lettering. Someone must have brought our guitars up while we were gawking over the balcony. My amp was nowhere to be seen. When I opened the door to my room, I decided that royalty could have stayed here, and probably had. A canopied bed stood against one wall. Blue and crimson shrouds billowed from the valance circling the tester above the lavishly ornate bedposts.

Gold-trimmed tapestry dominated one wall, stretching towards the high ceiling, while beneath it, a massive armoire of dark wood had been converted into an entertainment center. A mirrored bar occupied one corner, crowned with crystal decanters and etched glasses. Over the bar stood the bust of someone who resembled me in an odd kind of way.

I decided to check out the bathroom. At its center lay a sunken bath of black tile and gold fixtures, while a bidet and toilet waited nearby. I peeked behind the door of a lavish, multi-jet shower booth the size of my bathroom in Florida. Alongside the shower, twin sinks scalloped like seashells perched atop a marble counter. Mirrored walls reflected my image in freakish echoes, and I noticed that my reflection could use a shave. Within the well-stocked medicine chest I found toiletry items neatly laid out.

I closed the bathroom door and tried the bed. Pillow soft. Beneath a renaissance painting, an artificial fireplace cast warmth upon a chaise lounge crafted from gold-woven fabric. The things that must have happened in this room.

I opened the camera bag and carefully removed the pistol. The nickel-plated automatic gleamed in my hands. Was the hammer frozen? The gun didn't seem that old. I tried the safety latch. It refused to budge. What if I needed a weapon? What a weird gun. An antique? I gently tested the trigger. It moved easily, but the trigger didn't pull back the hammer, and without a cocked hammer, no bang.

I pulled a little farther on the trigger. Nothing. I pulled a little more.

Click.

Flame shot out the barrel. A cigarette lighter!

I collapsed on the chaise lounge, laughing so hard that tears streamed down my face. I slapped my knees, hooting and hollering at myself. A damned lighter! I had to admit it was an excellent replica— it could fool anyone. Each time I pulled the trigger, a polite butane flame erupted from the barrel.

The little red car had tumbled from my shirt pocket and I picked it up. Colorado dirt clung to one wheel, soil from a world so far away. I touched my clothes. So out of place.

I put the gun lighter and toy car on the bed stand. Opposite the bed sat another armoire, this one with a faded hunting scene painted on its face, cracked and ancient. I swung it open.

Clothing! Suits, sports jackets, and sweaters— I opened a drawer at the bottom of the armoire— folded shirts, socks, and underwear. I took out a royal-blue polo shirt and selected gray trousers, 34x32— a perfect fit. Several pairs of new shoes lined the bottom, and I picked a pair of loafers— size 11— a perfect fit. Were all these clothes, with their up-scale labels, supposed to be for me?

After a lingering shower and a leisurely shave, I got dressed and went to look for my amplifier. My front door's heavy brass latch had no means of locking, which gave me a creepy feeling. Down the hallway Mitch's door sat ajar, and when I swung it open, cigarette smoke caught my throat. His room had been styled in a modern motif with a chrome bed and art deco furniture. Abstract paintings and drawings circled the walls which were finished in stylishly textured plaster. Mitch emerged from the bathroom.

"Brad! Ain't this something? They even have my brand of cigarettes, the best booze, and ashtrays! My room is a smoking room, thank you very much." He said as he patted his chest.

"Have you seen my practice amp?"

Mitch looked amused, as if I had asked him about a discarded toothpick. "It's gotta be somewhere. Check Jon's room."

I went to Jon's door and knocked. I knocked again. The door opened a few inches. Jon peered out.

"What?"

"Looking for my practice amp."

"Haven't seen it." He started to close the door.

"Great. Somebody stole it?"

"It's around. Don't sweat it." Jon shut the door.

I shook my head. What was Jon's problem? Sometimes he seemed stranger than Danny. I walked through Danny's doorway, which stood wide open. His room was done in earth tones with the décor of an old English men's club. From wood-paneled walls animal heads gazed down upon overstuffed leather furniture, while rugs and animal skins were scattered over the hardwood floor. Danny sprawled on a mahogany four-poster, staring at the mosaic ceiling with god-knows-what running through his head. A bottle of Corona stood frosting on his nightstand.

"Problems?" Rudy Umber stood behind me at Danny's door, his eyes sharp-blue tacks. Biceps rippled from beneath his black T-shirt, as if he'd just been working out.

"No problems," I said. "Just wanted to see how everyone was doing."

"If you need anything, please use your phone."

Rudy lurked in the hallway, watching me while I returned to my room. The guy had the personality of a reptile. Probably a good security man, though. The gas fireplace in my room gave off inviting warmth, with its hearth of carved stone. I sat on the chaise lounge and leaned back, as perfect flames licked artificial logs. What would Carol be doing at this moment? And my shop, would someone be walking by, peering in the window, wondering where I had gone? And my faithful Honda, friendless and abandoned at the airport. South Florida seemed like a lifetime ago, years distant, and this overdone castle, this unfamiliar new land was where I now belonged, where I was supposed to be.

A low rumble like thunder came from beyond the latticed windows where clouds had lifted to reveal sunlight. When I swiveled the window outwards, birds sang from the rooftop and the air smelled crisp and rain-washed. My window overlooked the circular driveway and below me a red Maserati sat glistening near the front entryway. Nearby, a pair of gardeners worked on the well-manicured grounds with its neat shrubbery and pampered rosebushes, while a stone wall followed the gentle roll of the land to where iron gates stood guard across the driveway.

Another percussive crump echoed from afar. A distant thunderstorm? The two gardeners removed their hats, gazed off toward the sounds, and then shot a quick glance toward the house before they resumed working. Below me, a man with slick-black hair and flashy clothes emerged from the front entrance. Adrenaline jolted through me. Pablo Lupa?

He spoke in a strange language, addressing someone out of my view, and then made a frustrated gesture. He jumped into the Maserati and squealed down the driveway, speeding past the nude statues toward the gates which had already begun opening.

I closed the window. None of my business. I was here to play music and make money. Someone knocked. Jon held out my yellow practice amp, and explained that it was in his room after all.

There was still time before lunch, so I set up the amp intending to get in some practice. As I began tuning my guitar I noticed a sheet of paper lying at the foot of the door. Someone must have just slipped it through the gap above threshold, since it wasn't there when Jon had dropped off the amp. I checked up and down the hallway. Empty. Blinking heavily, I read and then reread the handwritten message: "Beware. Go to lunch, but do not eat the food. Say you are not hungry. It is poisoned."

17

The table looked gorgeous, considering it was laden with death. I stood before it, forcing a swallow. I should have known something would go wrong, it always did, after all, wasn't this just another pathetic scene in the sick movie of my life? Who would want to poison us? Pablo Lupa? His enemies? A few minutes ago I had called a band meeting in my room, where after much shouting and arguing we all agreed to go to the table but not to eat, and then see what happened next— after all, what else could we do, where could we go? Danny wanted to bolt, scatter out the door like frightened birds, but then what? Walk home?

The sumptuous table, loaded with food in silver bowls and platters, occupied the center of the cavernous room. Tropical plants made it seem as though we were outdoors, and the air smelled of life. Birdcalls came from hidden speakers, while sunlight poured through the translucent roof, illuminating the massive chamber in a rich glow. Set into the stone-lined walls, smoked windows and glass doors circled the massive chamber. From somewhere out of our view a woman laughed, and the stone corridors reverberated with her strange, tittering echo.

The rest of the band stood around the table, fidgeting, their faces reflecting the same gruel of apprehension that churned in my stomach. I let out a deep breath as we sat at our assigned seats. Mitch, still unshaven, wore a tan blazer with a white shirt, open at the collar to display his gold chains. Jon was preppy in his pressed T-shirt and new jeans. Danny's old boots clumped across the tile, but he wore fresh camouflage fatigue pants with a brown military shirt. His eyes resembled two wounds— strange, angry slits that seemed best avoided— and he had his bandaged thumb tucked into an armpit. I wore clothes from my closet, which bore top-line labels— a royal-blue YSL shirt with gray Brioni slacks and black Gucci loafers. Maybe we should have shown up naked for lunch. At least that would have helped to take our minds off the tainted food.

Roast beef, squab, and steaming dishes made my mouth water. Breads of all descriptions sat heaped next to slabs of butter and pitchers of iced tea. Which was poisoned? Poisoned with what?

"Hey, guys." The Escalade driver sauntered over to the table with a conspiratorial grin. The poor fool seemed so out of place with his crumpled Yankees cap, he'd probably be in serious trouble if he got caught hanging around with the guests.

"Grabbing some lunch, huh?" the driver said.

No one spoke.

"Having a good time so far?"

Everyone murmured.

"Oh, wow, I love this stuff." The driver glanced about like a thief, a glint of mischief in his eyes. He dipped a serving spoon into a dish of spongy orange pudding.

"Don't eat that," I said.

"This? Why not?" He held the spoonful of orange glop to his lips.

"What's your name?" I asked, hoping to distract the idiot until someone from the household staff came to chase him off.

"My name?" He asked, grinning and nodding at me. "Wow. My name. Flash. Yeah, Flash, that's my name." He let out one of his short, abrupt laughs. "Flash!" He widened his eyes at the sound of his name, and then took a lick of the orange stuff.

"Stop. It's poisoned," I said in a hushed voice. "Put it down before someone comes. OK?"

"Poisoned?" His eyes narrowed, but his elfish smile intensified.

"Yes. Someone warned us with a note under my door." I produced the note from my shirt pocket, but he apparently couldn't read.

"That's crazy. No one would poison the food here. Besides, it tastes so good." He put the spoonful of orange pudding in his mouth, making yummy sounds. "See? Umm, good. I love pumpkin and white-chocolate soufflé." He licked the spoon clean and put it into his shirt pocket, glancing around as if aware of his palatial surroundings for the first time. "Must take a real asshole to live in a dump like this, huh? Don't tell anybody I said that, OK?"

Where was the halting accent we had heard on the way in from the airport? He almost seemed and sounded American.

Abruptly, Flash's smile faded. He puffed his cheeks, as if trying to release a belch. He stumbled forward, grabbing my shoulder for support, and then sank to his knees.

"Oh, Jesus, no," I heard myself say. I eased Flash onto his back. The man's eyes blinked rapidly and his breath labored. That horrid poison must be ripping his guts apart, and it wasn't even intended for him.

"Only cyanide works this fast," Jon said, standing calmly over the driver, his head cocked inquisitively. "We've got us one dead jackrabbit."

I wanted to curse Jon's coldness. Flash's body trembled beneath me, convulsing, the blood draining from his face.

"Help," I yelled, "someone, help!"

A pasty-skinned man wiping his hands on an apron emerged from what must have been the kitchen door. He stopped cold, stared at Flash, frowned, then smiled stiffly, then frowned again and hurried back into the kitchen, shaking his head.

Flash tried to speak. He grabbed me by the neck and pulled me down, as if he wanted to whisper into my ear, his breath hot and damp. Specks of pumpkin clung to the corners of his lips. I gently removed Flash's Yankees' baseball cap.

"Tell my mother I love her. OK?"

"Yes, yes, I will."

"Tell my dog, I love him."

"Yes, yes."

"Promise me you'll kiss him for me, please." Flash's lower lip trembled, and his eyes were pools drained of their last, precious drops of life.

"Your dog, yes, of course."

"Kiss him on the nose, he likes that. OK?"

"Nose. OK"

"And tell all the— all the women—" Flash's eyes let go and he released a long, last breath. His expression finalized in a death mask.

"He's dead, dead, dead, and we're in deep, deep shit," Danny said, cradling his injured thumb. "I'm bustin' out of here while I can. They'll play hell catching me."

Someone towered over me. Red mustache. Large folded arms. Black T-shirt. Rudy's blue eyes glared down.

"This guy just collapsed. I think he ate something from the table," I said.

Rudy's eyes narrowed.

"It wasn't our fault," Mitch said. "I think we need to talk to Pablo Lupa, right now."

Rudy shot a disgusted glance at Mitch and then looked back to Flash. The poor man's eyes gaped, and the incriminating spoon hung out of his shirt pocket.

"You have a call," Rudy said coldly, and held out a portable phone.

"Who could be calling me here?" I asked.

Rudy pressed his eyelids together, as if my response severely tried his patience. He glared at the ceiling for a moment. "It's your brother," he said dryly.

"I don't have a brother," I said.

"It's Domingo. He says it's important."

Flash said, "Domingo is a brain-dead dick."

Danny let out a shout of surprise.

The impish grin had returned to Flash's face.

"Tell him I'm having lunch with my new friends," Flash said, blinking at the skylight.

"As you say, Mr. Lupa." Rudy turned on his heel.

"Lupa!" I said. "Pablo Lupa?"

He cocked his head, grinning like a skull, and then howled and laughed with such intensity that we recoiled. His roaring hilarity filled the chamber with layers of bizarre echoes that swarmed throughout the room like crazed bats. Giggling wildly, he rolled onto his belly, slapping the marble floor.

Pablo   Lupa!

"Oh, God, I can't stand it, oh, you guys!" He broke into another bout of cackling laughter, and drew himself onto his knees, tears in his eyes. He pulled his cap on backwards, the bill pointing down his neck.

"You're Pablo Lupa? The food wasn't poisoned?"

"Oh hell, this is so funny!" Pablo Lupa staggered to his feet and collapsed into a chair. "Oh, God, you guys, you should have seen your faces. Especially you." He pointed the serving spoon at Danny, mimicking his ferocious expression. "Like the big bear, ready to eat the hunter." He burst into another peal of laughter, rapping his spoon on the table.

"You got that right," Danny said.

"And you, Brad Wilson, you were going to kiss my dog's nose! And I don't even have a dog. Ha! I got you guys good, didn't I?"

I forced a laugh. A part of me was angry at the deceit, but the rest of me was relieved that no one was trying to kill us. Pablo

Lupa, posing as our driver! I wondered, had we said anything to offend him?

"Hey, everybody, chow down." Pablo Lupa waved his serving spoon like a baton. "Eat, drink, and if you want to make Mary, hey, I'll send for her, too, ha! Afterwards, I have something special for each of you."

Rudy strode briskly to Lupa and held out a portable phone. Pablo whispered something to him, glanced at me, and then took the phone.

"Hello, Lupa residence," he said in a nasal British accent. His smirk faded and he blinked while he listened. Turning away from the table he spoke in short, snappy sentences. Then Pablo tossed the phone to Rudy and his smirk returned.

"My brother, he worries too much."

"Where is he?" I asked.

"In his villa in Maserta," Pablo said, noisily scooting his chair up to the head of the table.

"How many brothers do you have?" Jon asked.

"Two. I am the youngest and the smartest. Best looking too. My brother Aldo was just here, but he had to go home to have his wife change his underwear. Ha!"

I recalled the loudly dressed man standing below my window, looking toward the distant thunder.

"Was that Aldo I saw driving the Maserati?" I asked.

Pablo Lupa's smile flattened. "So. You must be the smart one." His gaze drifted away from me and he nodded his head. "Let's eat!"

Danny's eyes were more subdued now as he looked over the food. Jon seemed cooler than ever, and Mitch cocked his head, studying the banquet, as if examining a fellow chef's craftsmanship. Pablo Lupa loaded his plate, reaching across the table and stabbing great slabs of beef. Soon, we lost ourselves in the food. I heaped my plate with curried vegetables, wild rice, squab, and several dishes I'd never seen before. I put a fork full of vegetables into my mouth, and a marvelous flood of flavors made me grin.

Mitch had the best table manners, using his utensils properly, not gorging himself the way I expected him to. Was this the same man who could wolf down a burger and fries in ninety seconds? Pablo Lupa ripped a squab in two with his hands and took a huge bite, chewing while he nodded to the beat of an unheard tune. Danny hunched over, his fork making quick trips from the plate to his mouth, his other arm protecting his food. Jon nibbled slowly, seeming more interested in observing than eating.

"This is very nicely done, the *pate de foie gras*," Mitch said. "My compliments."

Pablo Lupa let out a short burst of laughter. "You guys look exactly like I thought you would, even the mountain man," he said, gesturing at Danny with a fork. "And there, Jon, the thoughtful monk, concerned always with the welfare of others, while Brad, the photographer with the eye of the artist, misses nothing. Then of course, there's Mitch, who could make the pope a whore and the devil a saint."

Mitch raised his iced tea in salute.

"Jon, you drive a Mustang Mach II, competition yellow. I have to show you my collection. Cruisers. Muscle cars. Cool wheels."

"I'd like that," Jon said.

"Now I understand how you know so much about us," I said with a laugh. "You had that white-haired guy following us around the last few days. He works for you, doesn't he?"

"What's this?" Pablo asked, looking around the table.

Jon scowled at me, slowly shaking his head.

"Nothing," I said, "I was just talking."

My pulse quickened as Jon gave me a dirty look. What was Jon's problem? How else could Pablo Lupa have known so much about us? Didn't it make sense that White Hair had been sent by Pablo to report back to him?

"How do you like your rooms?" Pablo stopped in mid-chew, his eyebrows arched expectantly.

Everyone murmured their approval.

"How about you, Jon?"

Jon put his fork down and sat back. "It's interesting. In a good way, of course, I like it."

Pablo stared at Jon as if he'd seen something unclean. He took another bite of squab and spoke with his mouth full.

"You guys ready to rock and roll? Wait till you see the rehearsal studio. It's going to blow your minds."

Everyone murmured again.

"We haven't played in a while, but we're up for it," I said.

"Good." Pablo dabbed his mouth with a linen napkin. "I'll show you around after lunch. Introduce you to some of the ladies.

Hey, we've got plenty of time to party, have a good time, kick out the jams, you know? This is gonna be so cool." Golden rays spilling from the skylight reflected off Pablo's high cheekbones, giving him almost a saintly quality.

Some saint. And Rudy, his bishop. I smiled and took a deep drink of my iced tea, amazed how it tasted of cream and roses, and resisted the temptation to guzzle the whole glass. I'd arrived. Delicious food. A mansion. The good life. I could get used to living like this.

"I saw a heliport on the way in. You have a chopper?" Jon asked.

Pablo leveled his gaze at Jon. "Yes I do. One of my brothers borrowed it. Perhaps tomorrow I'll take you guys for a ride." Pablo glanced upward, and then got to his feet. "Check it out. There's something for you in each of your rooms."

I caught a glimpse of Rudy walking along the second floor hallway.

"I gotta go take care of some business," Pablo said. "Eat, drink all you want. If there's anything you need, it's yours!" He let out another short burst of laughter and patted my shoulder as he walked past me.

I took my time pouring more tea, waiting till Pablo Lupa was out of earshot. "Why didn't you want me to mention White Hair?" I asked Jon.

"It'll just complicate things," Jon said. "Besides, White Hair is history. Let's go to our rooms, see what's up there."

"Before you do," Mitch said, "I gotta say something. There's been a change in plans. Well, not really a change, but the actual deal—" He looked at me for help, then blinked and shook his head. "We were supposed to get half the money upon arrival, paid in cash, and the other half upon departure. It's the best I could do. The money, half of it, should be in each of your rooms."

Jon pushed away his plate. "Bastard. You did it again."

Mitch took a deep breath and his eyes bulged. "Like I said before, if I didn't say what I had to say to get you guys down here, you'd still be scratching your butts in Colorado. I did what I did to make this deal happen. C'mon, a half-million dollars should be sitting in your rooms right now."

Jon flexed his jaw.

"Screw this," Danny said, tossing down his fork. "Let's go see what the hell we got up there."

Chad Peery

* * *

In my room, a large, blue suitcase sat upon my bed. I snapped open the latches. Leafy, glorious-green cash! Neat rows of bundled hundreds stared out at me, identical to the packets Mitch brought me in Florida, only now a whole suitcase full! I began spreading the bundles out on the bed and the powerful smell of money made me giggle. How amazing, how insane, to be sitting on a bed in South America with a cash-filled suitcase!

I laughed out loud. So many packets. I had no idea there would be this many. If this were half a million dollars, how would I ever get twice this much back with me? Layer after layer of cash came out of the suitcase, yet still there was more. Was this right? I counted the packets already on the bed. Ninety. I'd barely made a dent, the suitcase was still loaded with cash! Each packet held fifty, one hundred-dollar bills. Five thousand dollars. One hundred packets would make one-half million dollars.

God! I rubbed my eyes. There must be four, maybe five million dollars here. Someone made a mistake. Maybe they'd given me the full payment for all four of us, four million dollars. That had to be it. I left the suitcase on the bed and went into the hallway, closing the door behind me, wishing it had a lock.

I knocked on Mitch's door. His shiny pate glowed as he opened the door, and the hair along the sides of his head formed a broken halo.

"See? You guys thought I wouldn't come through. Here we go, man, the real thing." He shuffled toward a black briefcase on the bed, arms outstretched, as if pleading for a woman's favors.

"You get your money?" I asked.

"One-half million dollars, casharoonie. Ain't it something?"

He sat on the bed, his arms around the briefcase, his eyes gleaming at the cash. "We're halfway there, Brad! A toast!"

He hopped over to the bar, an uneven cabinet of modern swirls and gentle edges, done in distant blues and yellows. With a clink of glasses he returned carrying two, half-filled tumblers. He held one of the chilled glasses out to me.

"Ice-cold Stoli. The best. To the Jammies!"

I stared at the glass. This was getting strange. What was all that cash doing in my room?

"C'mon, do it all! Clears out the cobwebs. Like this." Mitch gulped the vodka and gave me his cannibal stare, like when we first met at Wendy's.

"Now you," Mitch said hoarsely.

I took a swallow, then another. The chill masked the burn. I downed the glass and exhaled fumes, the sting in my throat giving way to warmth in my belly.

"Yeah! Back in the saddle. On our way!" Mitch said.

I handed him my empty glass. "Everybody else get their money?"

"Danny did. I don't know about Jon, I suppose we'd have heard about it by now if he hadn't. Ready for another?" Mitch carried the glasses to the bar.

"No, thanks, I'll— see you in a bit."

As I entered the hallway, someone downstairs let out a yelp and there was a splash in the pool. I didn't have time to check out whoever was frolicking in the water. I had problems. This was too weird. And I shouldn't have taken that damned drink, I needed a clear head. The latch to my room opened easily. The suitcase sat on the bed just as I had left it.

Was this another of Pablo Lupa's practical jokes? Maybe he was testing me, like when he pretended to eat poisoned food, to see if anyone would warn him. I chuckled. This guy kept you on your toes, at least. But what now? I opened the case. Glorious, green millions stared out at me. Men and women would kill for it, die for it. What would I do for it?

I laughed. This was another of Lupa's tricks. Had to be. Giggling like a madman, I watched the craziest thoughts pop into my head. Why not? I lugged the suitcase into the bathroom, snickering all the while. Now, I understood Pablo's ways. Yes! I stripped down to my boxers and snapped open the suitcase. My insane face mirrored between the reflective walls, echoing my madness and I grinned, delighted by my craziness.

I dumped the contents of the suitcase into the sunken tub. There! An ocean of cash! I stepped into my money bath, spreading the packets of bills around with my feet.

"All I need now is one of Jon's cigars," I said with a laugh. I rolled in my bed of cash, rooting about and tossing money over me, giggling like a lunatic. Burrowed into my nest of cash I soaked it in, the inky essence of freshly printed currency against my skin.

Chad Peery

    A voice inside me asked what I thought I was doing, bathing in a sunken tub full of money. Did I fancy myself some sort of Scrooge McDuck, rooting about in his cash vault? I laughed. What was I doing in South America? What was I doing anywhere? I laughed again, silly with giddiness and vodka. So what? Nothing to be done, now. I lay still, contented, staring at my bizarre reflection in the ceiling mirror— a naked man wrapped in a blanket of affluence.

    With a huge crash, the bathroom door burst open.

18

Rudy stood in the doorway with folded arms while a sarcastic grin flirted with his lips. Pablo pushed past him into my bathroom and put a palm to his forehead. The scene stood frozen, until Pablo erupted in a cackling fit of laughter, slapping his knees and stomping his heels. Rudy scowled, iceberg-calm in a sea of madness. Heat rushed to my face. Should I laugh too? Be serious like Rudy? Act innocent? Still giggling, Pablo Lupa fell to his knees and wiped tears from his eyes.

"What the hell? What are you doing?" Pablo waited, his mouth open, an expectant little bird waiting for a worm of levity.

"Just laundering some money," I blurted.

Pablo reared back, roaring with laughter, slapping his face. Mirrored reflections followed his movements like drunken puppets. More tears formed in his eyes and he could barely speak.

"I done a lot of things with money, but— this?" He picked up several bundles of money, tossed them into the air, and then held his sides and he convulsed with laughter,. Rudy remained silent, glaring with steely blue eyes.

"There's been a mistake. This suitcase was not intended for you," Rudy said, his German accent stiffening.

"No, no, look what he did, this is too much," Pablo said, cradling his cheek in a thoughtful pose. "This guy, I knew it when I first saw him sitting in my plane, he was the one!"

Pablo's eyes glistened with mischief, and he shuddered through another comedic giggle. "Brad, Rudy will pick up this stuff, *your* briefcase with *your* money is on the bed. Get dressed and we'll go have us some real fun!"

I gathered my clothes and squeezed past Rudy, with his imposing muscles and stern, red mustache. On the bed, as Pablo had promised, sat a black briefcase. I supposed that it would be rude to count the money in front of him. I pulled on my trousers while Pablo sat on the chaise lounge, plucking my guitar. I was struck by how ordinary he seemed in his running shoes, worn jeans, plaid shirt, and floppy Yankees' cap. He could have easily been one of the bronze-skinned gardeners, except for his impish smirk. And so barrel-chested. Was he full-blooded Inca, I wondered?

"My mother was Indian, my father European. Spanish, actually."

"How did you know what I was thinking?"

"Your eyes say much." He laughed and strummed a chord. "This the same guitar you had in the Jammies?"

"No. Bought it in Denver," I said, tucking in my shirt.

Pablo picked up the poison-food note which had fallen to the floor. He grinned as he read it. "Really had you guys going, huh?"

"You're a good actor."

Pablo chuckled, fingering the guitar strings. I switched on the Taxi amp for him. When Pablo played a few bass notes, the amplifier buzzed and rattled.

"What's the matter? Is it broken?"

I discovered a screw protruding from the amp's back panel. It tightened easily with my fingers.

"Just a loose screw," I said.

As Pablo resumed noodling on my guitar, I wondered who could have messed with the amplifier. Why would someone remove a screw? Pablo strummed an E power chord, smiling and nodding his head.

"You play keyboards?" I asked, as I slipped on my loafers.

"I play around a bit, just for fun, you know. My mother made me take lessons." He laughed and strummed an open C chord. "What's wrong with Danny's hand?"

"Had a little accident, it's just his thumb."

Pablo's fingers formed an open G chord. "Can he play OK?"

I felt uncomfortable under Pablo's gaze. "Sure, he's fine, it's nothing."

Pablo strummed. "Good. Clothes fit? I tried to get everybody's size."

"Fits great," I said, closing the armoire. "How did you know my size?"

He grinned.

Something beeped, and Pablo removed a palm-sized device from his belt. He flipped it open, spoke Spanish, listened for a moment, and then returned it to his belt.

"Wow," he said, pointing at my bed stand, "my lighter! Lost it on my plane." He picked it up, aimed it at me and pulled the trigger. Flame sprouted from the barrel and Pablo laughed, nodding his head. "Cool. My friend Iggy Krotch gave me this." Pablo tossed the gun-lighter back on the bed stand. "What is this?" He picked up my red toy car from the bed stand.

"Just something a kid gave me."

"Your kid?"

"No."

Pablo held my toy car up to the light. "How about old cars, you like 'em?"

"Sure."

"Let's go check out my wheels."

I shrugged OK. With a sly flick of his wrist, Pablo slipped the red car into his shirt pocket. I wasn't about to say anything, after all it was just a toy car.

Rudy noisily shoved open the bedroom door and lugged the blue, cash-filled suitcase into the hall. As Pablo and I followed him, I glanced back at my briefcase on the bed.

"Wish my room had a lock."

"Why?" Pablo asked. "Nothing's happens in my house that I don't know about. You lock the bedrooms in your home?"

"No, I guess not."

He swept his hand through the air. "Then why should I? Everything here is safe, you have no idea." Pablo let out an odd chuckle.

"Well, hello there," Mitch said, standing in his doorway, smoothing his semi-circle of blond hair. "I'm Mitch Damian, the band's manager. I don't think we've been formally introduced. May I say you have a fantastic home?"

Pablo ignored Mitch's outstretched hand. "If you need anything, pick up your phone, it'll be taken care of."

"Thanks, I will, and by the way, we appreciate the payment."

"I pay my bills, nobody can say I don't."

"Right. OK then."

"Brad and I have business. I'll send for you and the others later."

Mitch gave me a questioning look, and I gave him a quick shrug as I followed Pablo toward the stairway. When we walked across the center of the great room, a woman in the pool splashed water at us and called out, "Hey Pablo, aren't you going to introduce us to your new friend?"

Three women's heads bobbed in the water, all blondes, not young and not old, their hair pulled up in buns. I smiled back. They were all attractive, and I guessed that what remained hidden underwater wouldn't disappoint, either.

Pablo waved the women off with a laugh. "Hey, Brad, see one you like? She's yours— she'll do anything you want. They've all been checked out, no HIV, no nothing, and they're here just for you guys. Maybe we'll go swimming later." Pablo giggled. "Ever get an underwater blow job, huh?" Snickering, he puffed his cheeks and then roared with laughter. I smiled to be polite, embarrassed that the women might have overheard. This could be an interesting couple of days.

We strolled between large tropical plants to the rear of the great room. Pablo held open a glass door for me, and I realized he must been seven or eight inches shorter than my six feet. But the man was thick chested and powerfully built, which gave him an imposing presence.

"You haven't seen out back, have you?" He led me through an ornate hallway, and we entered a drawing room where floor-to-glass windows looked out onto the rear of the estate. We walked past furniture that could have graced a museum, and then exited through an ornate door onto the back terrace. The balcony was elevated above the grounds, and Pablo stood at its carved-stone railing.

"My little world," he said with a smirk, holding his arms out, his broad face raised to the sky.

I stood by his side, amazed by the vastness of the grounds. To my left, not far from the mansion, stood a structure resembling an aircraft hangar. Probably where he kept his cars, I guessed, since it had multiple garage doors. Beyond that sat a two-story apartment building with children playing nearby— probably where the help lived.

To my right lay a tennis court, basketball court, and soccer field, all looking brand new and unused. The manicured grounds had a perfect carpet of grass, bordered by neat rows of bushes and flowers, as one would expect to find at an English manor. Forested mountainsides surrounded the small valley, and beyond that, to the west, a white-peaked mountain dominated the skyline. The scent of fresh-cut grass hung sweet, and gardeners trimmed a hedge with an unhurried air.

"So, what do you think of my little paradise?"

"Amazing. All that's missing are carnival rides."

"Carnival— oh, you mean like Michael Jackson?" Pablo spit over the edge into a manicured bush, and then laughed.

"What mountain is that?" I asked, motioning toward the snow-capped peak.

"Paxicoto, the old man volcano. The Inca God Venalocha lives there, deep inside the mountain. When someone unexpectedly disappears, that means they've been taken by Venalocha, down into the mountain, through secret tunnels that lead to the center of the earth."

"Wow. What does this god, Venalocha do, when he gets them down inside Paxicoto?"

"Do? He turns them into statues like in the wax museum, that way, they live forever." Pablo froze in mid-stride as if to demonstrate, a smirk suspended upon his face.

"Like an Incan version of mummies?"

Pablo laughed. "Yeah. Inca mummies. Right. That's good." He cackled and shook his head.

"Then what?"

"Then? They come back to life as lazy-assed revolutionaries, that's what!" Pablo threw his head back and laughed at the sky. "Let's check out the cars!" He loped down the broad stone stairs onto neatly clipped grass, still wet from an earlier rain.

I fell into step with Pablo Lupa, amazed to be walking along side one of the richest men in South America. He seemed so normal, almost goofy in his old Yankees' cap, which probably once belonged to Mickey Mantle.

"You seem to like a lot of American stuff. And your English is excellent."

"Should be. Had English tutors when I was a kid, and went to the University of Miami for six years. Lotta good parties, good times. Yeah. So, tell me about this white-haired guy."

My stomach tensed. I recalled Jon's warning about keeping White Hair a secret. Screw Jon, he was always getting weird about something. Pablo scowled and slowed his pace as I told him about White Hair and his partner dogging us all the way to the Colorado airstrip.

"To hell with them," Pablo said, as we continued toward the garage. "They're both a long ways off. Probably cops. Tell you what— if the coca plant grew in America instead of here, cocaine would be legal and they would export it all over the world just like they do with tobacco. North American tobacco kills way more people than South American cocaine, and doesn't even get you high. Talk about a rip-off. You Americans are no different than us, just more arrogant. And you're hooked on the biggest drug of all— money. It gets you strung out faster than anything. And those people in your government— man, they have a bad case of the jones. The Americans had my father killed. You know about that?"

I expressed my regrets, while my lunch became a lump in my stomach. Time to change the subject.

"Got any kids?" I asked.

"Three. Live with their mother in town. I don't think she likes me very much." Pablo's laugh came out like a sorrowful hack. "And you?"

"No, no kids."

"How come?"

"Just happened that way, I guess." I felt Gjerna's essence for a moment, as if her spirit walked alongside me. If only we could have had a child together.

As we approached the hangar-like building, Pablo pushed a button on his transceiver. One of the garage doors rolled upward, exposing a well-lit interior. Inside, ten or twelve cars were parked to my left, side-by-side in a line— some covered with tarps, others gleaming under the lights. Several men in coveralls worked beneath the hood of a vintage Jeep in the next stall. They looked up and quickly nodded to Pablo. In another part of the building an engine revved into a tight whine.

"Check out this one," Pablo said, and pulled the tarp from a white, '57 Chevy Nomad wagon. "Restored, perfect, stock, just like the day it came from the factory."

I ran my hand over the glossy paint and opened the driver's door. The courtesy light came on, illuminating a spotless, authentic interior.

"Over here," Pablo called out, skipping to the next car like a kid in a toy store. "This one's my favorite, my street rod." The roadster had a deep purple finish and its roof had been chopped, giving the hotrod a squat appearance. A chromed V-8 gleamed beneath the hood bonnet. Slicks on the back and compact front tires tilted the machine into a raked attitude. Pablo jumped in behind the steering wheel. The hotrod started with a roar, and Pablo sat with his left foot on the running board, keeping time to the throbbing engine. Exhaust fumes filled the air.

"Wait," Pablo said, shutting off the engine. "You'll love this one." He hopped out, ran to another car, and with a flourish, cast the tarp aside, revealing a powder-blue GTO. The Pontiac gleamed, its bold lines and massive chrome bumper appearing so new that the sixties might have been yesterday.

"This is my baby," Pablo said. "C'mon, we're going for a ride."

I opened the passenger's door and slid onto the spacious car. No seat belts. The Pontiac had much more interior room than the Cadillac Escalade, and it seemed strange how the GTO's windshield was so far away. Pablo twisted the key and the engine throbbed to life. He pressed a button and the GTO's garage door began lifting. Pablo pulled out his radio and spoke a few words, and then clipped it back onto his belt. Whom did he call, Rudy? Pablo shifted the four-on-the-floor, as if practicing going through the gears.

"GTO, man, 1967, best muscle car ever made. Four hundred twenty-five horses, and none of that smog bullshit. There's only a few of these in mint condition like this one."

"Where do you get these cars?"

"A buyer up north ships them to me. Money buys anything. Cars, people, anything."

Pablo revved the engine and the GTO rumbled forward. Where were we going? Out to challenge another roadblock? As the GTO surged past the garage door, the engine suddenly fell silent and the gage needles dropped to zero. Pablo slammed on the brakes and cursed.

Two mechanics came running, jabbering amongst themselves. Pablo leaped out and slammed the door with such ferocity that I thought the window might break. He screamed and slapped one of the mechanics with his Yankees' cap. The man cringed and fell to his knees, raising his arms in a defensive gesture. Pablo kicked the mechanic so hard it bowled him over. The other mechanic jerked open the hood as if the engine were on fire. This distracted Pablo, and he began yelling in Spanish while gesturing toward the engine. It was like being a spectator at a family squabble. I joined Pablo and the mechanic at the front fender, where a pungent smell of burnt insulation hung in the air. Pablo hissed more curses, jabbing his finger at the mechanic with each word. Whatever he said caused the man to shrink back, his face a grimace of horror.

So. Was this the other side of Pablo Lupa— the spoiled brat indulging in a temper tantrum, the bully enabled by his riches? Or was this only the tip of a far-more dangerous iceberg? My face reddened. I wished I were back in my room.

Pablo adjusted his cap. "Sorry, Brad, like these guys, I told them, there's a short! There's a short in there! But like, do they listen? No! They just don't get it. You can't find good help down here— nobody knows these old cars. Know any good mechanics? Ha!"

Pablo's radio chirped. He snatched it from his belt and walked out of earshot. He glanced towards me with a look that stiffened my neck, before he turned away, gesturing wildly and shouting in Spanish.

Someone slapped my back and I jumped.

Jon!

"Hey Brad, what's happening?"

"Dammit, Jon, you scared the crap out of me. What are you doing here?"

"Thought I'd check the place out. What's up with Pablo?"

"Got really pissed about this car a minute ago, then he took a call."

Pablo spotted Jon, but there was no friendliness in his recognition. He turned away, an ear pressed to the transceiver.

"Who's he talking to?" Jon asked.

"Don't know."

Jon leaned into my ear. "First chance you get, come to my room, we need to talk."

"So," Pablo said to me, walking back and clipping the radio onto his belt. "We have news about your Mr. White Hair and his friend. He just flew in to Maserta on a private plane. This White Hair asked lots of questions about you, Brad. Wanted to know where you were staying and who you were with. I told my brother to take care of it, to call in the cousins. You are my guest, and my cousins, they are very good at making problems disappear."

19

I walked alongside Jon and Pablo, ignoring their idle chatter about vintage cars. I couldn't believe White Hair had come all this way and seemed interested in me instead of Mitch. What the hell? Why would anyone want me, and for what? I had no enemies. I didn't deserve this. Pablo's cousins would deal with this White Hair, which probably meant the guy wouldn't live to see sundown. Anger boiled with each step across the manicured lawn. Why would this son of a bitch follow me to South America? Who sent him?

"Pablo, I've been thinking," I said, "what if I talk to this White Hair? I'd like to find out what he wants with me."

Pablo put his arm around my shoulder and fell in step. "My cousins will take care of the problem. This man does not exist, he has never existed, he's fish food. C'mon, we're musicians, we don't have to worry about shit like this! Let's go check out the rehearsal studio. I feel like jamming!"

I figured Pablo must have called ahead to have Rudy bring Danny downstairs, because the two of them now waited at the mansion's front entrance. Rudy was his usual, surly self, while Danny stood with the arrogant pose of a truant, grinning behind his gray beard. Pablo led us through the mansion's double doors and into the first antechamber, where Napoleon's bust, piggybacked atop a headless nude statue, guarded a stone archway. As we passed the Frankenstein-like thing, it wasn't hard to imagine how someone, in a bit of drunken devilry, might have lopped off the statue's head and replaced it with Napoleon's bust, cackling and giggling like a madman all the while.

With a conspiratorial air Pablo unlatched an ironclad door, which creaked open. Beyond the doorway a bare bulb illuminated what could have been the threshold of a medieval dungeon. Cool, dry air rushed past us, and my imagination pictured a great blade swinging from the ceiling below, while iron maidens yawned, hungry for flesh.

A procession of bare bulbs lit the way as Pablo descended the winding stairs, glancing back with a sneaky grin. The cool air seemed dry, not damp as I expected, and I caught the faint odor of formaldehyde. The stone stairs and walls were smooth and well aged, as if this walkway to the inner belly of the mansion had been in use for centuries.

I glanced over my shoulder. Rudy, his face hard with shadows, followed Jon and Danny. Why was Rudy tagging along? There was a sinister aura about him, and it wasn't because of his powerful body or cropped hair. When we reached a hallway at the bottom of the stairs, Pablo stopped at another thick door and looked back, grinning.

"Hope you guys like it."

Pablo pushed the soundproofed door open. Chilled air greeted us as we followed Pablo into the room. From the ceiling, a lone bulb glowed like an intense, blue star. On the stage sat a gleaming drum kit, while to its left was a Marshall amp, a half-stack. I recognized the bass amp on the other side of the drums— an Ampeg SVT, its monolithic cabinet holding eight, ten-inch speakers. Next to the bass setup stood a Hammond B-3 organ— a massive keyboard on legs, which always made me think of a polished, hardwood casket. The Hammond came with two Leslies— cube-shaped wooden amplifiers containing revolving speakers.

An electronic keyboard, one of the newer synthesizers, sat atop the Hammond. Microphone stands and floor monitors cluttered the stage. The speakers of a JBL sound system faced the room's leather sofas and chairs. I laughed. The studio even had soda and candy machines.

Pablo turned up the stage lights. The equipment lineup looked like a reproduction of a stage shot I'd seen on the insert sleeve of our second album. The vintage Rogers drum kit had the same sparkle-blue finish as Danny's old set, and the new cymbals gleamed. The coarse grill cloth on the Marshall amp brought back memories, as did the dark-green Ampeg bass amp with its fat, tube-powered head and glowing-red light, which resembled a one-eyed robot. Carpeting covered the floor and stage, while tapestries, gold records, and posters of Fillmore concerts hung from the walls. Behind the stage, smoked-glass windows looked in on a control room packed with recording equipment and computer screens.

Suddenly, a man burst through the control-room door and hopped onto the stage. His lanky build reminded me of a spider. Nervous black hair ringed his bald crown, tumbling down his back,

Smoking Jimi

and magnified eyes blinked behind wire-framed glasses. He fussed with a microphone that stood in front of the kick drum.

"Milo, this is the Jammies," Pablo said. Milo adjusted his glasses and nodded toward us, and then vanished into the control room.

"Milo used to do sound for the Stones and Pink Floyd, and he's come out to help me set up my studios. Rudy, let's go, we need those guitars!"

Rudy disappeared into the hallway. Pablo shook his head and grinned as he opened a liquor cabinet set into the wall.

"First a toast. To good times and good vibes." From a bottle of Crystalle, he poured clear liquid into four small glasses, half-filling each one except for mine, which he filled to the top. "To the Jammies. To rock and roll." He raised an eyebrow at me and winked.

What was Pablo's game, why was my glass so full? Screw the wiseass. I downed the whole drink in one shot, anticipating a mild burn like the Stoli.

Wrong.

I gasped for air, while Jon coughed and Danny growled. Imaginary flames streamed from my breath.

"That's some serious shit," Danny said, while Jon nodded in exaggerated agreement.

"Go ahead," Pablo said, glancing at the drum set. "Get a feel for it."

Danny sat behind the snare and picked up the drumsticks, favoring the freshly bandaged thumb on his left hand. He twirled the other drumstick in his right hand, and slammed it down on the floor tom, the booming percussion as deep as a gunshot.

Milo's reedy voice came through the floor monitors: "Some bass drum, please."

Danny slowly pumped the bass drum pedal, the wooden ball striking the transparent drumhead, which blurred with each deep, forceful thud. Danny brought his left drumstick down on the snare, cracking out a crisp beat. Bass drum and snare began marching in a steady rhythm. The room seemed acoustically live but not too noisy, and the drums were being fed into the sound system, just enough to fill the room.

Danny added the closed high hat, tapping the twin cymbals with his right stick on the eighth notes. I smiled. Even with a bandaged thumb, Danny still had that rock-solid beat— there was a good feel to his playing, and despite the years away from music, he was still the drummer he had always been. I sensed Pablo observing the three of us, watching closely, like the time he pretended to be our driver.

"OK," Milo said through the floor speakers, continuing our sound check. "Now the overheads."

Danny's sticks moved to the large ride cymbal, which had a clear, ringing tone, then on to the splash cymbals— saucer-sized brass disks that crashed easily and decayed fast. He moved to the floor and mounted toms, establishing a heavy, walking groove and then integrated the whole drum set, laying down a foot-stomping, steady beat that brought a grin to his face. It was an expression that Danny wore well— the bliss of a man riding a drum kit, taming it with a powerful gallop— a geometry of simple complexion.

Melodies and chords ran through my mind, creativity rippling with every crack of the snare and body-moving crump of the bass drum. My foot pumped and my heart raced.

Finally, the studio door swung open and Rudy arrived with our guitar cases. Jon and I donned our instruments and adjusted the shoulder straps. I plugged into the Marshall amplifier. Heart hammering, I switched the amp off standby and began tuning. Pablo stood behind the Hammond organ and held down an E note, a tuning reference for Jon and me.

My guitar was a good one, the tuning pegs tight, the strings fresh, and the tremolo bar worked well, far better than my old Stratocaster. My mind raced and my heart revved like the engine in Pablo's GTO. What should we start with? Pablo's level of playing was probably rudimentary, so I figured we should begin with a simple blues progression. Danny had stopped playing so we could tune, and now waited, sticks in hand.

Pablo laughed and reared his head like a crazed hyena. From the Leslie cabinets flowed a pulsing chord pattern. I found it in the key of A, not the easiest for a keyboard. Pablo's riff was jazzy, cool, and laid back in a cooking sort of way, not at all what I expected. Danny began keeping time on the high hat, nodding his head to the beat. Jon softly pedaled his bass on an A note, using the E as a syncopated counterpoint. I calmed my pounding heart, and slowly strummed an A-minor sixth, letting each string ring out like the piper at dawn's gates.

Pablo really could play! His technique was simple but tasteful, and his eyes gleamed with mischief. Danny kicked out a steady beat, and Jon locked his bass pattern into Danny's bass drum. It was happening! My heart picked up, not from anxiety, but from joy, the way it used to when the band played freeform and we would explore our best musical landscape. I strummed the upper notes of the chord, stroking the two highest strings, and then worked my way up the neck to the next inversion, following the harmonic intervals of the scale. Like a sweet kiss, I held the highest chord, drawing it out before repeating the climb.

Danny began clicking a stick on the edge of the snare, and then everything just took off. My knees pumped to the beat and Pablo grinned as his head turned from side to side, keeping pace with the snare drum. Jon smiled in a way I hadn't seen in so long. Still, the volume was polite, far below the roar the amplifiers were capable of producing.

Something clashed.

Pablo had gone into a chord change— B-minor seventh, up a full step. Pablo nodded to me, and then modulated to a C major. Back down to the A. Jon followed, walking his bass lines along the chord changes. We repeated the changes several times, and then returned to vamping on the root chord.

Singing. Jon! I couldn't tell what the words were, or even if there were any, but it was a melody, a distinct melody, and dammit, we were playing a song! We hadn't played, really played in years, and here we were, jamming, creating a song from nothing!

Danny embellished his drumbeat, fitting tom fills in around the chord changes, his chops as solid and steady as ever. Jon stopped singing and nodded to me. Solo! I arched a finger around the guitar's volume knob and cranked up the level to where a single note would sustain itself, full and slightly distorted, the way a good tube amp should.

I let a long, sweet note hang in the air and massaged the string, vibrating it gently. Suddenly, my fingers came alive, moving over the strings, not going for the fast or flashy licks, just keeping it tasteful and melodic. I changed my chord position, inverting the solo's patterns higher and higher, exploring variations of melodies that flowed from somewhere far beyond me, entering through my heart and finding their way to my guitar.

The romance of playing! How I had forgotten the magic, when your body, mind and soul become the music, flowing in a beautiful ribbon, filling the air with exquisite images in a language anyone could understand! I focused with such purity that I heard only the music— I felt the music— I was the music— my music, and my solo soared, flying upon the broad wings the band had unfurled. Finally, I hit one last, sustained note, and then allowed it to descend slowly like a waterfall over a bridge of rainbows.

What a sweet rig, that Strat and Marshall! I returned to the original chord pattern, my heart pounding out the cadence of a young man's euphoria.

Pablo nodded hugely, smiling bigger than ever. With his left hand, he pedaled a chord on the Hammond organ, while his right hand went to the synthesizer's keyboard, and made the most amazing sound. I backed down my guitar volume enough to leave space for his keyboard solo, and Jon seemed to sense what was happening too. Pablo's face softened as if he were becoming someone else. I nearly forgot to play— I was so taken by Pablo's graceful, sensitive phrasings, his near-genius combination of simple lines and seductive melody.

Incredible! How could a rich eccentric and three has-been musicians make such awesome sounds? It was as if this strange combination of individuals held a key that unlocked musical secrets that held no answers— riddles of mind, air, and sound. I laughed at such a notion, stumbling over my own joy, as little fishes of merriment swam across my vision. This was the happiest moment I'd experienced in so long.

Pablo's patterns evolved into something that wasn't a solo, but still improvisational, and I followed his thoughts on my guitar's fingerboard, lending a few softly played notes to his synth patterns, as one would add a small blossom to complete a bouquet of flowers. Pablo gazed at me with the face of a child shining at the stars, and he connected with me, for we began weaving a string of pearlescent notes that intertwined, hanging in the air in a rainbow mist of harmony. My essence began to dissolve, as if I were becoming the music, coalescing into the being that I had always been, this multicolored soul— the musician, flashing most brilliant, shimmering with life and love.

I was stoned!

Wasted!

My lips tingled, the core of my chest hummed, and startling flashes glossed my vision. Had Danny's tempo slowed? The beat of his drums receded, and Jon stared at the floor, playing one note over and over, like a moron. I inhaled with a gasp, realizing I had forgotten to breathe. My heart slammed and my hands had gone weak.

I stopped playing.

Was someone toying with the lights, switching them on and off? Unfamiliar people stood in the room. Where had they come from? Had our music created them? They hovered like statues near the wall, salt pillars staring at my strangeness. I closed my eyes. Whatever was happening, I wouldn't allow it, not this, not now. I'd done acid years ago, smoked dope like everyone else, but I'd never had any ill effects. This couldn't be a flashback, could it?

I opened my eyes. Everything was watery, velvety, soft, like the complex texture of air that I drew into my lungs. Pablo had stopped playing. The silence hummed with pent-up tension and energy. No, it was my Marshall stack, buzzing. Pablo stared at his keyboard, nodding as if he'd just finished reading the last chapter of a great book. The engineer stuck his head out the door of the recording studio. He was a spider, a human spider. He seemed puzzled, as if something had suddenly gone wrong, or maybe the power had failed. Power. I found that word funny, but I didn't know why. A laugh erupted from my throat.

The statues by the wall moved, settling like butterflies into the sofa and chairs. I couldn't look directly at them, and only dared give them a vague glance. Pablo's cheeks flexed as he let out a big breath, and he smiled towards the statues. Statues. I giggled. Had Pablo painted their genitals red?

"What did you guys stop for?" Danny asked. He looked ten years younger sitting behind that drum kit— no, maybe twenty, if only he didn't have that beard. Someone farted. No, it was Jon, thumping a bass note. I laughed. Danny responded with an explosive cannon shot from his kick drum. How loud, how freakishly immense was that sound, towering to the sky and back. Suddenly, Jon's bass and Danny's drums were in lockstep, marching with a majestic beat as tall as the Rocky Mountains, powerful and terrifying as the forest with all its impossible vastness. Jon's expression was that of the shepherd, his eyes fixed on Danny with the gaze of a mentor, a father, a brother.

I closed my eyes. Shapeless forms danced. I forced my eyelids open. The ceiling shimmered, flexed, and breathed. This had to be a drug! What drug? Something in the drink? Pablo must have spiked our drinks. He had no right, damn him. No right? I chuckled. Pablo had a million rights. And what of it? Yeah, what of it?

Spider brought out two stools, one for me, the other for Jon. Danny and Jon seemed lost in this cool, solid groove, and Pablo made birdlike sounds on his synthesizer, looking like a crazed wizard tapping his finger on a magic stone.

Who were the statues, sitting quietly, watching us? My face tingled. This was one incredible drug— it wasn't like the acid I'd taken back in the old days, it was smooth, almost transparent. Either that or I had finally lost my mind. I laughed out loud. It had been so long, so long. Pablo was grinning and nodding, his eyes sparkling with the gleam of the mystic, the guru, leading the neophytes into his chamber of illumination. My fingertips vibrated with incredible energy, and I asked my speeding mind to concentrate on playing the guitar.

Danny and Jon settled into this subtle yet insistent groove, and Pablo's synthesizer effects were the perfect canvas for the broad strokes my guitar splashed and swirled into beautiful spirals and forms. I found that I was playing the guitar without force of effort or thought, almost as if I were an external observer. I sensed everyone in the room focused upon me, especially the statues on the sofa. They were captivated by the bending of strings, the subtle technique of the pick, the cascade of emotions flowing from my amplifier in a kaleidoscopic stream of color and love.

How long I played, I had no idea, it was simply over when it was over, and the music built to a finish as if this grand, involved piece had been rehearsed for years. As the last few notes died out and silence reclaimed the room, mild exclamations erupted from the statues. I forced myself to look at them. They were women— beautiful women, all blondes, wearing the stylishly ragged clothes of wealthy people. A boy sat on the floor, gazing at his shoes with an air of disgust.

"Wow, you guys, heavy stuff!" Pablo said, grinning. Was he stoned too? I couldn't tell. Danny seemed confused, examining the tip of a drumstick, and Jon carefully leaned his bass guitar against the amplifier, slowly shaking his head. He made eye contact with me and turned away, blinking thickly. Jon had rarely done drugs, at least not with us. Did he understand what was happening?

"Got it all on tape," Spider said, sticking his insectile head out of the doorway.

"What was in that drink?" I asked no one.

"Drink? Oh, man!" Pablo started laughing. "I can't believe, oh shit, are you guys OK? Wow, man, all this time I thought I was getting high from the music, like it was so good, man, did we get all that on tape?"

"Didn't I say yes?" Spider asked.

"Right, sorry, you guys, I forgot, a couple of weeks ago Iggy Krotch came down from London, and we were like partying and jamming, and we must have put some jungle juice in the Crystalle. Wow. You guys OK?"

"OK isn't the word," I said. "What's jungle juice?"

"Indians brew it up in the jungle. It's a holy sacrament, 'cause it's the same stuff the Incas used. Jungle juice isn't as heavy as acid or anything like that, so don't worry. You'll be OK." Pablo laughed again, colors flashing across his face, as if his skin were flushed with neon blood.

"I can't believe this," Jon said.

Danny giggled and threw his sticks into the air. They crashed and tumbled across his drum kit with a life of their own, their one opportunity for self-expression. Danny's face was gentle and childlike, the exact opposite of his other persona.

How long had we played? My watch made no sense, the hands pointed in crazy angles at numbers without meaning. Spider stood, arms crossed, scowling at the drum kit, pondering something. I marveled at his shiny black hair.

"How long were we playing?" I asked.

Spider looked up. "Dunno, a while. Got it all on a DAstick." His British accent made me giggle.

"DAstick?" Jon asked thickly.

"Yeah, everything here's digital. I can save a whole recording session onto one of these babies." Spider held up what resembled a credit card, and then dropped it into his shirt pocket. "You guys played some pretty far out stuff," he said, puzzling over the drum kit.

One of the women approached Pablo. "Rudy needs to see you when you're finished," she said. My mind flashed that these women were spies, then mothers, then sisters, and finally sumptuous women, here to please Pablo's friends. I wished they would all just leave. I didn't want an audience, not like this.

"We're going back upstairs," another woman said, running her hands through the boy's auburn hair. The boy scrunched up his face, making himself look like a little old man.

"We still doing dinner?" another blonde asked.

"Yeah, sure, what time is it?" Pablo asked with a giggle.

"Almost four."

My mind raced. Four! How could that be? I gingerly placed the guitar into its stand and waited, hand outstretched, to see if the instrument would succumb to some weird twist of gravity. While Pablo chattered and giggled, my mind wandered insanely. I just wanted to rest in a quiet, private place.

"I'm going upstairs, I think I need, I don't know," I said.

"Cool, man," Pablo said, nodding and grinning. "Candy, take Brad upstairs, you know, be done by six, bring him down for dinner, OK?"

The woman had shoulder-length hair, and seemed a young forty with loving, gentle creases. She was beautiful, but I found her flame-blue eyes frightening. Her boy followed her to the stage, dragging his feet across the carpet.

"Pablo," she said, "you told me Derek and I were—"

Pablo held up one finger, cutting her off in mid-sentence. He smirked and pointed upwards.

She pursed her lips into a thin line and then quickly flashed me a smile.

"Hi, I'm Candy Floss, and this is my boy, Derek."

"And I'm still me," I said.

Pablo broke out in his hyena laugh.

"I'm hungry," the boy said, tugging at the turquoise belt around his mother's jeans.

I was aware of Danny and Jon huddling together, backs turned, discussing a drumbeat judging from their motions. How could they not be as stoned as I was? And then I realized that I had drunk twice as much of the drug-laced Crystalle than they had. That was sometimes the way these things worked. Once you get over a certain threshold, you're really out there.

Pablo put a thick hand on my shoulder. "Hey, man, you're going to be OK, Candy will take care of you, know what I mean? You'll come down off the jungle juice in a little while, no sweat, OK?"

Smoking Jimi

I nodded numbly and negotiated the enormous six-inch chasm from the stage to the floor. Candy grinned at me the way a nun smiles at a naughty child before the punishment begins.

"Follow me," she said. The boy and I trailed her through the studio door, and she glanced back at us as she mounted the stone steps. I intended to follow her, but Derek cut in front of me, nearly tripping me, and then scurried down the corridor past the stairs. Suddenly, I too was a child, sneaking away from adults to find secret places and hidden doors. Snickering, I followed the boy down the hall, where I caught the cloying odor of formaldehyde, mixed with the sweetness of beeswax. As Candy's ascending footsteps echoed from the stairway above us, the boy pushed open an ironclad door.

"This is where they go when they're finished," Derek said.

The room's darkness induced drug-induced flares and alien images. The boy clicked on the lights, blinding me.

I blinked.

Was I hallucinating? Life-sized, human statues. Playing guitars. A drummer in mid-stroke. A platinum-haired singer with a leather-clad fist poked into the air, his bare chest in stark contrast to the black leather vest.

Iggy Krotch? I rubbed my eyes, trying to clear my vision. The statues of Iggy and his band almost looked real! They stood on a compact stage, like a movie set with the actors frozen in place. Iggy was in his trademark pose, with his left hand clamped over his crotch. The room was similar to the rehearsal studio we had just played in, right down to the snack machines and amplifiers. But this room held the persistent smell of chemicals.

A powerful hand grabbed my shoulder and jerked me backwards. I stumbled into the hallway.

Rudy!

"You! What are you doing here?"

Before I could answer, Rudy shoved me against the corridor, cracking my head against stone. My ears rang and vomit surged against my gullet. Derek screamed as Rudy lifted him into the air by one arm.

"Derek!" Candy cried out from the bottom of the stairs. "You put him down! Now, dammit!" With the fury of a mother bear she advanced, baring white-knuckle fists. Pablo burst into the hallway as Rudy put the boy down.

"They were in *there*," Rudy growled, slamming the door to the statues' room.

"That door was *unlocked?"* Pablo hissed, his voice as viperous as when his GTO wouldn't start. Derek ran to Candy, but she never broke her glare at Rudy.

Narrowing his eyes, Rudy turned his gaze upon me and said in his German accent, "Yes, it was unlocked, and I caught these two in there."

Like an oil slick, a smile spread across Pablo's face.

"So, Brad, you saw my little wax museum, pretty cool, huh? I just had these statues made of Iggy Krotch and his band— looks like the real thing, huh? I was going to show you guys, make it a surprise, you know?"

20

    Although I didn't recall walking up the stairs, I found myself following Candy into my room. I could easily see her wake— delicate waves trailed behind her, colored with the incense of patchouli and sex. She strode across my room as if she lived there and drew the drapes across the window. I almost giggled as spikes of colored daylight, like naughty children, flirted and peeked around the edges of the antique cloth, playing tag with one another.
    "I can't believe that fascist pig, how dare he touch my boy?" she growled.
    "I wanna go play over at Maria's," Derek said, toeing the priceless rug with a worn sneaker.
    "Just a minute young man. What were you doing in that room downstairs?"
    I suppressed a giggle.
    "Nothing. Just wanted to see my friend Iggy," Derek said.
    "Have you been in there before?"
    Derek looked to me, as if asking for help. "Sort of."
    "Tell me." Candy crossed her arms, mimicking Rudy's pose.
    "I was just playing. Wasn't hurting nothing."
    "Don't you ever go in there again, understand?"
    He lowered his head and nodded.
    "Now you go to Maria's and stay out of trouble. And don't give me that look, young man."
    Derek glanced at me and then disappeared through the doorway.
    I sat on the bed, blinking, my mind not keeping up with my thoughts. I touched the knot on the back of my head where it had smacked into the stone wall. My pain had an odd sensation, as if it didn't really hurt. I closed my eyes. Stubborn flashes and striking visions pried my lids open. I blinked, as if seeing the room for the first time.
    "You OK?" she asked.

I nodded, and then realized my mouth was hanging open. I rubbed my face, wishing everything would just stop. "What was that stuff he gave us?"

"Pablo's jungle juice? Sort of like mescaline." She sat on the bed and leaned over, whispering. "I have to tell you. He's a damned liar. Giving you that doped-up Crystalle was no accident, he did that to me once, the bastard." She rummaged through her purse and produced a blue pill. "One of these'll take the edge off."

I swallowed the pill. It tasted like her. She went to the bathroom door, peeked inside, and then crooked a finger, motioning me to follow. The room was much too bright and I shielded my eyes as she closed the door behind us. She dimmed the lights. I became fascinated by the opposing mirrors, and how our images teased one another, playing leapfrog, regressing infinitely into a mind-melting haze. In this light, her eyes weren't frightening anymore— they now held the soft, blue depth of quiet water.

She fidgeted as if she needed a cigarette. "Maybe it's none of my business, but are you guys totally clueless? Don't you know what you've gotten yourselves into? Tell you what, from what I heard today, I'm getting me and my boy out of here, maybe tonight or tomorrow at the latest. I think the bastard's running out of time."

Holding onto the counter I leaned over, peering into the bathtub, almost certain I'd see it filled with bundles of cash. I blinked, annoyed by the incessant flares of light. I sat on the toilet next to the bidet, while Candy leaned against the sculpted counter, peering down at me, and I again had a sense of imminent punishment. Multiple reflections in the mirrors mocked and mimicked her, and I tried to avoid looking at them— I might lose the real her. Had she just said something important? I couldn't recall, and besides, what did it matter?

I gazed into her face and truly saw her for the first time. Such a beautiful woman. Her loving features fit together with such a soft, feminine harmony. Blue eyes and easy lines defined her, revealing her sensibilities, her loves, her fears. Blonde hair tumbled around her face, playing about her earlobes, cascading along her graceful neck, inviting me to love her, to worship her, to taste her sweet skin. She was in that rare class of woman that a man could love totally, unconditionally, his ego discarded like worn-out shoes.

"Gjerna."

"What?"

Smoking Jimi

"Huh?"

"You said something."

"I did?"

"A weird word," she said, amusement in her eyes.

"Gjerna?"

She nodded with a curious twist and shrugged. "You're such a beautiful man. How did you end up here?"

I grinned at the floor like a bashful idiot.

"Damn," she said, shaking her head, "none of you people are hardcore, except maybe that manager of yours. This ain't right. Pablo's one sick piece of shit." She put her hand to her mouth, inhaling, as if taking a drag from an imaginary cigarette. "So, what's your name?"

"Brad Wilson, I'm from Florida."

"I'm Candy Floss. My real name's Sherri, but around here, you'd better call me Candy." A cloud passed over her face, making her look old and serious, yet still very beautiful.

"Why?"

She laughed. "That's the name they gave me when I was a Playboy centerfold, back in the seventies. Believe it or not, that was me, Miss July. Pablo still has a copy— he likes to do that dirty-boy thing while he looks at my foldout picture, just like when he was a kid. Likes to have me watch him do it. Makes me want to puke. Doesn't seem interested in touching me, he just gets off making me watch him make love to my picture. He's one sick bastard."

I giggled as I drew a mental picture. "Why did you come down here?" I blurted.

"He found me a few years ago, probably like he found you. I was living on my own in California, needed money, so I took Pablo's AIDS test and got on his plane. This is the third time I've come down here. The money's unreal. But I had to take Derek with me this time, his birth father flaked out at the last minute."

I opened my mouth but had no words.

Her eyes met mine. "Poor baby," she said, stroking my hair. "Brad, can I trust you?"

I chuckled. "I don't know. Can *trust* trust me? Can trust be trusted?" I laughed at my cleverness.

"No, Brad, I mean it. Can I tell you something I shouldn't?"

I nodded— an idiot who understands nothing.

She lowered her voice and leaned forward. "You and your friends have got to get the hell out of here. If you don't, you'll end up like those guys in the basement."

I stared at her, this beautiful woman who had just blurted a Chinese phrase.

"Brad, wake up! Do you really think you'll live to spend any of that money Pablo promised you? I don't know where he gets his sick ideas— maybe he thinks he's some sort of Inca god or something. What I do know is that you're going to end up like—"

"Like Jimi Hendrix?" I said, grinning, holding an imaginary guitar, impressed by my flash of creativity.

"Yeah. He's dead."

The front-door latch clicked. Candy scowled as the bathroom door squeaked opened. Pablo stood there, motionless, his eyes twinkling with the sparkle of a malicious prankster.

"So, it's the bathroom, is it? Pretty kinky. You guys doing something I should know about?"

"Pablo, honey," she said in a different voice, more as a child's. "I was just trying to help Brad come down off the jungle juice." Candy glanced at me as if I were a cadaver.

"No sweat, the doctor is here," Pablo said, patting his shirt pocket. He wore his Yankees' cap backwards and with his black T-shirt, he looked like a frat house reject.

"Why don't you go hang out with little Derek for a while, sweetie?"

Candy nodded, took a pitiful glance at me, and was gone.

I needed to urinate and so I got to my feet, swaying like a man thirty feet tall. As I reached way down to raise the lid, Pablo said something and closed the door. I did my business and the water came alive with the colors of the rainbow, as if the psychedelic drug wanted to dazzle me one last time before I sent it to the sewers below. My heart said Candy. I missed her already. Didn't she try to warn me about something? What could happen here, besides getting stoned out of your gourd? Maybe I was crazy. Maybe everyone was crazy.

I laughed as I flushed the toilet. My mirrored reflections teetered, but I avoided looking at my face, I knew that would be way too scary. I kept my eyes on the floor tiles as I carefully found the door.

Pablo sat on the bed, smirking, with a gun in his hand. I laughed. It was that stupid lighter pistol. He put my briefcase on his lap and placed two tiny bottles on it. He patted the bed next to him, his smirk so large it disfigured his face.

"Here, man, sit, just you and me, I'll set you right." Pablo opened a vial, and tamped some green leaves into the bowl of a silver pipe. "Look, I'm sorry about the jungle juice, you gotta believe me, I didn't know it was in the Crystalle. What did Candy do, give you some stupid pill? Man, that won't do anything. Now this, it'll take off the edge and bring you down off the jungle juice nice and easy. Always works for me. Know what? You played heavy today, man, those were some killer riffs. So I went and got my special stash, something I hardly ever share."

I sat on the bed as directed, and Pablo held up the other container, a smoked-glass bottle with a finger-sized, dark-brown object inside. Probably hashish, I figured. I took a deep breath. I hadn't been high in so long, and smoking dope was the last thing I needed right now. Why couldn't Pablo just leave Candy and me alone? Her warning haunted me, but I couldn't recall the meaning behind her words. A laugh erupted for no reason.

"Look, Pablo, I don't need, I mean, maybe it's best I just mellow out on my own."

From Pablo's reaction, I had just asked him to chop off a finger. A shocked stare replaced his smirk. Then, Pablo laughed, as if he were puking up a hunk of indigestible mirth.

"Brad, man, you don't want to insult me, baby, I've brought out my best stash, I don't do this for just any swingin' dick. Besides, you'd piss off the rock-n-roll gods." He broke into another jag of laughter. Pablo took the finger of brown hashish from the bottle and crumbled a portion into the pipe's bowl.

"There, that's just enough so the Great Spirit will breathe inspiration into our souls. You first."

I held the pipe in my hands, examining it. The dark-brown powder in the bowl partly covered crushed, green leaves. What would it hurt if I took one hit, just to placate Pablo? It would be the polite thing to do. I put the pipe to my lips. Pablo pulled the trigger, producing a flame from the gun barrel. I inhaled. The taste was mild, almost sweet, not the sharp, spicy bite of hashish. Pleasant. Familiar. I drew the smoke into my lungs, held it, and slowly released it. Pablo smirked and nodded as he put the pipe to his lips. He took a long drag, puffed up his chest, and then passed the pipe back, pushing it toward my mouth. A curl of smoke twisted from the bowl.

What the hell. I took a second hit. This one burned my lungs with the sharp sting of high-grade weed. My eyes watered and I coughed out the smoke. Pablo laughed, snickering and snorting as smoke escaped from his nostrils.

"That's all, man, no more," I said. Already, I felt woozy, my heart raced, and each breath come fast and shallow. What a dumb idea. I should have remembered how pot intensifies the effects of psychedelics. Stupid! What else had I forgotten?

"Good shit, huh?" Pablo said, his face turning serious. He tapped the bottle containing the chunk of brown hash, holding it to the light. "Who was the greatest guitarist of all time?"

I shook my head. "Hendrix?"

"Yeah! Jimi, man, Jimi! And he ain't dead. He lives, man, he lives right now, in you and me." Pablo gripped the skinny bottle in his fist and held it aloft as if he were saluting the stage at a rock concert with a full-open Bic lighter.

I was in no mood to salute. Those two hits off the pipe had stirred up the effects of Pablo's jungle juice. Colors flashed across my vision with renewed vigor. Wordless, vengeful things floated before my eyes, taunting me.

I cursed for no reason and exhaled loudly.

Pablo laughed. "Hey, man, I brought Iggy's guitar up for you." He pointed at a guitar case near the door. "Iggy Krotch gave me his axe. Go ahead and play, see how it feels."

"Play? Guitar? You gotta be kidding."

Cackling like a gnome gone berserk, Pablo fetched the guitar and plugged it into my Taxi amp. I closed my eyes and wished he would just go away. What was his trip, anyway? We'd already played, jammed heavy and all that crap. The whacked-out bastard got his money's worth. I opened my eyes as the guitar amp buzzed and Pablo placed a black Les Paul guitar into my lap. It felt heavy compared to my Stratocaster, and my left hand hung useless on the strings like a piece of meat.

"I'm stoned out of my head."

Pablo laughed so hard he gagged himself. "You're more than that, man. You're experienced!"

I stared at the guitar and then at Pablo, with his red-rimmed, insane eyes.

"Don't you understand what's happening? Can't you feel the power? I'm going to tell you what I've never told anyone before. But you— you of all people should understand." He held up the jar with the finger of dark hash. "When Jimi died, I paid a half-million dollars for this."

"That's a lot for hash. Was it Jimi's?"

Pablo snickered. "No. Not Jimi's hash. It's more. A holy sacrament. Remember? Do this in memory of me, and all that shit? Some of the heaviest musicians in the world have smoked this with me. Just last month, Iggy Krotch sat right there on the bed where you are now, getting blown away. None of these cats ever knew what this stuff was, but man, it took them places they'd never been. I always told them it was just hash, but really, I was spreading Jimi's magic to the world. Now, this is all that's left."

"What is it?"

"It's Jimi, man. It's him. His finger."

Pablo shook the thing in the bottle. "At one time, I had his whole hand, man, it was freeze-dried, you know, preserved and everything like that. But we done a lot of partying over the years, man. Did you know you could even smoke the bone? Sometimes it makes these really cool sparks. But now, this is all that's left, and when it's gone, there ain't no more. It's the most special thing in the world, and I'm sharing it with you, my friend. Let's do another hit."

I sat, clenching the cold guitar as Pablo's vile words replayed in my mind like a tape loop. Had I really smoked a dead man's finger? This had to be another of Pablo's jokes, right? Ghoulish soot gripped my lungs.

"I'm going to be sick."

Pablo leaned back and roared with laughter.

Salivating heavily, I slid off the bed to my knees. A tortured sound erupted from the amp as the guitar fell to the carpet. Could I have smoked Jimi Hendrix's finger? An ugly taste clung to my mouth— sticky and sickening and evil and then the vomit came.

Pablo chanted strange words over me as I puked, then laughed like a crow, all beak and black feathers and beady eyes. I staggered to the bathroom. An old, disheveled reflection stared back from the mirrors. That couldn't be me. How could anyone look that bad?

I leaned over the toilet and purged myself. When I flushed, a strange part of me observed that the water circled in the wrong direction. Or did it? A long-forgotten teacher began lecturing on the Southern Hemisphere. I rinsed out my mouth over the sink. At least the horrid taste of the finger smoke was gone. Jimi Hendrix's finger? God. I had to straighten up. Had to maintain . . . maintain . . . maintain . . . I repeated the mantra as I wandered back into the bedroom.

I almost tripped over a throw rug that covered where I had gotten sick. A cool breeze touched my face. Pablo was standing inside the frame of the open window— the crow, preparing to fly? No, he was pissing! His urine stream glittered in the evening's light, and his head nodded to an unheard beat while his left knee kept time.

"Aaooo," he howled out the window, and then laughed when he saw me. He hopped down, stuck out his tongue, and holding his arms aloft, shook his body like a zany scarecrow, rolling his eyes.

"Brad, man, where else can you piss out the window of a mansion, huh? Ever done it? Want to? You gotta go? Huh?" He cackled and crowed like a maniac, but then the rumble of thunder from the open window interrupted him. The radio on his belt chimed and he answered in Spanish. He went to the bed and sat, facing away from me.

I wandered to the window, my vision perverted with bizarre colors, my mind fuzzy and raw. Dribbles lay spattered where Pablo had pissed over the sill. Magic dribbles. Cool air washed over me, and for the first time, while admiring those dollops of enchanted piss, I understood what being alive really meant. It was the precious ability to see, think, and feel— to be, and every moment was to be— what? My great epiphany vanished as quickly as it had come. Magic piss? I looked again. It was only urine dribbled on a windowsill by an insane idiot.

I wished I were back in Florida. I missed my life, my studio, my car, I even missed Carol. My Nikon! What ever happened to my camera? I turned to ask Pablo, and at first, I thought he was chuckling, as his shoulders seemed to convulse with laughter. Then he turned to me, and tears streaked his cheeks. The impishness had vanished.

"Why are they doing this to me, Brad, I never did anything to anybody, did I?"

What was I supposed to say?

"Somebody here. That's it. Somebody here's helping them. Aren't they?" He wiped a tear.

Heat spread across my face. Why was Pablo losing it?

"Help?" I mumbled. More thunder rumbled in the distance.

Pablo stared at the window. "Just forget it, man. Forget it. Everybody's in it for themselves. It's all about money, isn't it? Fucking money."

Pablo batted my briefcase to the floor. "Fucking goddam money!" Pablo leaped to his feet, cursing in an unfamiliar language. He kicked the briefcase, slamming it into the wall, and then stormed out the door.

I rubbed my burning eyes. What just happened here? More of Pablo's insanity? A great wave of fatigue washed over me, drowning the drug-induced light in my belly, soaking my core with a thick, seeping darkness. I fell face down on the bed, not wanting to ever see again. The antique bedcover's ancient dust invaded my nostrils and I surrendered, allowing exhaustion to smother me in its merciful blanket.

Chad Peery

21

Resting on the bed, I tried every trick I knew to escape the recurring hallucinations, but the neon-edged perversions triumphed, tormenting me to madness. My tightly wound insides shuddered at the thought of what had just happened on this bed. I couldn't have smoked Jimi Hendrix, could I? God! No one would make another human being do anything that sick. Not even Pablo.

Something grazed the back of my neck and I flinched. Could it be? I was back, I'd made it! I was whom I used to be, and always wanted to be, in a time and place I desperately longed for. Gjerna gazed down at me, the drowsy light casting her in a golden mist. We were in our Copenhagen hotel room, and the illumination dimmed because the Scandinavian day was ending, or perhaps the sun had gone behind a cloud. Either way, it didn't matter— I'd never seen anything more beautiful than my Gjerna. I rolled onto my back as she sat next to me. The open fields of her skin glowed with the warmth of endless summers, kissed by the essence of paradise.

"Gjerna."

"Sure, baby," she cooed, stroking my hair. I closed my eyes as her soothing hands played across my face. She kissed my forehead.

"You're such a beautiful man." Gjerna pressed her lips to mine, sweetly and softly. Her breath was familiar and warm as she snuggled next to me. How I loved being with Gjerna in our hotel room, where from beyond the window came the exotic sounds of a Scandinavian city at dusk— children calling, traffic flowing, gentle people going home to their loved ones.

I opened my eyes. My dream evaporated. I stared at the strange woman next to me. She was beautiful, but she wasn't Gjerna. The sweetness on her breath came from vodka. I glanced about the room and was taken by a horrible emptiness— the terror of not knowing who I was, or where I was, or when it was.

Suddenly, I was hit with a bracing splash of reality— I was Brad Wilson, washed-up rock star— this naked woman was Candy Floss, washed-up model— and we were together on a bed in some rich asshole's mansion in South America. I let out a great sigh.

"You OK?" She whispered.

Five answers came to my mind simultaneously, and then evaporated.

"I think I got sick," I said. "Pablo had me smoke this stuff, I don't know why I did it— I thought it was just hash, but it was really Jimi Hendrix's finger."

She laughed so hard it angered me. How could she be so heartless?

"Oh, Brad," she murmured, "I can't believe he did that to you. Pablo is such a dick, he pulls that trick on everybody. They get all freaked out, thinking they've just smoked Jimi Hendrix's finger, when really, it was only hashish. It's just another of Pablo's lame jokes. I suppose he thinks it's funny."

A thought flashed through me— sometimes life is wonderful and it's good to be alive. I kissed this beautiful woman who had just freed me from Pablo's hell, and her pliable body responded, pressing against mine. She smothered me in so many pleasuring kisses that soon I forgot about the ridiculous notion that I had smoked Jimi Hendrix. I lost myself in her blonde curls and swirling moans, drowning myself in multicolored oceans of pleasure, intoxicated to my core by her sensual body. We entered into a slow, perfect embrace, and lay motionless for the longest time, minds and bodies joined within the aura of our pleasure. And then began the most beautiful jam, and we played the melodic lines of our bodies into a pure, sweet song of bliss.

Afterwards, holding each other as the echoes of ecstasy faded, we collapsed within ourselves. I drifted off as a thunderstorm grumbled in the distance, a million miles away.

* * *

Candy Floss stood over me, shaking me awake. She had dressed, her tight jeans and loose blouse fitting her so perfectly that I wanted to take them off for her. I sat up, feeling almost normal again. I began fumbling with her buttons.

"Brad," she whispered, cradling my hands against her breasts, "you and your friends— look, I can't let Pablo do to you what he did to Iggy."

"Why are we whispering?" I whispered back.

Her face hardened and she leaned into my ear. "Because the sick little fuck has every room bugged, could be watching right now on video. And he'd kill me if he knew I was telling you this."

"Telling me what?" I whispered, struggling to keep up with the conversation.

She grabbed a vodka bottle from the bar, grabbed my clothes and led me into the bathroom where she sat me on the commode. She kicked the door shut.

"How do you know the bathroom isn't bugged?" I asked, still whispering, as I started to dress.

"You don't have to whisper in here. I've seen his monitoring setup. He doesn't have the bathrooms bugged so Rudy can't spy on him while he does kinky things with his guests. Brad, he's really gone off the deep end. You should hear the stories I've heard the past few days. If I would have known I would have never come back down here, and Christ, I brought my kid!"

She leaned heavily against the counter and took a long swig from the vodka bottle, swishing the booze in her mouth before she swallowed.

"If you don't get your ass out of here tonight you'll end up dead." She took another swallow and stared at me. "When I found out what those sick bastards did to Iggy and his band, it made me want to puke."

"Did? Who did what?"

She studied me. "Pablo collects people. That creep Rudy does the dirty work." She burped softly into her fist. "Iggy and his band turned up missing after they visited here last month. Yesterday, one of the girls told me a story I couldn't believe. So, last night I stole a key and went down to that room to check things out. Iggy and his friends were there all right, every last one of them."

My mind raced to the room with the wax figures of Iggy Krotch and his band.

"You mean, well sure, I saw wax statues down there."

"Why do you think Pablo and Rudy got so freaked when you and Derek found that room? Those aren't wax dummies. They're the real things, covered in some sort of waxy chemicals. God knows what Rudy did to them. Couldn't you smell the formaldehyde? There's a couple of other rooms down there too, locked up tight. It's anybody's guess who he's had stuffed and mounted. Remember that studio you played in? I'll bet that was going to be your display room, and you guys were going to end up just like Iggy's band. The only reason Pablo brought you guys down here is to be a part of his trophy collection. Thank God he doesn't seem interested in collecting women."

I shivered. A cold draft trickled down my back. Carol's dolls flashed through my mind. Thunder rumbled, closer than before.

"Thinks he's an Inca god," she continued, "believes he's descended from royalty and he's immortal. Thinks he inherits the powers of those he kills. Read it in some stupid book about Incas. Got shit-faced drunk a couple of nights ago and told me all this weird crap. Steals things from people because he thinks it lets him control them. Took a gold chain from me when I first got here, said he'd kill me if I told anybody."

She put her hand on my shoulder, her warmth anchoring my scattered thoughts. More thunder.

"Hear that? Some heavy people are pissed at Pablo and his brothers. There's a bunch of fighting going on not far from here, and it's heading this way. Brad, what am I supposed to do? I got a little boy. God knows I should never have brought him down here." She leaned into my ear. "I'm getting me and my boy out of here, tonight." She slowly unscrewed the cap of the vodka bottle as if waiting for my response, and then screwed the cap back on without taking a drink.

My mind finally linked the sound of thunder to something more ominous. "How are you getting out?" I asked.

"My little secret. I can take you along, but only you. Understand? I'm taking a big chance on you baby, and I'll make sure there's room for you. Your choice. Meet me by the pool in one hour." She gave me a forlorn look, and then the hardness crept back over her face. She walked through the bathroom door and tossed the vodka bottle toward the bed.

"Good luck baby. You'll need that bottle more than I will."

* * *

I stood at the latticed bedroom window, gazing toward distant rumbles. Occasional flashes blinked in the distance, outlining the hills beyond the front gates, which stood shoulder-to-shoulder across the road. Multi-colored haloes circled the streetlights along the driveway, and I blinked, trying to rid my eyes of the last effects of Pablo's psychedelic drug. Beyond the well-lit grounds, darkness encroached from all sides, while stars glowered like white-hot embers. My breath steamed in the night.

As I started to close the window, a man carrying an assault rifle jogged down the front driveway, and shouting in Spanish, ran off toward the garages.

I flinched as loud music blared from the stereo behind me. Mitch!

He held a finger over his lips, his face a haggard mix of new shadows and old perversions. He carried his briefcase under his arm.

"What are you doing? Why the music?"

"Someone could be listening," Mitch said, speaking above the jazz music. "They got our rooms bugged. Weird shit's coming down."

"What time is it?"

"Seven-thirty. You missed dinner, Pablo said to let you sleep. Too bad, because this afternoon I cooked up *Puenta Fujoles a la Maison*. Worked on it all day, wanted to show you guys what I could do. Man, you should see that kitchen."

A rumble came from the distance. The lights dimmed, and then recovered.

"Where's your money?" Mitch asked.

I gestured at the black briefcase Pablo had kicked against the wall.

"Keep it close Brad, we've got bigtime problems."

"I know," I said, as the jazz music picked up intensity.

"Rudy and Pablo were talking downstairs, and I just happened to be on the other side of the door. Remember White Hair, that guy who followed us down here? Rudy said Pablo's cousins never did find this White Hair dude and his partner, and they're still out there somewhere. White Hair's name is Alex Krell, and he's a major European dope dealer. Rudy wants to know what Krell's doing here and why he's been asking about you. Thinks Krell may be connected to one of the other cartels."

"European dope dealer? Following me? Makes no sense." Acid surged through my stomach at the thought of this White Hair bastard, Alex Krell, out there asking questions about me. It was probably because of my involvement with Pablo, or Mitch, or both. Would Alex Krell dare come to Rancho Vizcaya?

"Rudy thinks Jon used one of those satellite phones to make some calls after we got here. Rudy searched our rooms today, but couldn't find anything. Said we're nothing but trouble. Wants us gone, one way or the other."

Mitch cast a paranoid glance toward the window.

"I just talked to Candy—"

"Never mind those hookers. We gotta get our asses out of here and fast. Me and the chef got to talking, and he told me that a war has just broken out. The fighting could be working its way toward us."

"I just heard the same thing," I said.

"Remember the Golden Path, those soldiers at the roadblock on the way in? They've been fighting all day with some hard-core communists called the SLA. From what I heard, this SLA intercepted a shipment of guns the CIA sent to the Golden Path with the help of the Lupa family. SLA came out of the hills today, thousands of them, and raided a Golden Path town. Caught 'em off guard, killed a bunch of people."

"And all this time I thought that sound was thunder."

"That's not thunder, pal. The chef also said to forget the government soldiers— they won't set foot in this part of the country. Said he's taking his family out of here tonight, heading to a village in the mountains, got a sister up there. Says it's gonna get real ugly around here real quick."

My head moved like a rusty wheel. "Where are Jon and Danny?"

"I heard about the drugs Pablo gave you guys. Set Danny off really bad. He's over the edge, freaked, made a bad scene at dinner. Jon's with him now in his room."

I lowered my head to my hands as the ceiling swooned. "I don't understand any of this, we were just jamming and everything was OK, and Gjerna came to my room, and then it was Candy, and she told me Pablo's going to have us all killed, turned into wax statues." I went into her story about Iggy Krotch.

"Who's this chick?"

"Candy Floss. One of Pablo's girls."

Mitch picked up the near-empty vodka bottle from the bed. "Yours?"

"Hers."

"Sounds like a drunk's story. Iggy Krotch stuffed and dipped in wax? C'mon."

Hallucinations invaded my skull, trying to steal their way back into my brain.

"Brad, you OK?"

I nodded.

Smoking Jimi

"Let's get over to Danny's room, figure out what to do next. And bring your money. Don't let it out of your sight."

Chad Peery

22

The scene in Danny's room was worse than I had imagined. Glass sparkled below a shattered mirror. An antique table lay smashed, and shreds of drapery clung to the windowsill as if someone had tried to claw their way to freedom. One of the posts on Danny's antique bed leaned precariously, while animal heads on the wood-paneled walls gazed with sightless eyes. Danny sat on the bed staring at nothing, his face drawn with paranoia.

Sitting next to him, Jon glanced up and shook his head warning us away. On his face, a fresh bruise caught the light. Two black briefcases sat on the bed next to Danny, and I sat mine down near the door. Mitch held on to his briefcase, like a child afraid of losing his lunchbox to bullies.

The lights dipped and dimmed, and then died entirely, thrusting the room into pitch-blackness. A distant rumble came through the open window. Dirty rainbows flickered across my vision. Danny howled and moaned while Jon tried calming him.

From outside came the grumble of a diesel motor starting up, and the lights glowed again, in a dim, haunting way. As we stood looking at each other, a popping sound erupted in the distance. It reminded me of firecrackers, but then I recognized the staccato snap of small-arms fire.

"Need my gun, where's my goddam gun?" Danny sat erect on the bed, his eyes fixed on me. "Government's coming, ain't they? General Ray warned us, man, he warned us!"

Jon sprinted to the window. "This isn't supposed to be happening, something's gone wrong." Jon turned to us, holding his hands aloft like a preacher. "You two come with me, we need to talk."

"Life sucks, and then you die," Danny growled after us, as we filed into the hallway.

The three of us stood at the railing that overlooked the main chamber. Recorded birdcalls drifted from nowhere, while muffled shouts came from below. Quiet returned, except for the canned chirping.

Jon said, "Guys, I'm only telling you this because— we're friends, I can trust you, right?"

Mitch and I looked at each other. Jon heaved a sigh, and then spoke in hushed tones. "I'm not really a monk, not like you think. I'm with the ATF. We've worked with the Vituscans for years to get information on the Trotts and groups like them." He looked back and forth between Mitch and me, as if waiting for a reaction.

I blinked in disbelief.

"ATF?" Mitch asked. "You're a damned cop?"

"Keep it down, Mitch. What's important is that you do exactly what I tell you, understand?"

"Should have known something was wrong with you, man." Mitch glanced at me for support.

Jon gave Mitch a hard stare. "Wrong? You two guys came to Colorado and dumped this thing on me, remember? I was doing just fine, setting up General Ray and those damned Trots. Besides the usual machine guns and grenades, those idiots were stocking up on nerve gas and heavy explosives. We were getting ready to raid Deadwood Camp when you guys came out of nowhere with this Pablo Lupa thing. The big shots in D.C. ordered me to go down here with you guys. Rumors had it that the Lupas and the Golden Path were putting the Oro Cartel back together. These Washington buttheads cooked up some scheme to start a ruckus, then convert Pablo by offering him protection. But now, looks like those shit birds have triggered a war between the Golden Path and the SLA, and we're right in the middle of it."

"You stupid little . . ." Mitch growled. "Your government bullshit just got me killed." He turned his back and rested his briefcase upon the stone railing. "I gotta— you know— we, gotta get outta here. Even the chef's jumping ship."

My soggy mind recalled Candy, who said to wait for her by the pool. She and her son would probably be escaping with the chef. Should I tell Jon about Pablo's plans to have us stuffed and mounted?

Mitch turned to Jon and frowned. "I heard 'em talking downstairs. Pablo's hip, knows you've got a satellite phone."

Jon blinked.

"You hid that phone in my Taxi amp, didn't you?" I asked.

Smoking Jimi

Jon nodded. "I stashed it out here, so they wouldn't find it if they searched my room," he said, glancing at a statue. "I just tried using it, but something's jamming the signal."

A crash and thud came from Danny's room. We rushed through the door.

"Christ, he jumped!" Jon yelled, bolting for the window.

The three of us crowded into the casement. I expected to see Danny's broken body sprawled upon the cobblestone. Instead, the flowerbed lay crushed where Danny must have landed, before sprinting off into the shadows. A guard, holding an assault weapon aloft, stood alongside the fountain, gazing towards the line of nude statues and the gate's distant lights. He spoke into his handheld radio, took another look down the driveway, and then rushed off in the direction of the garages.

"Dammit! I knew something was going to happen, I should have never left Danny alone," Jon said

"C'mon," Mitch said, "the guy's a flake. He's wiggy."

Quick as a cat, Jon whirled and landed a punch, cracking Mitch square in the face. Jon's second blow missed because Mitch was already reeling backward, stumbling over a broken table. He landed on his back, just like that day at Wendy's.

I grabbed Jon's shoulder, but he didn't need restraining. He was frozen in place, staring at the door.

Pablo Lupa!

Followed by Rudy, Pablo approached us with the intensity of a jaguar. Pablo held Jon's satellite phone in his hand, while Rudy stood behind Pablo, aiming a pistol at us, his grin laced with venom.

"So," Pablo said quietly, contemplating the thick phone in his hand. "This is my reward? I take you into my home, I treat you like brothers, and what do I get? WHAT DO I GET?" He glared until we looked away.

Pablo thrust the satellite phone at Jon like a sword. "You. Did you call your friends, the cowards who tried to kill me? Or maybe you talk with your comrades in the American government. Or your white-haired faggot friend from Europe? How stupid do you think I am? You really think you were going to kill me tonight? Maybe cut my throat? Shoot me?"

He laughed and abruptly hurled the phone out the open window. It clattered on the driveway, clacking like old bones.

I couldn't take my eyes from Rudy's gun, an angular weapon with a cruel barrel. Should I make a break for it, maybe leap out the window the way Danny had? Rudy stood on a long, narrow carpet, and if I moved fast, I could pull his feet out from under him, bowl Pablo out of the way, and be out the door. Who was I kidding? One of the bullets in that gun was destined to rip a hole in my chest. We were all going to die. Jon jerked his arm free of my grip.

"Pablo," Jon said, his voice unsteady, "I'm your only hope of living through the night. I can—"

"You can't do shit," Pablo snapped. "You're a dead man." He spit on his Yankees' cap and threw it into Jon's face. Blinking, as if trying to focus, Pablo whipped a small pistol from his pocket and aimed it at Jon.

"One is missing," Rudy said, "the crazy one"

"He's gone," I said, glancing towards the smashed window.

Rudy leaned over the transom, shook his head at Pablo, and then returned to his station, posing like a wrestler, arms folded and muscles rippling. But now, Rudy seemed edgy and nervous, his eyes returning to the window.

"You threw Danny out the window?" Pablo asked with a vile smirk.

"He jumped. He's totally crazy," Mitch said from the floor, wiping a bloody lip, still clutching his briefcase of money.

An ugly silence passed, and I felt Pablo's stare. "And you, I thought you were my friend." I glanced away from Pablo's gun long enough to look into his hideous eyes, rimmed with hate, or drugs, or both.

"Oh yeah?" I said. "You mean like Iggy Krotch?"

Pablo glared at me the way a snake stares at a mouse. "So? You like Iggy? Wanna play in his band? Just yesterday, I was talking with my friend Iggy and he said, 'Pablo, I could use another good guitar player. Somebody who plays like Jimi Hendrix.'" Pablo's scoffing laugh made me despise him even more.

The sound of a helicopter came from the open window, its rhythmic whump settling into a chopping whine as the aircraft touched down on the helipad. Rudy whispered something to Pablo.

Jon said, "There's your copter, run while you can."

A skeleton grin crept across Pablo's face. "Rudy, kill these two now. I'll meet you at the helicopter in ten minutes. Me and

Brad here, we have a special gig to do first. We're gonna jam forever."

With his pistol, Pablo motioned me towards the door. I glanced back, and Jon's pallor reminded me of Iggy Krotch under wax. Mitch groveled on the floor, gesturing and whining nonsense. As I walked through the door, I felt the eyes of the doomed upon me.

"Stop here," Pablo said, slamming the door behind us. "Those two, they're not special, and that's why they're going to die now. But you, didn't I always say that you were the one? Didn't I? That's why I want you to live forever, like my friend Iggy." A moment of silence passed, and then a horrid thump rattled the door— a jarring thud deeper than Danny's kick drum. Another explosive gunshot reverberated in my chest, then a quick third. The mental impact of Rudy's murderous gunshots slammed into me. I collapsed to my knees.

"God dammit, no!"

Pablo kicked me and I collapsed face-first onto the stone. I pounded the floor with my fists, cursing Pablo and welcoming the pain.

"Stop!" Pablo shouted.

I continued pummeling the floor, pain flaring through my hands and wrists.

A horribly loud shot.

I looked down, expecting to see my blood pooling on the stones.

Nothing.

From the great room came the crash of glass. Then from above me, Pablo's cackling laugh. He gestured at the ceiling.

"Look! Look at that! Now we got us some real air conditioning." Pablo laughed again. I went to the railing, and saw glass scattered on the floor below. Apparently, he had fired a shot upwards and struck the skylight. Snickering, Pablo raised his gun, and another thunderous shot rang out. More glass tumbled and smashed against the floor tiles. Pablo roared with laughter.

Candy Floss! She stood with a heavyset man, two other women, and her boy, pressed against the far wall beyond the pool. She spotted me, and even at this distance her eyes told me of her escape, my death, and sorry, but there was nothing more she could do. I envisioned shoving Pablo over the rail, imagining the satisfying thud his body would make. As if he'd heard my thoughts, Pablo snorted and backed away, leveling his gun at my chest. When I glanced back over the rail, Candy and the others had vanished.

As Pablo marched me down to the basement, my pounding heart reminded me that Jon and Mitch lay dead, their hearts forever still, while my own death waited for me below. What could be going through Pablo's mind? Did he think the SLA rebels wouldn't kill him? Why wasn't he escaping with Rudy right now, getting on that chopper? Was he completely insane? Stoned out of his mind?

I stepped onto the basement floor, where the air held the distilled scent of death and rancid vapors. The hair on the back of my neck stiffened. How would this maniac kill me? A gun? Too messy. How had he killed Iggy and his band? Poison?

"Iggy boy, oh Iggy boy," Pablo called, cackling like a crow. He jabbed the pistol into my ribs, forcing me towards Iggy's studio door. Pablo threw me the keys. The musicians' wax-cased bodies stood onstage with Iggy's fist poked into the air, forever frozen in a ridiculous gesture of rebellion. He had his head tilted back with eyelids closed, but the other band members' eyes glistened, as if their sockets held marbles of glass.

The air reeked of formaldehyde. I figured somewhere down the hall that bastard Rudy had a workroom filled with vats and volatile chemicals. That's where I would end up, if the SLA rebels didn't kill Pablo and me first. I never hated anyone more than I hated him.

"Sit." Pablo indicated a couch in the middle of the studio. I remained standing. Pablo laughed. Keeping a wary eye on me, he went to a bar, grabbed a bottle and tossed it to me.

I caught it. He laughed.

"Looks like another bottle of Crystalle, that crap you spiked with jungle juice."

"Maybe it's the same bottle," Pablo said, snorting a laugh.

I was really getting to hate his laughs.

"Drink," Pablo said.

I refused. I didn't need to get stoned again on Pablo's psychedelic booze.

Pablo snickered. "You think it's poisoned, like lunch today?" He roared in laughter and snatched the bottle from my hands. "I drink first!" While holding the bottle sideways so he could keep his vile gaze on me, he took three big swallows. He wiped his mouth with a shirtsleeve.

"Now you." He thrust the bottle toward me. I didn't take it.

"Brad, man, do I have to shoot you? Ever been shot? Hurts like hell!" He snickered. "I don't wanna give you forever death, man, I want to give you eternal life! Remember? You asked me what happened when the Inca God Venalocha took those souls down inside Mt. Paxicoto, the old man volcano. They're still there, still alive. The Incas understood how to live in the moment of death forever. They knew how to freeze time. Venalocha's waiting for you, he's holding a place for you in eternity right now, and you can jam heavy every day, just like Iggy here. Think he's not happy? Just look at this dude, man, he's got his attitude. He can never die, never."

"You're fucking crazy. Out of your mind insane."

Pablo sneered, corrupting his eyes. "Insane? Me? I bought you. I paid for you. I own your ass. You came to me with a big, fat boner for all that pretty, green cash. Who's crazy now? Drink!"

I grabbed the naked neck of the bottle from Pablo, and calculated how fast it would happen if I threw it at his face and lunged for the gun. Maybe he was stoned enough that I'd have a chance. Again, Pablo seemed to read my eyes and let out a stubby laugh as he backed away to a safe distance.

My options were none. I figured if I could get him high on his damned jungle juice, then I might get a break and somehow escape. But I also remembered how messed up I got on the drug this afternoon. I still didn't feel like myself. Putting the bottle to my lips, I pretended to take a drink.

"I ought to blow your damned brains out," Pablo hissed, his eyes so vicious I had to look away. "How dare you disrespect me? Drink, now!"

Screw him. I could maintain as well as anyone. I took a swallow. The alcohol burned my throat and I had the urge to puke, knowing what it contained.

"Again!"

I took another swallow. My only chance would be to fling the half-full bottle at the punk and grab his gun. But not at this distance. Pablo would shoot me before I got halfway there. What the hell, he was going to kill me anyway. I was destined for his sick collection of dead rock stars. As I tensed my legs for action, Pablo's radiophone chirped.

He poked a button. "Rudy?" A cloud came over his face. "Hey. Rudy?"

"What's going on, Pablo?" I asked. "Heard your buddies in the Golden Path got their asses kicked by the SLA. Really bad. Fighting's getting closer. Didn't you hear? Better get your ass on that chopper while you can. Hey, crazy bastard, they're coming for you. Everybody knows it."

"You don't know shit," Pablo said with a leer. "Drink!"

"I already did. It's your turn." A spurt of adrenaline raced through me as the drug began coming on and my heart accelerated. I would have to move fast before the jungle juice really hit me or I'd be too far out of it to do anything. I held out the bottle. Pablo snatched it, and standing at a safe distance, downed a swig. He thrust it toward me.

"Now you! Do it!" I took the bottle and swallowed again. I handed it back. Pablo took another drink and slammed the bottle down on the bar. A demented grin crept across his face as he produced a small wooden box. Handling it carefully, he opened the lid, revealing a row of glass vials.

"I've just opened the door to forever," Pablo said, with a sly smirk. "You ready to receive Venalocha's gift of immortality?"

A thump came from the studio door. Fear flashed in Pablo's eyes. With another thump, and the latch slowly turned. Was the SLA here to kill us? I looked around, searching for a hiding place. Maybe I could talk them into killing Pablo and letting me go. Would they understand English?

The door swung open.

Rudy stood in the doorway, his eyes stretched into wide, disconnected circles. Bloodstains soaked his clothing. Had the pig soiled himself dragging Jon and Mitch's bodies down here? He blinked like a man under water. Groping the air, he sank to his knees and twisted onto his back. His body shuddered.

Pablo rushed to Rudy's side.

"No! Man, no! They shot him!"

Rudy writhed and bared his teeth. Pablo gently lifted Rudy's torn shirt. I looked away from the gaping hole in his abdomen. No gun in his holster. Had Jon and Mitch gotten the jump on him? More likely, the SLA had overrun Vizcaya's defenses, shot Rudy, and would soon hunt us down.

"See, they're here. You're going to die, freak bait. Run while you can."

"Get back," Pablo growled, "or I'll kill you right now." Keeping an eye on me, Pablo snatched the wooden box and removed a glass vial. He pulled the cork stopper from the vial and pressed the cork to Rudy's neck. Instantly, Rudy's face went slack and a long breath hissed from his mouth. His lifeless gaze reminded me of the guys in Iggy's band.

"See, man? He's at peace, he's in Paxicoto, he's found his forever." Pablo held forth the cork stopper. A short pin protruded from the bottom. Whatever was on that needle had put Rudy down instantly.

"Hold out your hand." A rumble shook the floor. "Now. I got no time for your shit. Give me your hand, or I'll shoot you. Now." The look in Pablo's face was that of the Inca sacrificial priest about to shove his victim into the steaming volcano. My heart pounded. Pablo edged closer. Adrenaline surged. I wouldn't die without a fight. Instinctively, my hands flew up as Pablo lunged. I grabbed the gun barrel, turning it away from me. It exploded in my hands and my ears screamed from the gunshot, but I held my ground. Something pricked my left hand. I recoiled in horror. A spot of blood formed on the back of my left index finger. I gripped it and squeezed hard. A drop of blood fell from my finger.

Pablo sneered as he retreated. Hoping to force the poison from my wound, I squeezed my finger so hard it turned deep red. Holding the gun on me, Pablo leered with an infected smirk and slinked backwards, glancing over his shoulder towards the door.

"Forever, man, you can't deny forever. It's done. You're there, man, you're there. See you in forever."

"Eat shit and die."

Pablo nodded his head, as if I'd uttered some great truth. More dark-red blood dripped from my finger. Could I squeeze out enough poison? I felt lightheaded, and the colors were all wrong, as if I were viewing the room through a broken video monitor. I took a deep breath, vowing not to give in to whatever was invading my body.

Pablo's radio chirped. He answered in Spanish, then cursed and flung the radio aside. Gripping his gun he floated backwards and paused at the door, where a thousand things passed between us as we locked eyes.

Shots!

The gunfire came from upstairs, reverberating in horrid green waves, bathing Pablo in a vile light, this misbehaving child whose father waited for him with a belt. He vanished into the hallway

Muffled shouts and gunshots echoed from above. Clenching my finger in a tourniquet grip, I stepped over Rudy. Could he still be conscious, paralyzed by Pablo's drug dart, crying out in the silence of his mind? More yelling and horrible racket came from upstairs. As I hurried down the hallway, I prayed that the tightness in my chest was fear, and not Pablo's death drug.

Wood splintered at the top of the stairs. Spanish words spewed forth in staccato bursts. I darted into the studio where we had jammed. No inside lock. With the door closed the room was dark except for the amps' pilot lights and the dim glow of the recording booth window. Behind the windows something flashed, accompanied by a soft whump. Another hallucination?

Like the ripples of a pond, waves of luminescent color passed before my eyes, flashing in patterns so sharp and clear I could almost touch them. I blinked hard in a futile attempt to clear my vision. In moments the soldiers would discover Iggy's studio—what would they think of the waxed bodies? And when they reached this studio, what would they do to me? And Pablo—where had the murdering bastard gone?

Moving carefully I made my way towards the recording booth door, but my foot caught on something and I stumbled forward, falling heavily onto the carpeted stage. Musical notes rang out, tinny and thin next to my ear. My Stratocaster! I could just make out the instrument, resting in its stand, and inches from my face. My fall must have set the strings vibrating.

My finger!

When I fell, I had let go of my injured finger! Fear seized my heart in a death grip. The remaining poison in my wound would now reach my bloodstream. What did it matter? The soldiers would eventually find me and it would be over. So be it. I would end my life with peace and love in my heart. I would die with my guitar in my hands.

Sitting against the Marshall speaker cabinet, I held my guitar, my old friend. The amp's power indicator glowed a soft red and I opened up the guitar's volume knob, just enough to hear. I leaned my head against the amplifier. The guitar felt good in my hands and my fingers formed a chord pattern. Before I lost control to the numbing poison, I wondered if I should crank up the volume and play one last screaming solo— after all, hadn't I just smoked Jimi Hendrix?

I laughed, but it was short and bitter. No, I would spend my last moments thinking of Gjerna and the family we never had. How I wished we could have spent our years dancing life's dance, to have held her in my arms forever. Maybe she waited for me now, on the other side of death's door.

I thought of her and gently stroked a minor chord. The speakers at my back came to life with the most beautiful, sparkling voice I'd ever heard. The guitar, with its strings slightly out of tune, gave the chord an honesty all its own. It was my chord— it spoke of my life, my joys, my hopes, my loves. It sustained, just as my life had sustained, and then faded to an end, just as my life was about to end. I would sit peacefully, strumming my life's chord, and when the soldiers found me, they would gather around, entranced by the beauty and love streaming in colored ribbons from my Marshall amp— it would envelop them, wrap them in the most beautiful hues, and the love in their hearts would blossom— they would lay down their weapons and we would forever live in peace in the green fields of Mt. Paxicoto.

I strummed again.

Idiot!

What was I thinking?

Something told me to get my ass into the recording booth, right now. Carefully, I lay my guitar into its stand and got to my feet, swaying. My body felt as if I'd suddenly gained fifty pounds, while my breaths came in quick, shallow gasps. Numbness crept across my face and lips. Don't stop moving. I heaved open the recording booth door. Hallucinations obscured my sight with obnoxious flashes of colors. The only true light bled from a glowing computer screen and a few red dots from an equipment panel. I could just make out a shape on the floor. The thing made a gurgling sound. I knelt down, trying to peer through a dense fog of colored obscenities.

Pablo?

No.

Spider!

The English studio engineer lay on his back, his eyes staring. He had something in one hand. I pried open his dead fingers and removed the DAstick from his palm. Someone had scrawled "JAMMIES" in white ink on the credit-card sized device.

Chad Peery

Or was I hallucinating? I thrust it into my shirt pocket and rubbed my eyes, trying to clear my vision. A massive hole occupied the center of Spider's chest and blood pooled on the carpeted floor. He'd just been shot! That *was* a gun flash I saw moments ago. Pablo must have shot him, while standing on this very spot.

But where was Pablo now?

Watching? Hiding?

Finger on the trigger?

Something growled. Not me. Not Spider. Pablo? The growl turned to a roar, and then became a screeching howl. My guitar! In my confusion, I must have turned the guitar's volume knob the wrong way, and now my instrument sat in its stand at the foot of the amp, feeding back in a screaming, grating howl that would have made Jimi Hendrix proud.

23

As the guitar wailed and screeched, the door to the hallway opened, spilling a shaft of sour milk into the studio. Soldiers! Outside the studio the lights flashed on, and despite the recording booth's smoked glass I shielded my eyes. A teenager's face came into view, painted with green-and-black war paint, his head wrapped in an olive-drab bandanna and his eyes glazed with murder. The grating feedback from my amplifier seemed to baffle him— he probably reasoned that sounds such as this don't just happen, so someone in here must need killing.

Holding his automatic weapon at the ready, the youthful soldier advanced into the room, while an older, bearded man appeared behind him, wearing a red beret. Their predator's eyes fixed on the recording booth glass. I ducked. Did they see me?

My heart hammered madly and I made a quick promise— I would not die here tonight. Not this way. Drugs or no drugs, I would not let this happen. I peeked over the window ledge. The teen approached me, his gun snug against his hip, its barrel aimed in my direction. How many had this boy killed tonight? I tried not to think of the orgy of bullets and blood upstairs. I retreated into a corner behind the equipment rack. It occurred to me that if I sat very still the soldiers would think I was just a piece of equipment, and they would leave me alone.

Stupid!

I cursed my violated mind. Hallucinating heavily, I could just make out my surroundings through a frustrating medley of colors. My arms tingled, but at least I could still move— the paralyzing drug from Pablo's sting hadn't completely taken control. Where had that vile bastard gone? Neither of us could hide in this small room.

A nearby equipment rack sat askew, as if it didn't like the wall. I crawled over to it and leaned my cheek against its cool metal. Surely, it would pity me and give me sanctuary. I made the ridiculous attempt to fit my body into the tiny gap between the rack and wall. How pathetic. How futile! Frustrated and angry, I punched the floor. It boomed, resonating like a drum. I pounded again. The floor reverberated like a muffled tom-tom.

I pinched the carpet and pulled. A neat square came up. The flooring was hinged at one end— an escape hatch! Beneath it a ladder tapered into darkness. I lowered my legs into the cavity.

The howling of my amp ceased abruptly. The door to the recording studio creaked open. Not ten feet away a soldier's hand reached around the doorway and felt for the light switch. Panicking now, I forced my sluggish body the rest of the way down the ladder and pulled the trap door closed. The pitch-blackness intensified my hallucinations, while the ladder seemed rubbery and alive, as if I were descending into the bowels of some ungodly monster.

The place reeked of dankness and death. Gravity increased its pull, nagging and tugging, drawing my body to its bosom. I resisted, holding tight to the ladder, struggling to survive this life-and-death contest.

Suddenly, I slammed into the ground, a sack of cement split open, lying flat on my back. I gasped like a fish out of water, desperate for oxygen, but no air entered my lungs. A dark vacuum drew me into the newly formed cocoon, trapping me inside a body of clay, while horrid flashes of mental lightning reminded me my brain had not yet died.

Pain rippled across my torso like cracks on a vase. I lay broken, unable to breathe, suffocating on my own breath. From somewhere above I looked down upon my pathetic body in this earthen coffin. I had seen my own death, and now there was nothing more for me here.

Blackness, sweet blackness came, and I floated, floated.

A racking, sobbing gasp pulled me back into my body. Like the waves before an advancing tide, life ebbed into me with each breath. Sweat misted my body. I become aware of the cold surface beneath me, and the grip of paralysis receded from my chest. I tried regrouping, to get my mind to comprehend something, anything. My mental process was like tuning a radio dial across the static, occasionally finding a coherent station, but then losing reception before I could hear a completed thought.

I licked numb lips. Pablo. Think of Pablo. My hatred for him might give me power. He must have come this way. Would the soldiers find the tunnel? Did they see me escape? Did Candy Floss and her boy get to a safe place? Would the paralyzing drug kill me? Perhaps the needle didn't have a full dose on it, since it had been first used on Rudy. A faraway sound echoed down the tunnel. Light pierced the darkness. Its orb danced like a firefly, and firing off frightening halos as it stabbed towards me. Larger and brighter it came, distorting my vision. A flashlight! Someone approached! Pablo? I could barely move, and even if I could, what would I do?

Time must have fast-forwarded, for now someone towered over me, their flashlight casting out razor-edged rainbows that sliced at my eyes. The intruder kicked the sole of my foot and then shined the light upwards, illuminating his face.

A bearded ghost.

Danny!

Chad Peery

24

Danny helped me to my feet leaned me against the earthen wall. Keeping his voice low, he explained how he had injured his ankle in the jump from the window, and had been hiding in the garage. Moments ago, he had seen Pablo emerge into the garage from the other end of the tunnel and drive off in his Cadillac Escalade amidst a hail of bullets.

"Some bad shit was going down so I came back to get you guys, couldn't leave you and Jon behind. Where's Jon?"

"Rudy killed them both," I blurted.

"Jon? Dead?" Danny spat on the ground. "Can't be dead."

"I saw, man."

Danny released a low, cursing moan. He wiped at his eyes. "Where's that goddam Rudy?"

"He got shot by the SLA, I saw him die." I shuddered at the gruesome image.

"There's a bunch of crazy sons of bitches out there. I need a goddam gun."

The colored bands of light that had been fidgeting above me now coalesced into a net, which swirled down and pinned me to the ground. I found myself curled in a ball, my eyes at the level of Danny's boots. They reminded me of when I first saw them as I lay upon the ground near his cabin. I closed my eyes, wishing I could will us both back to Colorado. Maybe if we rolled up like potato bugs and burrowed into the dirt, we'd be safe.

"What's got into you?" Danny asked.

"I'm messed up bad," I said to Danny's boots. Picking through the clutter of my ravaged mind, I told his boots about the hallucinogenic alcohol Pablo had forced me to drink, and how he stabbed me with a drug-tipped needle. Danny's grizzled face replaced his boots. I told him about the soldiers in the rehearsal room, and the trap door in the recording booth. I let Danny know how my body tingled, my lips were numb, and I was so God-awful scared.

"Hey, we're gonna be OK," Danny said, helping me to my feet. "That Pablo dude's dead meat. I figure they got the road blocked, and his fancy-assed Escalade is toast. There was a chopper out there, but it took off a while time ago, they didn't hang around." Danny glanced down the tunnel. "We gotta get our asses out of here."

A thump came from above us. The trap door from the studio had opened, spiking our sanctuary with a blade of light.

Suddenly we were running. I stumbled along behind Danny, holding onto his belt, and all the while I was blinded by electric streaks of colors— gruesome patterns that vibrated menacingly everywhere I looked. Surely, the SLA soldiers would spot my noisy hallucinations and shoot us dead.

Danny propelled me up a short ladder at the other end of the tunnel where I emerged into the stench of gasoline and grease. Panting, I crawled onto the cement floor and found myself next to a hulking beast that must have been one of Pablo's hotrods. Ambient light drifted through an open garage door, which illuminated the outlines of cars and toolboxes. My drugged mind animated the scene in a flowing, sinister way, as if the world were melting and reforming into something depraved. I closed my eyes, trying to coax my brain back to sanity.

Danny emerged from the tunnel and began kicking at the manhole cover. The iron plate clanked into place, flush with the cement floor. The sound sent shivers through me, causing horrid, neon waves to cascade through the air like ripples upon a fetid pond.

"Don't move," Danny said. In moments, the car next to me rolled silently backwards until a tire rested over the manhole cover. Danny set the parking brake.

"There," Danny said quietly, "no mother's coming out of there, don't matter what kind of firepower they've got." I sensed him searching the shadows for intruders. I covered my eyes with my hands, wishing my cool palms could wipe away the damnable hallucinations. My heart was still beating so rapidly that it made me sick.

"I know what you're going through, man," Danny whispered, rubbing my shoulder. "Just hang in there, buddy, I'll get us outta here."

He helped me into a crouch, and then led me along a row of vehicles. Danny opened a car door and its interior light flashed on. Spitting a curse he shut the door, and we moved to another vehicle. As he opened the door, hinges creaked, but the car remained dark.

"This one's got keys," Danny whispered. His words send sent shards of greens and reds cascading across my vision. Danny led me to the passenger's door, but when it opened, the courtesy light ignited brighter than the sun, shooting arrows of fire to the back of my skull.

Danny cursed, shoved me into the seat, slammed my door and then hobbled around to the driver's side.

"Come on, baby," Danny said, as he cranked the starter. The beast screamed in agony. Danny stomped the gas and the starter cranked again. The creature's mechanical cries echoed through the garage. God! The soldiers? How long before they came running?

Gravity ceased.

In silence, bullet holes exploded in the windshield. Glowing steams of life leaked from my punctured chest and floated before my eyes, while sparkling shards of glass from the shattered window tumbled in place like dazzling diamonds. The vision exploded into a thousand pinpricks of light, and faded, like dying fireworks. I cursed the vile hallucinations and blinked, trying to clear my eyes and find reality.

I saw that the windshield was intact, and so was I. The engine roared to life. Danny crunched the gearshift and cranked the wheel toward the open garage door. With us in its belly, the metal creature leaped forward. I glanced at the dash. GTO. God! Was this the same GTO that Pablo tried to drive earlier in the day? If so, the vintage Pontiac wouldn't get twenty feet before lurching to a stop.

So. This is where I would die— in the front seat of a muscle car with Danny at the wheel, our blood mingled on the floor mats, while teenage murderers gawked through the windows.

We hurtled past the garage door, the rear wheels churning madly, screaming and burning rubber as Danny guided the big car toward freedom. The engine howled, inhaling night air, its twin exhausts roaring like deep-throated cannons. Nude statues hurtled past the windows, as if they too were running for their lives.

"Get your ass down and stay there," Danny yelled.

I curled into a ball beneath the dash. Everything changed— I now rode in an old-time, iron-bellied train, secure and safe in its metal womb. From far away, glass crunched and crackled. The universe swooped and swerved. Lights of the front gate flashed past us as the big train bucked and swayed over the uneven tracks that led away from the hellish station of Rancho Vizcaya.

In the vague light Danny's face frightened me— I suddenly realized that this train's engineer was fading from this world and becoming translucent— an insane ghost retracing some long-forgotten journey that always ended badly.

I forced myself to take a sharp breath which returned me to the Pontiac, where I found myself sitting erect in the passenger seat. Behind us, rudely formed haloes gathered around the lights of Vizcaya's gate, which was fading into the distance.

Several small holes had been punched in the rear window, and the cracks surrounding them sparkled with a life of their own. Despite the smears of madness that were feeding upon my eyes, I could now make out even the tiniest detail in the cracks, as if examining the damaged glass with the superior optics of a mechanical being. My arms and legs tingled. I couldn't feel my face and my body wasn't mine. The jolting tickle of blood through my veins seemed foreign and pointless.

Danny cursed and slammed on the brakes. The road ahead abruptly snaked into a vicious curve, and gravel pinged as the Pontiac lurched, sliding broadside. The GTO rotated full circle like a berserk carnival ride, and then caromed to a stop at the lip of the road, inches from a plunge into darkness. The engine quietly chugged at idle, a patient beast waiting for its next command. Its headlights glared upon trees and bushes, casting garish shadows up the hillside which kept moving and shifting position, even though we were motionless.

"Gotta slow down," Danny said to himself, wiping a hand across his face as if it were a dirty windshield.

I laughed, slapping myself with perverse glee. Danny was every bit as out of his mind as I was, and he was going to save me? One whacked-out musician rescuing another? Hopeless irony twisted through my mind, screwing itself deeper into my hilarity. As if on cue, hallucinations gleefully flooded back— jealous, loudly dressed creatures tugging for my attention.

Thumping. The car's engine? No, my hammering heart, rattling about in my chest. My vision devolved into flashes of color and senseless forms, but I remained remotely conscious of the trees, watching us with a disgusted air, gesturing in the night breeze.

Danny wheeled the GTO back onto the roadway and we roared off, our headlights chasing darkness, my mind speeding ahead of their beams. Did we have a destination? Was a roadblock ahead? Friend or foe? Did it matter? They would probably kill us anyway. Why not? Everybody hated Americans. It was our heritage and their right. Something inside me laughed.

Danny hit the brakes, only this time there was no curve. Or was there? The multicolored road had morphed into forms I couldn't understand. As the GTO lurched to a stop, Danny killed the engine.

"They're just up over that rise."

I nodded seriously, thinking he meant more hallucinations.

"General Ray warned us, man, he said this was gonna happen." Danny got out and sniffed the air. He was a bear, an intelligent beast, with animal irises that pierced the darkness.

I opened my door and staggered onto the graveled roadside. Steam rose from my breath, and as it drifted upwards, it sprouted terrible nodules of fear. I gazed skywards, deep into thousands of years of stars, picturing my soul lost among them— up there is where I belonged, and where I would soon be.

"Brad, get back." Danny cranked the big engine, which throbbed to life. He released the clutch and then bailed out as the car crept forward. It tilted at a weird angle as it passed the edge of the road, and then crunched over a thicket of bushes, disappearing with a horrible, crashing groan. Quiet returned.

Candy Floss! I'd forgotten! We should go back to the mansion, she would be there waiting for me— she would help, she would know what to do. Suddenly, the last thirty minutes came rushing back and slapped me in the face. I staggered backwards. Danny stood in front of me, glaring at me with beast's eyes. Had he struck me? My useless mind didn't know. I could only go with what I had, and try to translate the unreality of my sensations into a semblance of organic symbolism. I laughed at the nonsensical string of thoughts as they skittered away in madness.

"You all right?"

"No," I said. The word repeated itself like an endless tape loop.

"Man, you're losing it, tripping bad. Listen. We're going up the hillside. Always take the high ground, that's what General Ray says."

"Then why did he live in a cave?" I snickered at my brilliant quip.

Growling, Danny grabbed my arm and dragged me up the embankment. Partway up the hillside I fell, tumbling into a thicket of hallucinations and weeds. Danny said something I couldn't understand, stared at me as if I were dead, and then vanished.

Why did Danny leave? What did I do? No matter. I would become a mound of earth. Nobody cared about a mound of earth. I closed my eyes. A vortex of madness whirled inside my skull and my body had gone numb. Suddenly, I saw it all clearly— the mansion, lit up with garish light, soldiers roaming its grounds, mopping up, hunting down and executing stragglers. I saw Rudy, Mitch, and Jon lying dead, the smashed front gates askew. Pulling back from that view, I saw the GTO resting in the ravine below, a marvelous machine destined to linger in rust and abandon.

Pablo! The thought of that vile maniac inflated me with anger. In my heart, that hate burned with such pure ferocity that it caused the grasses around me to catch fire, filling the night with deep-red flames. My anger spread across the hillside like wildfire, a conflagration of vengeance which I sent racing toward the mansion. It reached Vizcaya, which become engulfed in the justice of my flames— a burning hell— the funeral pyre for my murdered friends and all the others sodomized by Pablo's madness. Smoke from the inferno rose upward, staining the sky and sooting the stars.

I shivered. Freezing cold. Clutching this new sensation, I retreated inward, relishing the chill and discomfort, a precious sign that my body still functioned, that I still lived. How long had I been there? Where was Danny? It seemed as if I had lost a huge block of time— or maybe not.

Perhaps if I tried remembering everything that had occurred in the past few hours, it would straighten me up. Instead, I lost myself in circular, obnoxious reverie. I calmed myself. Were the worst effects of the drug behind me? Yes, I told myself. But then came the crackling of imaginary flames. My madness would not be denied.

Madness?
No.
Shadows!

Coagulated clots of darkness floated beneath nearby trees— shadows with a life of their own, independent of my drugged consciousness. More dark forms bled from the line of vegetation, staining the open spaces, their auras pulsing with morose hues of reds and greens.

Soldiers.
Needful things, seeking me, coming to feed upon my death like hungry ghosts.

25

    I remained motionless, for I had become a mound of earth and nothing more. The shadows came, drifting balloons of darkness. Lightning bolts of madness flashed through my brain, snapping and crackling in the air above me, there for all to see. And how could anyone miss the noisy hammering of my heart? A spider web of fear embraced me as the ghosts of death crept closer.
    My mind screamed! *Run! Hide! Do something! Do what?* I blinked, trying to recover my thoughts. I discovered that the drugs that were inciting my madness also had a beneficial side effect— they had dilated my pupils, which enhanced my night vision. Through the distraction of flickering hallucinations, I could make out a soldier advancing towards me, perhaps ten yards away. If I didn't move, he would step on me. There would be a surprised shout, and then green death would spray from his weapon, sending me to join my friends amongst the newly dead.
    Weeds crunched beneath his boots. He hunched over like a bear, sniffing the air. He gestured towards the other soldiers, and while he did, his weapon made hungry little metallic whimpers as if it sensed my presence and wanted to spit bullets into my body.
    Perhaps if I closed my eyes my eyelids would dampen the hallucinations, and the soldiers wouldn't notice the laser-edged neon streaking from my skull. An eternity passed and still I did not breathe, for I was a mound of earth, nothing more. Grasses again crunched beneath soldiers' boots. I opened one eye. The shadow soldiers were now drifting down the hill towards the road.
    The GTO! They must have heard it crash into the ravine and were searching for Danny and me. Something told me to retreat, to get to the tree line. I slowly turned my head, and nearly cried out. A soldier's boot stood inches from my face! The boot's owner farted, grunting as if trying to cover up his flatulence, and then shifted his weight, making leathery creaking sounds.
    Mound of dirt. Be a mound of dirt. I closed my eyes. Mounds of dirt don't move, they don't run, they fear nothing. Greasy hallucinations streaked the mirror of my brain, horrible things that urged me to vomit, to scream, to flee. Something poked

Smoking Jimi

my belly, sending currents of horror rippling over my torso. I resisted the urge to run. Again, the thing prodded my stomach, like a boy testing roadkill with a stick.

I was dead. The soldier had found a lifeless mound of dirt, nothing more. If I kept my eyes closed, then how could he see the uproar inside my brain? His boot tapped the side of my head. My eyes flashed open. The shadow-man had no face, and my mind created something horrid in its place. My brain screamed. *Do something— right damned now!*

I grabbed his boot and twisted hard. The soldier let out a surprised yelp and toppled sideways.

Suddenly, a new shadow, snapping and snarling like a beast, pounced upon the soldier. With a gurgling, bubbling sound the two shadows merged and then collapsed to the ground. From that heavy mass of darkness a single shadow rose over me, hovering like a viper's hood of death.

26

I lay helpless and numb, knowing the killing shadow would take me next. Seconds passed, each moment filled with eternal imaginings beyond horror— hideously spiced terrors. My heart marked off the seconds with a string of pounding thuds. *Do something!* I forced my eyes open. The death shadow, which had been lingering over me, must have been waiting for me to open my eyes, for now it bent down, its monster breath heavy and labored.

It whispered a sacrificial chant in some alien language.

No, it was speaking in English!

Danny!

He told me to keep quiet, and then with surprising strength, pulled me to my feet. In the starlight, the soldier's torso glistened darkly. I didn't want to think what Danny had done to him. Muttering curses, Danny retrieved the dead man's rifle, and using it as a crutch, limped on ahead of me while I followed, crouched low, as if I might bump my head upon the sky.

We took cover in a grove of trees, huddled together in the undergrowth like kids playing army. Terror ratcheted its grip upon my chest, while malignant rainbows swarmed my pupils. I blinked at the scene down the hill, past the road where the soldier shadows had converged like insects around our wrecked GTO. A tiny blade of flashlight beam cut the darkness, slicing the car with prisms of color, revealing the crazy tilt of its death pose.

The light went out, leaving a remnant of razor-sharp wounds that swirled and danced to some unheard, insidious rhythm.

A moan came from deep in Danny's chest. "Man, oh shit, I told you guys, General Ray, man, why ain't he here, man, we gotta move, gotta keep goin', this is bad, man, like we gotta take these guys out, we gotta get to the high ground."

A blinding light stabbed me, and then a powerful blow struck my ribs, bowling me over. I lay in the grass, retching, while rough hands probed my body. Angry shouts crashed through the underbrush. Danny's angry growl became a hollow thump, like a log struck by a rock. Someone ripped my hair, jerking my head into a crushing light.

A gang of soldiers held flashlights on Danny. He had one eye closed, and a red trail streamed down his mouth and beard. They shoved him to his knees next to the dead soldier's corpse. Someone pulled a bayonet from Danny's belt, held it aloft like a trophy, and then waved the blade in Danny's face, taunting him. Danny wiped blood from his nose and sneered. These soldiers, with their heads wrapped in olive-drab bandannas, seemed so young. How could children find such glee in violence?

A clean-shaven officer in his early twenties shoved past the soldiers and stood with his arms upon his hips. With great fanfare, he spit upon Danny. Snarling, Danny spit back. The officer swung his gun butt in a vicious arc and struck Danny's face with a horrible crunch. Danny collapsed in a heap. I tried to get to Danny to help him, but a soldier stomped me down, grinding my face into the dirt. They wrestled my hands behind me and tied them with a cord. I retched into a clump of weeds, and tasted blood. Danny had come back to help me, and it had cost him his life! Someone laughed.

Stumbling, my hands strapped behind me, I was dragged and pushed down to the road where a battered van waited. Soldiers threw Danny's unconscious body into the floor of the van and shoved me in after him. I couldn't make out his face in the darkness or see his injuries. A soldier scooted into the van and sat opposite me, his stubby assault rifle aimed at my gut, his eyes gleaming with belligerence. I looked away before my ravaged mind created something horrible from his shadowy features.

Numbness tingled upward from my wrists, and my bound hands felt like pieces of meat behind my back. No matter how hard I focused upon the pain, I couldn't hold back the insistent hallucinations, blinding me with their perverse intensity. I tried bending over to see Danny, but the punk soldier struck me in the shoulder with the barrel of his gun and barked harsh words. The rear doors slammed shut, sealing us in a chamber that reeked of sweat, guns, and gasoline.

Metal walls closed in. Numbness pierced my heart. I wanted to puke but I couldn't, my stomach had become a numb void. My lips and face had lost all feeling. I figured that all this exertion had energized the paralyzing drug from Pablo's needle, and now it was coming full on, with deadly effect.

Two soldiers jumped into the cab and the van started off with a lurch. I sensed we were going uphill, and dust leaked through the van as we rattled along. Maybe if I explained to the soldiers that we were only musicians and just wanted to go home, perhaps they would understand.

"This is all a mistake," I heard myself whisper. I said it again, louder. Danny groaned. Our guard said nothing but I sensed his eyes raking me over, his mind churning out malicious thoughts.

Suddenly, the shuddering thud of an explosion shook the van and it slid to a stop.

Shouting.

Erratic pops of gunfire.

The soldiers up front bailed out. At first, I thought some maniac was beating on the van, hammering its metal walls. Our guard groaned and slumped sideways. The gunfire died down.

Shouting.

Running.

A distant explosion shook the van and debris chattered over its skin.

My body wouldn't respond and I silently cried out in frustration, struggling like an insect trapped within a cocoon. Our guard lay dead quiet.

"Where are we?" Danny croaked.

I opened my mouth but only a moan escaped.

"I'm broke up pretty bad," Danny said, stirring in the darkness.

* * *

I don't know what happened next, from a void of blackness I found myself sitting on a rock near the edge of the road, the old van glowing softly in the starlight. My body tingled in a vicious, frightening way, and my hands, now freed from the cords, rested in my lap, throbbing. Danny sat slumped over next to me, his long hair obscuring his face. All around us insects chirped, drowning my thoughts with their miniature screams.

"Danny?"

His head rotated. By the faint starlight I could see that his face was horribly disfigured. Or was I hallucinating? My mind conjured up vile smears of color, like a bad child messing with finger paints. I was losing myself again.

"Van's shot," he said. "Bastards are gone."

"I may not be here much longer either," I said, my words badly slurred.

"Heard that. Life sucks and then you die." Danny's voice had a beaten-down hollowness. The insects crowded in on our conversation, screaming ever louder, and infesting my brain with their vile notions, their insectile thoughts scuttling across my mind.

* * *

I don't know what happened next or where I went. When I returned from my kaleidoscopic torment, I found myself kneeling over Danny. Trees towered over us, blocking much of the starlight. Blinking, my vision deformed and horridly distorted, I vainly searched for the road or the van. Perhaps we had wandered deeper into the forest for safety.

"Kill me," Danny croaked. "Can't make it. Use the knife in my belt buckle. Just do it, man." Danny's voice, more than his words, frightened me to my core. He turned his head exposing the white of his neck. "Brad, look at me, I'm already dead. Nobody can change that. Don't leave me here. Not like this."

The wind cursed the trees and in the darkness an animal cried out at the thought of a man killing his friend. A wave of horror swept through me. I could no longer hear the insects— they must have been shocked into silence.

"Brad, please, help me. I never asked for anything before, did I?"

* * *

My mind must have blacked out again for I now found myself alone, stumbling along a rocky path. Tears streamed down my face. Sobs racked my body. What had happened? God help me, I couldn't remember! Stars swirled as I collapsed to my knees. I had the horrible feeling I had just committed the unspeakable.

"Danny?" I cried out.

The screaky voices of insects answered my call. I was alone. Where had I been? Was Danny dead? I searched my violated mind, rifling through the psychedelic trash of Pablo's drugs.

What time was it? I glanced at my wrist. No watch. What did it matter? I was in a time and place that no timepiece could define. Something told me that Danny was gone. He understood it all— how life sucks and then you die. None of us would be missed, especially me. My life had been a complete waste. I should give it back, return it to the heavens. The stars above and their cold light agreed. They wished upon themselves for my death. In their cold way, they told me to stay put, to stop wandering. I obeyed, shivering and alone.

I waited.

Why did the insects have to make that horrid racket? Why did they continue to scream at me? I forced myself to think of something else. Pablo? I wished him a horrible, lingering death. With a shudder I pictured what Pablo had done to Iggy Krotch and his band, knowing that we would have been next. Why did we ever come to this perverted hellhole? Lured to our deaths by greed. I should have known better. Actually, a part of me did. But another side of me knew a sad truth— I had nothing to lose except a life not worth living.

My clothes clung wet and cold. I throbbed and ached where I'd been beaten and kicked. Thirst sent roots deep into my soul. Fragments of hallucinations floated before my eyes, but I could now make out my surroundings, in a dusty, colorless way. The chorus of screaming insects retreated as the corruption of dawn found the horizon. The sky's bloody glow bore witness to last night's carnage. Danny! Could I have killed my friend? Was it an act of mercy? Vile insanity?

Pine trees stirred to life in the early morning breeze, whispering and gesturing at the hopelessness of it all. In the early light a small gray bird landed on a nearby branch, cocked its head and stared. Suddenly, it burst into an intricate song with melodies so complex and beautiful that it brought tears to my eyes.

A guitar formed in my mind and an imaginary hand fingered its strings, following the bird's musical journey. Its fluted voice sang the most incredible lyrics— lines of words with such deep meaning that I openly wept. Something snapped inside me, as if a dam had broken, and a rush of understanding flooded through me— a cleansing sorrow of tears.

Now, I comprehended the bird's every word, understood every nuance. Waves of remorse washed over me and I grieved for my empty life— a vast desert of missed opportunities and wasted talent. The bird stopped singing, gave me a disdainful glance, and then took flight. I thought of Gjerna, and how I, like that bird, had flown away.

I turned my head to look towards where the bird had flown. There!
Mt. Paxicoto!
Down the rocky path in the morning light, a magnificent snow-clad peak rose into the slate-blue sky, dwarfing the earth itself. Paxicoto! Yes! The glory of that spectacular mountain rushed through me like a warm fire on a cold morning. Now I

understood! I had not come to this place out of lust for Pablo's money. Pablo was nothing but a false god, a murderous little imp. There was a much higher purpose to my being here.

I stood, my arms outstretched, embracing the mountain's image. The power of Paxicoto flowed through me, strengthening me— it called me home. That Inca god, what was his name? Venalocha? Yes. Venalocha and I must have known each other in past lives, for he now awaited my arrival inside his great mountain, Paxicoto.

My body trembled as a great surge of energy flowed through me. I found myself walking, almost floating, drawn along the path toward Paxicoto and my destiny with Venalocha.

I hadn't gone far when a bolt of doubt stopped me cold. Was I doubling back from where I had come? A memory flashed in my mind— Danny's eyes, staring and glassy, just like when Rudy died.

I fell to my knees. Tears flowed. Fingernails dug into my palms. No amount of pain could erase the pictures stamped upon my memory. Danny dying! I looked down. Dried blood streaked the back of my hands. God, had I really done this? Did Danny die by my hand?

Treetops obscured Mt. Paxicoto and I hurried down the path to where I could see my mountain again, for without it, I would perish like Danny. Tears blurred my eyes but I would not stop, I could not, I owed it to Danny, to Jon, to Frank, and yes, even to Mitch.

27

I walked the trail until the sun hung hot and high. Sweat stung my eyes. The world swooped and swooned. I rested on a rock and closed my eyes a moment. Insects buzzed. *Tired, so tired.* A bird chirped. *So tired.* Suddenly, music blossomed in my mind, as if the bird had dropped seeds into my skull that now sprouted into a patchwork of roots and budding branches which flowered into a melody, repeating itself so insistently that even an idiot couldn't ignore it! The lines and counterpoints were pure genius! God! Could this dazzling melody have come from me? A byproduct of madness? No. It made perfect sense. Now, I understood why the band, why all of us had been called upon to make this sacrifice. We had a destiny and it was contained in this song. Now I understood! I was spared because I was the crucible that would receive this important new music!

I played the melody in my head, turning it over and over like a precious gem, memorizing every facet, every sparkle. Such brilliance! The song seemed familiar, as if the melody had always been there, bubbling just below my consciousness, waiting for the right moment to shine through. This song, bought and paid for by the lives of my friends, would stay with me forever. Our Paxicoto song.

With that beautiful melody playing in my head I arose, the incredible power in my body resonating with a slight trembling at the knees. Mt. Paxicoto towered before me with its jagged, white-clad peak reaching deep into the sky. The rocky path took me along a ridgeline and as I approached a clearing, a strange object caught my eye, fifty yards down the hillside.

Pablo's Escalade!

The big SUV lay on its side at the bottom of the meadow, its roof facing me. This had to be Pablo's Escalade with its chrome wheels and oversized tires. Its once-glistening black paint was now dull and sooty, and its broken windshield sparkled. How could the SUV be here? There were no roads, nothing.

"Brad."

I flinched.

Smoking Jimi

A man stood in the path twenty feet away, examining me with the calmness of a reptile. He wasn't old or young, tall or short, heavy or thin. He wasn't well dressed, but did not wear rags. I tried focusing but his face changed— the more I stared, the more his features morphed. Deep crevices, no crevices. A predominant forehead, then one that receded into thick, black hair. Blue eyes, brown eyes, no eyes.

Enough. I my adjusted my collar and straightened my back. Whoever he was, it was important that I made the proper impression.

Pablo! It was that bastard, Pablo! His smirking face sneered from atop the stranger's body, just like the bust of Napoleon perched atop the headless statue. The thing gestured at Mt. Paxicoto.

"You'll never get there, Brad, never. That's for me and only for me. Your place is with stupid little people who pray to their stupid little gods and live like stupid little sheep."

"I'll kill you," I said, my voice shaking with anger.

Pablo held up my toy red car. "Kill me? No. I possess you. Your weakness is my strength." His laugh was filthy and coarse.

I stared at the little red car while in my head, I played my Paxicoto song— louder and louder and louder. Suddenly, the red car exploded into flames. Pablo dropped the burning toy car with a cry of surprise. His eyes flashed fear. Yes! With a renewed sense of power I stared at Pablo's snake eyes, playing my Paxicoto song even louder. As if being consumed by an invisible flame, his hair turned white, his skin crumpled, and he held up his hands in a feeble gesture.

And then he was gone.

The Escalade had vanished, too. A thicket of undisturbed brush occupied the space where I had seen the SUV. I stood alone on the trail. What just happened here? Had I destroyed Pablo? Had the bastard really been here? Was I losing my mind? Had I forgotten my mission?

Mt. Paxicoto stood before me. Now, nothing blocked my path to the great mountain except for one more hillside, and perhaps a valley beyond that. I picked up a long stick and hands trembling with energy, I used it as a staff, moving carefully at first, and then quickening my pace. As I negotiated rocks, gnarled roots and trees, I felt giddy, almost lightheaded. I had defeated Pablo! Nothing could stop me now, nothing!

The trail took a steep turn down a stony hillside and I found myself descending a steep path where hooves had slid in the soft earth, leaving deep gouges. Patches of slippery moss coated the trail, and so I carefully made my way down the path until I reached a grassy shelf where I stopped to catch my breath. The musical chatter of water came to me. Water! It seeped from a rocky face, trickling into a clear pool in a protected alcove. I rushed to the water and knelt down.

My thirst! I wanted to immerse my face into the cool water and wash away the pain, the misery. Pebbles lined the pool's bottom and sweet grass grew along its edge. This had to be the cleanest, purest water on earth. I was about to take my first cool drink when something made me turn and look at Mt. Paxicoto.

With a jolt, it dawned upon me. This was a test and I had almost failed! I felt so foolish. When I reached Mt. Paxicoto, Venalocha would provide for all my needs— no thirst, no hunger, no pain. How could I trivialize such a gift in a moment of weakness? If I were invited to dinner would I stop for food along the way? Of course not. I couldn't insult Venalocha and spurn the great gift he was about to bestow upon me. Honoring my thirst would be my offering to him, a sign of civilized manners. I took one last look at the pool. No, I would not give in. My friends had died for me and I would not fail them now.

Venalocha must have been proud, watching over me as I hummed my Paxicoto song and continued my trek to the valley floor, leaving the pool of temptation untouched. Breathing hard, I worked my way down to a small valley where the trail played out near a dirt road that was bordered by tangles of weeds and grasses. I searched the stony hillside that arched toward Mt. Paxicoto, seeking a way through the jagged rocks and stubborn vegetation. What now? Another test?

A dizzying surge of Venalocha's energy coursed through me, causing my hands to tremble. Venalocha's power was so overwhelming that it brought on a dizzy spell, and I wiped my brow. Which direction should I take? The road to my left disappeared over a rise, and I felt Venalocha nudging me in that direction. As I approached the hilltop I heard a deep thumping. A heart beat? What heart could be that big? Venalocha's heart, calling me? Faint strains of accordion music joined the thumps, and the two sounds began weaving a hypnotic melody, watery and dissonant across the distance.

The road crested a hilltop, where I blinked in amazement. A village!

A surreal cluster of adobe homes with thatched roofs lay before me. Other than the faint odor of cooking grease, the place seemed deserted. Were the townspeople hiding from me? Had they run from Venalocha's heartbeat? The tall thumps and accordion music seemed to come from across the town, still far off but getting closer now, as if Venalocha himself were walking towards me in giant, booming strides.

Cautiously, I entered the village, with its shadowed alleys and crumbling adobe. Most of the structures had simple openings for windows, with old boards serving as shutters. A colorful Indian blanket stirred in the breeze. A potted plant sat upon a wooden stool— but there were no cars, no animals, and no people. I tramped along the dusty lane to where it opened into a town square guarded by a stone church.

A rough-hewn bench seemed like a good place to rest and gather my thoughts. As I sat listening to the odd, thumping strains of music, something caught my eye— movement in a shaded alley. I squinted toward the shadows. Lying in the street— crawling— what? Animals? No! People! Were they injured? Did they need help?

I hurried over to the prone bodies. Three, dust-covered men crawled slowly, mumbling to themselves. I could see no wounds or signs of injury.

"You OK?" I asked.

One of the crawling men turned his face toward me. His features mimicked Pablo's, then morphed into a much older man's, with a face like a gently crumpled beer can. He said something I couldn't understand and resumed his slow crawl, face down, muttering. What insanity was this? The alley curved beyond my view, and from somewhere beyond that the eerie music drifted ever closer, echoing from everywhere yet nowhere. I could visualize the music in my mind's eye: *boom, boom,* went a bass drum, as out-of-tune accordions chattered back and forth like gossipy old women.

Something teetered around the corner, reaching as high as the eaves.

Venalocha?

A statue!

Beneath and around it, people shuffled into view. The Virgin Mary! They carried her life-size likeness upon a platform, wrapped in strips of red and yellow paper. A black-robed priest headed the procession, leading a donkey draped in bright cloths and flowers.

One of the men lying in the street beckoned to me. Yes! Now I understood why Venalocha led me here! I lowered myself onto my belly and pressed my face to the soft dust, performing a gentle act of consecration. As the procession approached the men next to me stopped crawling but continued their soft chants. How brilliant! Venalocha had brought me here to be cleansed, the way these pilgrims were being cleansed! *Boom, boom,* went the drum, and the accordions replied with a mournful dissonance that resonated perfectly with the truth in my heart. I glanced up. The Virgin Mary statue towered high above me in a frightening way, her face stark and mysterious.

My heart quickened as the priest's black robes swirled past, and water droplets sprinkled the dust— tears from heaven, falling to earth to quench my sorrows. The donkey stepped around the prostate pilgrims, followed by sandaled feet coated with holy dust. These honest, simple people filled my heart with joy and cleansed my soul in ways they could never understand. The weight of my life's tragedies lifted from me and became emaciated shadows, dying in the daylight, their power over me lost forever. This was the greatest gift I'd ever received— I was free! My tears made darken ovals in the dust.

Then scuffed, black boots.

Then nothing.

Smoking Jimi

28

From far away, a steady *tick, tick.* Not a clock, not a machine. Irregular. *Tick... tick, tick... tick....* Awareness of my body faded in, like the approaching rumble of a thunderstorm. My eyelids wouldn't open and my eyes throbbed to the back of my skull. Through a fog of stale urine, I became aware of a stone-cold floor beneath my belly. Pain advanced, attacking my body from every angle. Memories came— dust, the chalky taste of dust— the Virgin Mary teetering past— and black boots! Had soldiers taken me, beaten me? Each breath made a rasping whisper through my teeth. I couldn't move my swollen tongue. Through closed eyelids I sensed darkness. The only sign of life was the *tick...*

tick, tick.... I tried to speak, but no sound emerged.

Tick, tick... tick....

Someone murmured. Pablo? My eyelids slowly parted. Gray haze. No foreign colors or hallucinations— that was good. My breath continued— rasping in, rasping out— as if my body were on autopilot, leaving me free to explore my senses. *Tick... tick, tick.* I blinked. By the dim light, I could see someone hunched over a small, barred window.

Jail! I'd been thrown in jail! My surroundings came into focus, as my cellmate worked at the base of the bars with something in his hand. *Tick, tick... tick.* He stopped, peered at the bleak sky, and then resumed his work like a naughty boy scribbling graffiti. His profile almost reminded me of that bastard, Pablo. I tried to remember what happened to him but my mind was thick and useless.

Tick, tick. Then a new sound. My cellmate froze. The tool in his hand fell to the floor. Hinges squealed and the door flew open. Blinding light. A scuffle broke out. My cellmate released a pathetic cry as uniformed men dragged him away. The light went off. The commotion echoed down a hallway, and then silence settled in.

My body trembled as I tried to lift my head and I was rewarded with sparks of pain. It must have been approaching dawn judging by the dingy light seeping into the jail cell. I could just make out the place where my cellmate had chipped at the cement around one of the bars. He had barely made a dent. The rusty bolt he had dropped was powdered with white dust.

I moved one leg, trying to force it towards my chest. Bullets of pain ricocheted through my body. Everything hurt. I touched my face. A scab clung to my swollen forehead just below the hairline.

Water. I needed water. I tilted my head and surveyed my cell. Mold darkened the cement walls. A wooden door with a rude metal window towered over me.

Couldn't there be a sink, a toilet, something? My mind invented the sound of dripping water and I pictured the delicate drops splashing upon my tongue, cooling my bone-dry despair.

Was it my imagination? Was that drop of water? And another? I fought my body's pain and turned my head.

A spigot! And below it, precious moisture surrounded a rusty floor drain. Water! Heart pounding, I crawled to the spigot and gripped it with both hands. Stuck! I struggled with the handle, my body crying out from thirst and pain. The rusty handle scraped my palms. My hands trembled. My cheek fell against cement. Even Pablo couldn't have invented something as perverse as this. Gallons of cold water, ready to fill me with life, yet I didn't have the strength, the valve was rusted shut.

Another beautiful drop of water splashed before my eyes. Maneuvering my aching body, I rolled beneath the spigot. A drop fell between my cracked lips. And soon, another.

As I waited for each precious drop, dawn glowered through the barred window. A truck rumbled. A rooster crowed. From far off came the occasional shout or even a laugh, the voices all young and male. The voice of an older man cried out. Three short pops in quick succession brought silence. Background sounds slowly resumed. My cellmate wouldn't be returning.

While I waited for each drop of water, the cold cement siphoned warmth and life from my body. At least I wouldn't die of thirst. Waves of exhaustion shivered through me. I focused on my ration of life-giving water. Another drop fell between my parched lips. They didn't even feel like lips— more like dried mud stuck to my mouth.

Why had I refused to drink water on the trail yesterday? I pictured that pool of water so pure and clean, all a man could drink— and I didn't touch it. How stupid! What was I thinking? Why was I even out there on that godforsaken trail? Trying to reach some imaginary deity on Mt. Paxicoto? Madness— pure, wicked madness. I cursed Pablo again and wished him a long, horrible death.

Boots thudded. A key scraped. The cell door opened. Hands grabbed my legs and dragged me from the spigot. Two teenage boys in ill-fitting fatigues stood over me wearing hard expressions. At least their faces weren't smeared with war paint, like the murderers who raided Pablo's mansion last night, or was it the night before?

It took both of them, grunting with effort, to lift me to my feet. Suspended between them they dragged me down a grimy hall. Thick doors lined the walls. From behind one came muffled sobs, from another angry voices, and from yet another the chant of prayers. My toes scraped along the cement. I wanted to laugh. Pablo Lupa's size-eleven Gucci loafers were getting all scuffed up.

They shoved me through an open door at the end of the hall. One of the soldiers kicked a wooden chair upright and they lifted me into it, sitting me before a battered desk. A bare light hung above me. A ceiling fan squeaked.

"Water?" I asked in my croaking voice.

One of the teens thrust his finger in my face and spoke in Spanish, lecturing me. Whatever he warned me of was not a problem— I barely had the strength to sit.

"English?" I asked.

The teen kept up his Spanish banter. I had the impression the desk before me belonged to someone important. Behind it, a cracked leather chair leaned to one side, white stuffing emerging from rips in the fabric. The room had no windows, and a door to my right sat slightly ajar. As the teen soldiers' footsteps faded down the hall I sat alone in the room, longing for that dripping spigot.

Food! The smell of cooking made my heart dance with joy. I breathed in the glorious scent of burnt toast and eggs— the aroma of life and comfort, the smell of home. My stomach stirred. I cautioned myself to take it easy at first, not eat too fast so I wouldn't get sick.

A skinny man carrying a tray of food came into my view and sat behind the desk. He studied the food before him. Toast, a plate of eggs with perfect yolks, and yes, a precious glass of ice water all sweating and wonderful, its frosty drops gathering into a precious puddle!

"Please, water," I croaked.

"Only water? You sure? All this is yours."

He combed a scrawny hand through his black hair, contemplating me. The man was perhaps thirty with a moustache and pockmarked skin. His green fatigues bore emblems on the collars, and a black band with SLA in white letters circled one arm. SLA! Wasn't that the militia that attacked Rancho Vizcaya, murdering everyone? His dark eyes rose to meet mine, drilling into me. I stared back with the mindless gaze of a zombie.

"I am Colonel Justacio. You are hungry, yes?"

A pathetic moan escaped my mouth.

"Good. We play cards." He produced a deck of well-used cards and spread them before me along the desk's edge. "You first. Double or nothing." He sat back and his chair groaned.

Hand trembling, I touched a card. He flipped it over. Queen of clubs! Thank God. Now I would eat!

He chuckled. "Very good, *Americano.* Now me." He flipped a card. Ace of diamonds.

"Bad for you, good for me." The Colonel shook his head, grinning like a rat as he gathered up the cards. He pulled the tray closer and devoured the eggs, pausing to stuff toast into his mouth, packing his cheeks. He chewed while staring at me as if reading a cereal box. He raised the glass to his lips, and then paused.

"Water?" He tilted the rim toward me, spilling precious liquid onto the tray.

"Please. My throat. Water."

He sucked his teeth and drained the glass to the ice, the blackheads on his throat bobbing with each swallow. The colonel heaved a sigh, wiped his mouth with a sleeve, and pushed the tray to the side.

"Now. Your name?"

I had to think for a moment. "Brad. Brad Wilson."

"Brad Wilson," the Colonel muttered, squinting at my driver's license.

"And you work for the American CIA," he said, jotting something on a note pad.

"No. Photographer. I mean musician." I coughed, my throat painfully dry. "Please, water. Can't talk."

He glared at me but I could only see the water glass. The ice settled with a ghostly click, reminding me of that South Florida Wendy's with Mitch decked out on the floor. I sort of laughed.

"Oh? You think I'm funny?"

I shook my head. He stared at me for a moment, the bare light reflecting in a white ball from his forehead.

"So. You take pictures for the CIA. Yes?" His eyes bored into me. Dangerous eyes. Pablo eyes.

I said, "No. No CIA." I coughed, pain ripping through my chest and throat.

"We found this at Rancho Vizcaya." He pulled my Nikon out of the drawer, dangling it by its strap. "Yours?"

I nodded.

From another drawer he produced a stack of photos. "Your pictures?" He held up the shots I had taken of the Montgomery House in South Beach, in what seemed like a lifetime ago. The film company would be angry. I'd forgotten that I had their photos in my camera bag. I should call them first thing—

"This is where you hide the Lupa brothers?"

"Hide? No."

"And these, your CIA comrades?"

He held up pictures of Danny and Jon arguing. Pablo must have printed the photos in my camera after his pilot had stolen it.

"No, not CIA."

"And this. You hide something here?" He held up a photo of the hole in the hotel-room ceiling.

"No."

He showed me the photo I had taken of the Trotts checkpoint. "And this? The Lupas' guards? You have soldiers?"

"No."

"Are there any other pictures?" he asked slowly.

I thought of Gjerna's picture in the safe deposit box. A shudder of grief passed through me, then ironclad resolve. He could torture or even kill me, but I would never surrender that photo.   Never.

"My men found many bad things at Rancho Vizcaya. Is this how you talk to your friends in the CIA?" From his desk drawer he produced Jon's satellite phone. It had scuffmarks where it had landed on Pablo's driveway, and its antenna hung by a wire.

"Not mine."

"No? And so why did the Lupa brothers pay you all that money? For nothing? Don't lie to me. We found your money."

"Water? Please?"

"Water? What will you give in return? We have all your money. Now, we want the Lupa brothers. We don't want you, *Americano*. Where is this CIA safe house?" He held up the Montgomery House photo. "I make you a bargain. Water for truth."

"Florida. Movie set. Not here."

"Liar!"

"Water." I reached towards the glass on his desk.

Quick as a snake Colonel Justacio slapped the glass, hurling it against the cement wall. It smashed with a dark splatter, scattering diamonds of ice and glass.

"Tell! Where is Pablo Lupa?"

My mind raced. Pablo? Alive? Didn't the Colonel's soldiers kill Pablo? The monster must be in hiding, somewhere. Anger welled in my chest.

"If I knew, I would kill him myself," I croaked.

The Colonel glared at me. "Draw a card. You win, you go free. You lose, you die." He spread the cards again, face down.

With an unsteady finger I touched a card. Nine of hearts. He drew. Ace of hearts. The bastard had a marked deck.

"Bad for you, good for me." The Colonel clucked his tongue and opened another drawer. He withdrew ordinary garden utensils, perversely twisted and sharpened to the service of torture. I averted my eyes.

"I hate Pablo. He killed my friends."

"Where are the Lupas?" he asked softly. "Perhaps we begin with this one." The Colonel selected a claw-like tool whose tips had been filed to vicious points. The door squeaked open and the two young soldiers positioned themselves at my sides. The Colonel rose from his desk and hitched his belt. The vicious tips of the claw tool glistened as he turned it over in his hands.

"You are a friend of Pablo Lupa. You are his guest at Vizcaya. You Americans think we are all stupid, yes?"

Wearily, I shook my head. Hands gripped my shoulders. Terror erupted in my gut. My mind swirled, trying to craft an escape scenario, but my thoughts collapsed, crashing into the rubble of Pablo's drugs. *Fight! How?* It was the end, time to die. That finality gave me peace for at some near moment, the pain, the fear, the hopelessness would all cease to be. My life's burden was about to be lifted. The Colonel sat upon the desk, his skinny ass scattering cards. His eyes glowed with sadistic fire, eclipsing even Pablo's malevolent gaze.

"One more time. The Lupas? No matter," he chortled, "we have fun before you talk. You will beg me to hear the truth."

"Kiss my ass," I croaked.

He sneered at the teens. One boy ripped open the top of my shirt— the stylish pullover from Pablo's armoire, now crusted with filth. The Colonel fixed his gaze upon my bare chest. The soldiers tensed. The Colonel put the tool to his lips and his dark eyes rolled under his lids, as if he were sending a quick prayer to his god, expressing thanksgiving for this bountiful feast.

A new soldier appeared at his side and interrupted his meditation. The aide whispered hurriedly to the Colonel and then stood back. A cloud passed over the Colonel's face and he snarled at the man in Spanish. The aide retreated, bowing and nodding.

The Colonel stared at me for the longest time, and then slowly traced the teeth of the claw along my bare chest, sending horrid shivers scurrying across my torso.

"Maybe I just kill you now."

With a snort of anger he tossed the claw onto the table and then drew a pistol from his holster. He pressed the gun barrel to my temple, its cruel metal hard and cold against my skin. The hammer made a delicate click as he drew it back to the firing position.

"The house. Where is the Lupas' house? No more chances, Mr. Brad."

Obviously he didn't have time to play with his torture toys. It would be quick and painless. I'd thought of dying many times and I always feared it, so now I was surprised to find myself strangely composed, almost aloof.

Somebody was going to have a mess to clean up! Most likely the teens. They probably would have to return with a mop and bucket. I wanted to laugh, to show them what assholes they all were, but I didn't have the strength.

I waited.

The hammer clicked again.

The barrel withdrew from my temple. I opened my eyes. The Colonel puffed his cheeks and his eyes drew into narrow slits.

"Take him. We kill him later." He barked something in Spanish at the teens and then waved his gun with a disgusted air as he turned his back.

Smoking Jimi

The soldiers dragged me back to my cell. There, my face against the cold cement, I heard the occasional drop of water. I knew I should crawl to the rusty spigot and let life-giving liquid drip into my mouth, but I didn't move. What was the point? All I wanted now was one last moment of peace, and I cherished this precious slice of time before my execution. God only knew how long I had before they would come to kill me.

I became aware of something pressing against my chest. I knew without looking— the DAstick. The soldiers must have missed it when they frisked me. That digital recording of our jam session held my solos, Jon's bass playing, Danny's drumming— it was us. Soon, it would be pierced by a bullet from a firing squad.

My mind wandered back to Colorado, to that Holiday Inn with Mitch and his hamburgers and his silly grin as he hustled up guitars for us. I conjured an image of Jon, the undercover monk living in that trailer house, running his game while his pal Danny lived in a mountain fantasy of slogans and isolation. Soon, I would be with my friends again. "Life sucks and then you die," Danny had said so many times. I smiled in his honor. It hurt, but I held the grin as long as I could.

Cold cement siphoned heat from my body. Feeble shivers echoed through me and my cell darkened. Gjerna. Thoughts of her would warm me. God, if I had it to do again! I would have dropped everything and spent every precious day of my life with her, no matter what the cost. Why didn't I? Because I was bewitched by the twin whores— wealth and fame— the same two bitches who lured me to my death.

A Jimi Hendrix lyric came to mind— the one about living his life the way he wants to, because when it's time, he's the one who has to die. Too bad I never lived my life the way I wanted to. But I would always keep Gjerna in the altar of my heart. Perhaps we would be together in death the way we had never been in life.

I could not feel my feet and my legs tingled in a scary way. When the soldiers came for me I wouldn't be here. They would find a cold body and nothing more. I'd show them! They weren't dealing with just any fool, and their stupid jail was nothing more than a child's playhouse. These idiots with their moronic uniforms and silly patches. Pathetic children, playing grownups' games. Games where people die. My body made one last effort at shivering and then seemed to surrender.

Chad Peery

    I would never relinquish my love for Gjerna. With my last breath I would say her name— my last image would be of her beautiful face and her golden hair. Together for eternity, Gjerna and Brad.

    My thoughts faded. The sounds of the world whispered away. The light ebbed. No fear, no hope, no pain, no anger. Nothing. Blessed nothing.

Smoking Jimi

29

Children laughing, playing— the sound of sunshine and peace, of childhood forever. Heaven! I visualized green fields, babbling brooks, and gentle people. I blinked my eyes open. I tried to focus. The form of an angel stood nearby.

"I made it," I croaked.

"Oh? And what exactly did you make?" It was a male angel. He didn't sound too friendly. Perhaps it was his accent. Did people get thirsty in heaven?

"Need drink. Please."

Water came to my lips, spilling a cool trail down my chin, and I took in a few precious swallows. Grinding pain folded into my consciousness. Everything hurt. This couldn't be heaven, but it probably wasn't hell, either.

"You'll live."

I squinted, struggling to see through blurred vision.

"More water." My voice sounded like sandpaper on a dry day. I took a few swallows. "More."

"Not now. Later."

"Where am I?"

"Where do you want to be?"

The man's accent wasn't Spanish, and his voice had a strangely familiar resonance.

He helped me sit up.

"Are you hungry?"

"Don't know," I croaked. I could only make out blurry forms.

Chicken soup! I slurped down the first spoonful that came to my lips, and then another and another. Food! My soul came alive. Life lit up my body again. This man had to be an angel. I closed my bleary eyes for a moment, and when I reopened them the room focused. A gentle breeze stirred curtains hung across an open window. Strong, simple furniture. A painting of birds in flight over mountains. On the dresser, a flat-sided pistol.

"Take a little more water."

I turned my head, almost expecting to see a face like a crumpled beer can.

I croaked in horror.

White Hair! I'd been captured by White Hair!

He laughed at my surprise. "Drink."

Staring in disbelief, I did as he ordered. What did he want? How did he find me in that prison? I should have known he'd be tied in with the SLA. Faded blond streaks laced his long, white hair. He was maybe thirty with stark blue eyes. His facial features haunted me.

I gathered my strength. "Who are you?"

White Hair put down the glass and gave me a cold stare.

"The name is Alex Krell."

"What do you want?"

"I don't want anything."

"But you followed me."

"So?"

"If you want Mitch Damian, he's dead."

Alex Krell scoffed. "Why would I want that loser?"

"Who sent you?"

"Why should I tell you?"

"It's the government. You're with the government."

He laughed. "No."

"Lupa, then. Pablo Lupa."

"He's an asshole, from a long line of assholes."

"Please, tell me!"

Alex's eyes narrowed. "My mother's name is Gjerna."

"Gjerna?"

The room swirled.

I gripped the bed sheets.

"But— you mean, my Gjerna?"

"Yes."

"That can't be. She's dead."

Alex glared at me. "She might as well have been dead, the way you treated her."

The earth fell. "Gjerna— how?"

"She's my mother and I'm your son. But you were never my father."

30

Alex Krell sat in a chair facing my bed, staring at me with blue eyes as hard as a winter sky. I swallowed, trying to stop the room from swirling, my mind a rudderless ship in a gale. Gjerna! Alive— after all this time! Waves of feebleness swamped my soul. Gjerna had a son? My son? That's why Alex looked so familiar.

"Wait. This can't be. Gjerna died. Suicide. It was in obituaries, I had the hotel check."

"What are you talking about? You got my mother pregnant and dumped her. She tried finding you after you ran off to America, but you had disappeared, gone."

Darkness swarmed me and I wanted to be sick. It suddenly came to me— her parents invented the whole suicide story to get rid of me, and had hidden Gjerna away. By the time she escaped from her parents and tried to find me, I had already moved several times. How desperate she must have been. And I wasn't there for her! Tears streamed down my face. I gathered my thoughts and did my best to explain to Alex how her parents faked her suicide in order to get me out of her life.

"My grandparents wouldn't do that. They always said you were American trash, and they were right. If they were still alive they'd tell it to your face."

My cheeks burned. "I always wanted— I tried to find her, but my letters came back unopened, marked deceased. I called, sent telegrams. What could I do? I believed what her parents told me, that she was dead."

"Liar. Sure, you wrote to her for a while, but then you dumped her when you found out she was pregnant with me. My grandparents showed me one of those cruel letters you wrote. You broke her heart. I hate you. I've always hated you."

"But I— how could this be?"

"She was seventeen, just a child, you piece of shit. She didn't know about people like you. After the big rock star went back to America, Gjerna's mother became ill and the family went to Switzerland. Gjerna wrote you every day but you ignored her letters."

Smoking Jimi

"I did not! Her mother faked the whole thing, don't you see? She must have intercepted Gjerna's letters, that's why I didn't get them."

An ugly silence filled the room and Alex shook his head as he stared at me.

"You still have no shame do you? After my mother returned to Denmark and found no letters from you, she called all over Hollywood— your booking agent, the record company, the Musician's Union— nothing. Brad Wilson— big, brave, rock star— was hiding from a pregnant, seventeen-year old. To you she was just some knocked-up groupie. After she had me she tried raising me on her own. Thank God she gave up on you and married my stepfather. He was a mean old bastard and he didn't live long but he had money, and at least he was there for us."

A suffocating cloud spread through my chest. The room darkened as the sun dimmed. Gjerna needed me and I had let her down. I'd even failed my own son. Other than his premature white hair, which he probably inherited from my grandfather, Alex bore an eerie resemblance to us— I saw Gjerna's and my features combined, young again.

"How did you find me?"

Alex grimaced at the question. "After my mother saw that stupid program on MV-1, she wouldn't stop talking about you. She became obsessed with finding you— she even bought a ticket to Florida. Since I couldn't talk her out of it I told her I'd go first, find you, and then let her know what to expect. If you had not left Florida so soon, I would have sent back a report that you were a drug-addicted, pornographic criminal with a prison record, and would have told her to give up on you. But when she learned you had gone to Colorado she insisted I follow you. I'll be sure to let her know what an interesting life you lead. Pablo Lupa? Ha! I should have known."

"Where is she now?"

Alex glared at me.

"Is she married?"

"No."

"Then, why can't I see her?"

Alex leaned forward and jabbed a finger at me. "You'll never see her— I'll make sure of that. You broke her heart once. You'll never do that again."

235

I wanted to curse him, to tell him what an arrogant little shit he was, but instead, the story of Gjerna came spilling out of me. I finished by telling him that as I lay dying in the prison cell, I held thoughts of Gjerna in my heart.

Alex scoffed. "The only reason you're alive is my mother, she begged me to buy your way out of that prison. If it were up to me you'd still be there."

I took a moment to think.

"I heard you were a drug dealer."

"Is that what you heard?" Alex went to the windowsill and gazed through the panes for the longest time.

"After I finished college in New York I returned home to Copenhagen. I guess you could say I was a little wild back then, I learned a lot in the States, things I'm not very proud of. I did some importing into Denmark, but never any hard stuff, only hash, maybe a little pot. Then things got— complicated, you know, with the cops. So I helped Interpol bust some heroin dealers which made the cops look good, and they let me ride. I retired and now I'm a legitimate businessman with a portfolio and friends in the right places. How do you think I was able to keep up with you across two continents? I still have good connections with all sides." He shook his head and laughed. "I couldn't believe you traded your rental car for that old pickup. And those Vituscan friends of yours. Clever."

"How did you find me in that prison?"

"Connections. I know people who know people. That militia would rather have money than some old musician. But understand— my mother saved your life, not me."

My head fell to the pillow, weighed down with heavy thoughts. I felt overjoyed that Gjerna was alive, but my happiness was smothered beneath a blanket of remorse. My son fed me more soup and then I fell into a perfect, deep cocoon of sleep.

* * *

After daybreak I awoke— alone, stiff and aching, barely able to sit up. Gjerna, alive! And how I had failed her. I forced myself out of bed and hobbled into the bathroom where I crumpled to the shower floor while fingers of hot water washed away the filth. As I toweled dry, I discovered stitches sewn into my forehead and I put on a fresh bandage from the medicine chest. Even after I shaved my reflection sill looked like hell, puffed with bruises and welts, my skin red from the sun. I found clean underwear in a drawer, wrapped myself in a blanket, and settled into a chair by the window.

The hotel overlooked a village square where the occasional moped passed by with a puff of oily smoke, and simply dressed people strolled and chatted. Wherever this place was it seemed unmolested by the madness that had enveloped Rancho Vizcaya. Did the last few days really happen? I shuddered as memories flooded back— visions of death and Danny's last hours. I pushed them away, I wasn't ready. The door squeaked open. Alex Krell stepped into the room, a package under one arm.

"Clothes for you. We leave this afternoon. My partner has a plane coming for us at the airport. We fly to Caracas, get on a private jet, drop you off in North America, and I go home."

"But wait, what about Gjerna?"

"She doesn't want to see you." He let the words hang in the air, as if enjoying the moment. "I called her, told her you're a total loser, she should forget you."

"You can't decide that. You're doing what her parents did. That's why I never had a chance to be your father."

Alex hesitated. "Want me to take you back where I found you? Get my two million dollars back? Makes no difference to me. You're just one more asshole."

"Two million? You paid that much for me?"

"My mother's idea, not mine."

"But I'm your father."

Anger twisted Alex's face, and he flung the package onto the bed. "You're not anyone's father. My father died when I was fifteen. I never had a real father— never wanted a father— never needed one."

"But I did— I mean, I always wanted a son."

"That's the problem with people like you. You think we are just playthings, like toys." Alex slammed the door on his way out. My stomach knotted. My son hated me. How could I blame him? In Alex's eyes, I was the rat bastard who abandoned his mother. As I dressed with the clothes he had brought me, I had to stop to dab my eyes. Gjerna probably hated me too. I blinked back tears and went to the dresser, wondering if Alex's gun would be there, not sure what I would do if I found it.

From the top of the dresser I picked up the DAstick, with "Jammies" scrawled over it in white. I almost threw the thing out the window, but decided not to. It held the digitized memories of the last music my friends would ever play, our jam session at Rancho Vizcaya. In one of the dresser drawers I found bread and cheese along with a liter of spring water. I ate mechanically and then sat in the chair, drifting a while, pondering why fate had cheated me from death. Why couldn't I have perished along with my friends at Vizcaya, the way I deserved? How completely, totally unfair.

Smoking Jimi

31

The executive jet leveled off into the early evening skies, leaving behind the glittering lights of Caracas. Alex Krell, my son, sat across the aisle from me paging through a sports magazine. The South Florida investigator who had accompanied Alex on his travels had flown us to Caracas on a small plane. I recognized his creepy voice as the one that made the porn offer on my answering machine— obviously an early attempt to discredit me. The disgusting man left us at the Caracas airport, where our arrival and departure took place in secluded area away from immigration and customs.

"Why Halifax? Can't you just drop me off in South Florida?"

Alex lowered his head and pressed the two halves of the magazine together, as if hoping to squeeze patience from its pages. "We're going where I say we're going, that's why. We refuel in Halifax because it's simpler than stopping in the States. You can make your way home from there. I'm being generous. I could have left you in Caracas," he said, his soft Scandinavian accent dripping with sarcasm.

"This is bigger than Pablo's jet. Is it yours?"

He chuckled. "Only egotistical assholes own planes like this. It belongs to a friend of mine."

I stretched my bruised body, searching for a position that wouldn't ache. A melody came to me and I rolled it around in my mind, enjoying its lines. I recognized it— my Paxicoto song! Not bad for something born from insanity on a mountain trail. Maybe the band could work up a good arrangement— and then I remembered. I took a deep breath. Something made me take the DAstick from my shirt pocket and I pressed it to my cheek. I didn't know if I'd ever have the courage to listen to it.

"What is that? You had it on you when I found you."

"A digital recording of the jam session at Pablo's studio. This is all that's left of the Jamrods. Everybody's gone, dead, except me."

Alex gave me a long, sardonic stare. "Oh. Did I forget to tell you? That manager friend of yours, Mitch, is back in Buffalo

Smoking Jimi

by now. And Jon, your federal-agent pal from Colorado, he should be back in the States too. They both made it to a Golden Path village up in the mountains, where some of Jon's friends got them out."

"Alive? But Rudy killed them. I heard the shots."

"Didn't I just say they're alive? They escaped with some hookers and a chef. That's all I know."

Alive! Jon and Mitch must have jumped Rudy, shot him with his own gun, and then escaped with Candy Floss.

Axel said, "I also heard that Pablo Lupa is still alive, hiding under a rock somewhere along with his stupid brothers and cousins."

I reclined in the seat and let out a long, sad breath as a heavy weight lifted from my chest. Thank God, my friends were still alive. All but one.

"Danny's dead. I know. I killed him," I said softly.

"You? Kill Danny?" Alex hooted and howled.

"Danny was a friend of mine, goddamit. Saved my life."

"Then why would you want to believe you killed him?" Alex laughed again.

"Because, that's why."

"They caught that lunatic friend of yours at the airport. Found him trying to stow away in the wheel well of a plane for America. By now he's probably back with the other crazy people in Colorado."

I stared at nothing for a moment, and then smiled the biggest grin of my life. Killing Danny was only a nightmare, a perverted delusion! So much of this whole episode now seemed like a horrible dream. Except the part about being on a jet bound for Halifax, Nova Scotia, with my son who hated me. And Gjerna hating me from afar. That was all too real.

"Why didn't you tell me about Danny and the others?"

Alex examined his fingernails. "Must have slipped my mind."

"Maybe it's a good thing I wasn't your father when you were growing up. I would have taught you a few things."

A smile crept across his face. "A rock musician for a father? As you Americans say, I think I'll pass."

We spent the rest of the long flight dozing and chatting. I told him he probably got the gene for premature white hair from my grandfather, who turned white in his twenties. Alex told me of his years attending college in New York, which accounted for his Americanized English. I asked questions regarding Gjerna but he seemed very protective of her. At one point, he did say, "She didn't get fat, if that's what you're asking," and laughed himself almost to tears.

It was good to hear Alex's laughter— I hoped that life hadn't done to his heart what it had done to mine. He said that Gjerna spoke of me often and worried about what had become of me. For years, she had scanned music magazines, searching for news of the Jammies. As I listened, tears welled in my eyes, but I didn't let Alex see them. It tore my heart to know that Gjerna longed for me as much as I had longed for her. *And I wasn't there for her!* And my son, a drug dealer! Although he seemed to have scruples, if I had raised him as my son, both of our lives would have been very different. Poor Gjerna, what she must have gone through. If only! If only.

Alex's demeanor hardened. He made it clear I would never be allowed to see his mother, ever. He would report to Gjerna that I was an undesirable, dangerous man, and that would be the end of it. No amount of pleading could change his mind. Years of hating me had built an impenetrable wall around his heart.

I resolved that somehow, someway, I would find a way to communicate with Gjerna, at least to explain myself and tell her I was so sorry. I dozed off and when I awoke, it was still dark. I cleaned up in the rest room and even though I looked as if I'd been dragged through hell, saw that some life had returned to my eyes. I grabbed snacks and a soda from the fridge. My body ached as I ambled back to my seat— I just wanted to land and get my stiff bones off that damned airplane.

"What time is it?" I asked, as I sat down.

"Why? You have an appointment?" Alex snickered and shook his head.

"Seems like we've been flying forever. Do we have enough fuel to make it to Canada?"

"You didn't notice the extra fuel tanks under the wings?"

"What at am I supposed to do in Halifax? I don't have a cent."

"You? The big millionaire?" Alex chuckled.

"You know all that money's gone."

"Maybe Mitch or Jon will help you. But I doubt if your friends escaped with any of Pablo's money. Did you really think

Lupa would allow that? The Oro Cartel, giving away money?" He smirked in a way that made me angry. "You're lucky my mother saved your life." Alex gazed out the window as dawn began smearing the clouds with a raspberry glow.

"Sure has been a long flight," I said, stretching my legs and rubbing my knees.

"Want off, now?"

I ignored his taunt. As we descended into Halifax, Alex went to the cockpit, and when he returned, he began lowering the window shades.

"Why are you doing that?"

"To keep curious eyes out," Alex said. "Never know who these ground crews work for."

I pulled down my window shade. I had to think. How far was Buffalo from Halifax? Perhaps I could call Mitch. Or maybe have Carol wire some money. My thoughts darkened as I contemplated Carol's insipid world of dolls, creeping sorrow, and clinging perversion. I would move out and live alone. And stay alone this time.

"What about immigration, what am I supposed to do when we land?"

"It's all been arranged," Alex said, staring straight ahead.

I wanted to grab him by the shoulders and tell him so many things, but I felt weak to my core. I had failed at everything. Worst of all, I had let Gjerna down. I'd even lost my dreams of her— Alex had buried them beneath a mountain of hate. I caught a glimpse of him smiling to himself. Smug bastard.

After the plane taxied to a stop and the door opened, crisp, clean air breezed into the cabin. Alex motioned with his head for me to exit the plane. No good-byes, nothing, just that damned smirk, which had somehow grown larger.

"Alex, I'm sorry we couldn't be —"

"Get off my airplane. Now." His smirk became a cruel grin.

The morning sun shone brightly as I made my way down the stairway, and I shielded my eyes. I stepped carefully onto the tarmac, my knees a bit unsteady.

"Brad?"

I knew that voice! Squinting against the sun, I turned towards her.

Gjerna!

I stood with my mouth open, blinking in amazement. Yes, Gjerna! And how beautiful! Her blond hair looked just as I remembered, and the gentle lines on her face made her lovelier than I could have ever imagined. Tears welled in our eyes. We hesitated, and then rushed forward and embraced, and embraced, and embraced. We held each other's faces in our hands, and cried, and laughed, and cried. I kissed the woman I had never stopped loving, and who had always loved me. As I held her I realized I had arrived— I had finally found my forever. Maybe Pablo was right about eternity— only mine was here in this precious woman, not at the end of a poison needle.

Laughter came from above. Alex had tears in his eyes too, and the most beautiful smile.

"Welcome to Copenhagen," he said.

"Copenhagen?" I wiped tears and looked around. Commercial terminals stood in the distance, far from the three of us and this deserted section of the airport. A black Volvo was parked near the airplane. I took clean air deep into my lungs.

"Welcome home," Gjerna said, her face expressing everything I had always longed for.

I stared into her eyes, this woman I had dreamed of for a thousand years, the woman I would love forever. "Home. God, yes, I am home."

I held Gjerna in my arms and in that precious moment, we drifted through the doors of eternity, a place where we have always been— a place we will always be— Our Forever.

Above us in the deep-blue sky, a bird cried out as it flew overhead. I'd swear it said, *"It's your time to kiss the sky."*

THE END

Excerpt from Stealing Margo *by Chad Peery*

~About the Author~

Chad Peery's rock years include bass guitarist for John Kay & Steppenwolf, and Fleetwood Mac's Bob Welch. Chad shared the stage with the Starship, Foreigner, the Cars, Eddie Money, Heart, Fleetwood Mac, and many others. Chad also repaired guided missiles, has been a published songwriter, won national recognition in radio programming, and spent a few interesting years as a private investigator.

What did a young Chad Peery look like performing at Cal Jam II in front of 300,000 fans? (Where DID he get all that energy?) Curious about the *Smoking Jimi* author? Go to **www.chadwrite.com**. There, you'll find videos and links to Chad's rock years, as well as excerpts from *Stealing Margo*, another Chad Peery novel with a similar theme to *Smoking Jimi* (with a female protagonist). You'll also find links to e-book versions of Chad's novels, his upcoming audio books, his photo gallery, information about adopted children reuniting with birth parents, tinnitus impairment, as well as explore Chad's connection to West Virginia and pre-civil war "Western Virginia."

~Author's Note~

I chose to publish *Smoking Jimi* through amazon.com to avoid sacrificing the book's character through the conventional publishing process. In so doing, I have made the book available through online distribution and select local bookstores.

By recommending *Smoking Jimi* to your friends and through your generous mentions, you earn my heartfelt thanks. You'll find links and more information at **www.chadwrite.com**. You're also most welcome to join my friends' list at the usual social networking sites.

~*~*~*~*~*~*~*~*~*~*~*~*~*~*~*~*~*~*~

As a bonus, please enjoy the following pages from *Stealing Margo,* a new novel by Chad Peery.

Excerpt from <u>Stealing Margo</u> *by Chad Peery*

(pp. 4-8) As Margo approached a red light, her fingers tapped the steering wheel. Time for a family meeting. Family. Some joke. Zack, Brent's son from a previous marriage, should have already accepted Margo as his mother— hadn't the boy's excessively groomed psychologist said so? Then, why did Zack cling to his aloofness towards her? And why was Brent being such a jerk lately? Tonight, they would have it out.

Oddly, traffic had thinned on Enterprise Avenue, and she was alone as her Lexus pulled up to the intersection. From the sidewalk, a bag lady stared in the Lexus' direction, and when her uneven gaze came to rest upon Margo, it caused a twitch of apprehension.

Margo looked away. Crazy people— there never seemed to be a shortage of them these days. She glanced into the rearview mirror. How odd. The only car approaching was a massive beater— probably from the mid-70s. The old Buick came to rest a few car lengths behind her.

Its hood trembled to the engine's beat.

No front license plate.

Missing teeth in its grill.

And the color!

What did that car do to deserve such a god-awful shade of orange? It looked as if it had been dunked into fermented pumpkin juice, and then endured some bizarre ritual of shame and abuse.

The broad sedan had an expansive front end that seemed to smile at Margo with an ill-fitting grin, which almost made her giggle. Perhaps the old car recognized her as a fellow traveler— another beat-up survivor of the 80's.

The sky dimmed and Margo found it strange how a broad, heavy mass of clouds had drawn itself across the sun. Then, she caught movement in her rearview mirror.

Movement that shouldn't be happening.

The light hadn't changed, of that she was certain, yet the old car had lurched into motion and was now accelerating forward. In a brief moment the beater closed the gap, and with a horrid, grinding smash, the Buick collided with her Lexus.

Margo sat, stunned.

"Dammit! I don't believe this!"

She unlatched her seatbelt and shoved the door open.

Not a pretty sight.

Excerpt from Stealing Margo *by Chad Peery*

The impact from the old Buick had crumpled the rear of her Lexus. Shards of taillight lens lay scattered across the old car's orange hood, which seemed undamaged, but who could tell? The driver's door croaked opened. Unfolding himself arm-by-leg, a very tall, very bearded, longhaired man emerged, wearing a somewhat tucked-in, green-plaid shirt, and topped off with a black baseball cap with a golden "AH" inscribed across the bill.

A hayseed! What was this hillbilly doing in the Baltimore business district?

"Oh, wow, ma'am, I'm so, so sorry." The man removed his hat. He raised his furry eyebrows and batted his eyes. "You OK?"

"I'm fine. But look! Just look at this!"

"My foot must a' slipped." He indicated a pointed, black boot.

"Beautiful. You got insurance?"

"Well, yeah, sure," the man said. He put his cap on backwards and leaned into the old Buick.

"Could've fooled me," Margo muttered, as she retrieved her purse from the Lexus' front seat. When she emerged, she noticed the man wore an olive-drab pouch slung over one shoulder in the style of a woman carrying a purse. She wondered if he knew how stupid that looked. A faded, U.S. Army emblem was stamped across the pouch's flap. Another immature mind in a grown-up body, she thought.

Behind them, both lanes were filling with cars. Horns began blaring from the rear of the line.

"I'd better call this in. I'll need to see your ID," Margo said, fishing in her purse for her cell phone.

The man opened the flap of his pouch and showed Margo the butt end of a mean-looking, large-caliber handgun.

Margo blinked.

He put a hand on the pistol grip, and lowered the flap over his hairy forearm. Fear splashed Margo's stomach. Reality check: yes, that was a large handgun she saw— and yes, she'd better do something, fast

"OK, well, you know what, I'm kinda rushed here, why don't I just write you a check, I mean, this wasn't really anybody's fault, right?"

"Get in my car. Do it now. Don't even think about it. Just get in, and you won't get hurt." Stepping back, he motioned to the

Excerpt from <u>Stealing Margo</u> by Chad Peery

driver's door of the old beater, which stood open at a sinister angle.

What now? Margo couldn't read his expression behind all that hair, and his voice was absent any emotion.

"Look, none of this is necessary, I'm sorry about the accident, it was totally my fault. I've got money, would you prefer cash, or will a check do?"

"We're gonna have us a little talk, you and me. Get in my car."

Heart pounding and blood rushing, Margo glanced about. Traffic had backed up as far as she could see, and more cars had joined the chorus of bawling horns.

No help there, not from those road-rage jockeys.

No pedestrians, not even the old woman.

No cops.

Should she run, and risk getting shot dead on the sidewalk by a hairy lunatic? Margo jogged five miles each morning and did laps in the pool every night, but with this guy's long, loping legs, she doubted if she could outdistance him, at least not in the short run. Margo took a deep breath. What was she thinking? She was a lawyer! Negotiate! Give him what they all want.

"Look, I've got three hundred in cash with me, and tell you what, let me write you a blank check, there's over forty thousand dollars in that account."

"I'm hoping I'm not going to have to shoot ya." He cocked his head towards the Buick. "In the car, or take a bullet. Now. You're driving."

"Why? I don't even know you. What do you want with me?"

His reply was a hard stare.

"Oh, hell—just, hell!" Margo kicked her Lexus' crumpled fender, and shattered plastic chattered to the pavement. She stormed past the man and slid into the Buick's upholstered seat. Margo tucked her purse under her feet, aware that the cell phone in it just might save her life.

Her abductor folded himself into the passenger's seat. Judging by the angle of his right arm, the gun he held inside the pouch was pointed directly at her midsection. He tossed his black cap onto the dash, which seemed large enough for a family picnic. The plushy, lime-green interior and faux wood instrument panel made her blink in disgust. The massive steering wheel,

Excerpt from <u>Stealing Margo</u> *by Chad Peery*

emblazoned with the Buick nameplate, seemed better suited for a boat. Cool air breezed from chrome vents.

"Close your door."

Margo pulled the heavy door shut. Odd, she thought, how the interior on this old car seemed new.

"Now, back it up nice and easy, and pull around your car. Go on."

She lowered the column shift into reverse. As she backed up, fragments from her crumpled Lexus slid off the beater's hood. The steering wheel seemed to turn itself as she guided the big Buick into the clear lane and powered away from the accident scene.

Her abductor must have planned ahead— the driver's seat had been adjusted so that she could easily reach the pedals and see over the wheel. That meant that the car crash and abduction were premeditated acts, and not the irrational impulses of a lunatic.

A maniac with a plan is never a good thing.

"Hey!" He raised his free hand and aimed a finger at her like a gun. "Buckle up! Safety first."

He helped her work the seatbelt clip into the large buckle.

"Alright. Good job, Margo. Just keep on going down this street."

"Wait! How do you know my name?"

"You kidding? You're famous. Everybody knows your name. You're gonna turn here, then you look for the freeway onramp, northbound."

She needed to think of something, fast. Things were kind of rocky with Brent, but he wouldn't hire a hillbilly hit man, that wasn't his style. He only bought the best, especially if it was with someone else's money. She would expect an assassin dressed like a priest with a small caliber pistol, not a hairy hick packing a hand-cannon in an army-surplus pouch.

She tried to keep her voice calm: "Bottom line, we're talking serious money. I can get you several hundred thousand, all we have to do is go to my bank, and I'll get it for you, OK? It's nothing to me, really. In fact, I want you to have it. Think of it as a gift. I'll sign a letter of agreement, it'll be your money free and clear. I'm an attorney, I can make it completely legal."

"You warned me that you'd do this. Here, take this onramp."

"What do you mean I warned you?"

Excerpt from Stealing Margo *by Chad Peery*

"You warned me, plain as day. Now, get on here." A big hand motioned toward the onramp.

"Warned you? I've never seen you before."

He gave her a look that chilled, as if he could see through her clothes, through her skin, through her soul.

"Don't miss your onramp, now."

The big car seemed to know the way as she pulled westbound onto I-70. She pressed the gas pedal and the Buick merged into traffic.

Her kidnapper grinned and shook his bearish head, as if he'd just recalled a really good joke. "You're gonna stay in the slow lane. Now, take your cell phone out of that purse of yours, nice and slow."

"Cell phone? What cell phone?"

"Just give me the phone."

"Would you like me to call someone for you? I could do that," she said as she withdrew it from her purse.

He snatched the cell phone and pressed some keys.

"I'm calling your number at work."

"My number? You'll just get my voice mail."

"Good." He handed her the phone. "Leave yourself a message. Tell yourself that you've been kidnapped by a strange man who says he's from Maine. You might mention that he's read a lot of Steven King novels. Ha! Explain to yourself that he has a gun. And be polite. You gotta respect yourself."

Margo did as ordered, but after she left herself a message, she pushed 1-2, which forwarded the message to the front desk. Assuming Ashley wasn't cornered in the conference room by the old groper, and assuming she would see the blinking message light before she left to have a candlelit tryst with one of the partners, she would hear Margo's message, release an operatic scream, and call the police.*

* See more about *Stealing Margo* at **www.chadwrite.com**. *Stealing Margo* is for sale in print at amazon.com and createspace.com. A list of select local bookstores that carry *Stealing Margo* is available at chadwrite.com.

Made in the USA